Changeling

Changeling

PHILIPPA GREGORY

SIMON AND SCHUSTER

First published in Great Britain in 2012 by Simon & Schuster UK Ltd
This paperback edition published 2013
A CBS COMPANY

Text copyright © 2012 by Philippa Gregory

Journey map, abbey plan and chapterhead illustrations © Fred van Deelen, 2012

Section break artwork © Sally Taylor, 2012

1 3 5 7 9 10 8 6 4 2

Simon & Schuster UK Ltd
1st Floor
222 Gray's Inn Road
London
WC1X 8HB

Simon & Schuster Australia, Sydney
Simon & Schuster India, New Delhi

A CIP catalogue copy for this book is available
from the British Library.

PB ISBN: 978-0-85707-732-5
E-BOOK ISBN: 978-0-85707-733-2

Printed and bound by CPI Group (UK) Ltd, Croydon, CR0 4YY

www.simonandschuster.co.uk
www.simonandschuster.com.au

CASTLE SANT' ANGELO,
ROME, JUNE 1453

The hammering on the door shot him into wakefulness like a handgun going off in his face. The young man scrambled for the dagger under his pillow, stumbling to his bare feet on the icy floor of the stone cell. He had been dreaming of his parents, of his old home, and he gritted his teeth against the usual wrench of longing for everything he had lost: the farmhouse, his mother, the old life.

The thunderous banging sounded again, and he held the dagger behind his back as he unbolted the door and cautiously opened it a crack. A dark-hooded figure stood outside, flanked by two heavy-set men, each carrying a burning torch. One of them raised his torch so the light fell on the slight dark-haired youth, naked to the waist, wearing only breeches, his hazel eyes blinking under a fringe of dark hair. He was about seventeen, with a face as sweet as a boy, but with the body of a young man forged by hard work.

'Luca Vero?'

'Yes.'

'You are to come with me.'

They saw him hesitate. 'Don't be a fool. There are three of us and only one of you and the dagger you're hiding behind your back won't stop us.'

'It's an order,' the other man said roughly. 'Not a request. And you are sworn to obedience.'

Luca had sworn obedience to his monastery, not to these strangers, but he had been expelled from there and now it seemed he must obey anyone who shouted a command. He turned to the bed, sat to pull on his boots, slipping the dagger into a scabbard hidden inside the soft leather, pulled on a linen shirt, and then threw his ragged woollen cape around his shoulders.

'Who are you?' he asked, coming unwillingly to the door.

The man made no answer, but simply turned and led the way, as the two guards waited in the corridor for Luca to come out of his cell and follow.

'Where are you taking me?'

The two guards fell in behind him without answering. Luca wanted to ask if he was under arrest, if he was being marched to a summary execution, but he did not dare. He was fearful of the very question, he acknowledged to himself that he was terrified of the answer. He could feel himself sweating with fear under his woollen cape, though the air was icy and the stone walls were cold and damp.

He knew that he was in the most serious trouble of his

young life. Only yesterday four dark-hooded men had taken him from his monastery and brought him here, to this prison, without a word of explanation. He did not know where he was, or who was holding him. He did not know what charge he might face. He did not know what the punishment might be. He did not know if he was going to be beaten, tortured or killed.

'I insist on seeing a priest, I wish to confess . . .' he said.

They paid no attention to him at all, but pressed him on, down the narrow stone-flagged gallery. It was silent, with the closed doors of cells on either side. He could not tell if it was a prison or a monastery, it was so cold and quiet. It was just after midnight and the place was in darkness and utterly still. Luca's guides made no noise as they walked along the gallery, down the stone steps, through a great hall, and then down a little spiral staircase, into a darkness that grew more and more black as the air grew more and more cold.

'I demand to know where you are taking me,' Luca insisted, but his voice shook with fear.

No-one answered him; but the guard behind him closed up a little.

At the bottom of the steps, Luca could just see a small arched doorway and a heavy wooden door. The leading man opened it with a key from his pocket and gestured that Luca should go through. When he hesitated, the guard behind him simply moved closer until the menacing bulk of his body pressed Luca onwards.

'I insist . . .' Luca breathed.

A hard shove thrust him through the doorway and he gasped as he found himself flung to the very edge of a high narrow quay, a boat rocking in the river a long way below, the far bank a dark blur in the distance. Luca flinched back from the brink. He had a sudden dizzying sense that they would be as willing to throw him over, onto the rocks below, as to take him down the steep stairs to the boat.

The first man went light-footed down the wet steps, stepped into the boat and said one word to the boatman who stood in the stern, holding the vessel against the current with the deft movements of a single oar. Then he looked back up to the handsome white-faced young man.

'Come,' he ordered.

Luca could do nothing else. He followed the man down the greasy steps, clambered into the boat and seated himself in the prow. The boatman did not wait for the guards but turned his craft into the middle of the river and let the current sweep them around the city wall. Luca glanced down into the dark water. If he were to fling himself over the side of the boat he would be swept downstream – he might be able to swim with the current and make it to the other side and get away. But the water was flowing so fast he thought he was more likely to drown, if they did not come after him in the boat and knock him senseless with the oar.

'My lord,' he said, trying for dignity. 'May I ask you now where we are going?'

'You'll know soon enough,' came the terse reply. The river ran like a wide moat around the tall walls of the city of Rome. The boatman kept the little craft close to the lee of the walls, hidden from the sentries above, then Luca saw ahead of them the looming shape of a stone bridge and, just before it, a grille set in an arched stone doorway of the wall. As the boat nosed inwards, the grille slipped noiselessly up and, with one prac-tised push of the oar, they shot inside, into a torch-lit cellar.

4

With a deep lurch of fear Luca wished that he had taken his chance with the river. There were half a dozen grim-faced men waiting for him and, as the boatman held a well-worn ring on the wall to steady the craft, they reached down and hauled Luca out of the boat, to push him down a narrow corridor. Luca felt, rather than saw, thick stone walls on either side, smooth wooden floorboards underfoot, heard his own breathing, ragged with fear, then they paused before a heavy wooden door, struck it with a single knock and waited.

A voice from inside the room said 'Come!' and the guard swung the door open and thrust Luca inside. Luca stood, heart pounding, blinking at the sudden brightness of dozens of wax candles, and heard the door close silently behind him.

A solitary man was sitting at a table, papers before him. He wore a robe of rich velvet in so dark a blue that it appeared almost black, the hood completely concealing his face from Luca, who stood before the table and swallowed down his fear. Whatever happened, he decided, he was not going to beg for his life. Somehow, he would find the courage to face whatever was coming. He would not shame himself, nor his tough stoical father, by whimpering like a girl.

'You will be wondering why you are here, where you are, and who I am,' the man said. 'I will tell you these things. But, first, you must answer me everything that I ask. Do you understand?'

Luca nodded.

'You must not lie to me. Your life hangs in the balance here, and you cannot guess what answers I would prefer. Be sure to tell the truth: you would be a fool to die for a lie.'

Luca tried to nod but found he was shaking.

'You are Luca Vero, a novice priest at the monastery of St Xavier, having joined the monastery when you were a boy of eleven? You have been an orphan for the last three years, since your parents died when you were fourteen?'

'My parents disappeared,' Luca said. He cleared his tight throat. 'They may not be dead. They were captured by an Ottoman raid but nobody saw them killed. Nobody knows where they are now; but they may very well be alive.'

The Inquisitor made a minute note on a piece of paper before him. Luca watched the tip of the black feather as the quill moved across the page. 'You hope,' the man said briefly. 'You hope that they are alive and will come back to you.' He spoke as if hope was the greatest folly.

'I do.'

'Raised by the brothers, sworn to join their holy order, yet you went to your confessor, and then to the abbot, and told them that the relic that they keep at the monastery, a nail from the true cross, was a fake.'

The monotone voice was accusation enough. Luca knew this was a citation of his heresy. He knew also, that the only punishment for heresy was death.

'I didn't mean . . .'

'Why did you say the relic was a fake?'

Luca looked down at his boots, at the dark wooden floor, at the heavy table, at the lime washed walls – anywhere but at the shadowy face of the softly spoken questioner. 'I will beg the abbot's pardon and do penance,' he said. 'I didn't mean heresy. Before God, I am no heretic. I meant no wrong.'

'I shall be the judge if you are a heretic, and I have seen

6

younger men than you, who have done and said less than you, crying on the rack for mercy, as their joints pop from their sockets. I have heard better men than you begging for the stake, longing for death as their only release from pain.'

Luca shook his head at the thought of the Inquisition, which could order this fate for him and see it done, and think it to the glory of God. He dared to say nothing more.

'Why did you say the relic was a fake?'

'I did not mean . . .'

'Why?'

'It is a piece of a nail about three inches long, and a quarter of an inch wide,' Luca said unwillingly. 'You can see it, though it is now mounted in gold and covered with jewels. But you can still see the size of it.'

The Inquisitor nodded. 'So?'

'The abbey of St Peter has a nail from the true cross. So does the abbey of St Joseph. I looked in the monastery library to see if there were any others, and there are about four hundred nails in Italy alone, more in France, more in Spain, more in England.'

The man waited in unsympathetic silence.

'I calculated the likely size of the nails,' Luca said miserably. 'I calculated the number of pieces that they might have been broken into. It didn't add up. There are far too many relics for them all to come from one crucifixion. The Bible says a nail in each palm and one through the feet. That's only three nails.' Luca glanced at the dark face of his interrogator. 'It's not blasphemy to say this, I don't think. The Bible itself says it clearly. Then, in addition, if you count the nails used in building the cross, there would be four at the central joint to hold the cross bar. That makes seven original nails. Only seven. Say each nail is about five inches long. That's about thirty-five inches of nails used in the true cross. But there are thousands of relics. That's not to say whether any nail or any fragment is genuine or not. It's not for me to judge. But I can't help but see that there are just too many nails for them all to come from one cross.'

Still the man said nothing.

'It's numbers,' Luca said helplessly. 'It's how I think. I think about numbers – they interest me.'

'You took it upon yourself to study this? And you took it upon yourself to decide that there are too many nails in churches around the world for them all to be true, for them all to come from the sacred cross?'

Luca dropped to his knees, knowing himself to be guilty. 'I meant no wrong,' he whispered upwards at the shadowy figure. 'I just started wondering, and then I made the calculations, and then the abbot found my paper where I had written the calculations and—' He broke off.

'The abbot, quite rightly, accused you of heresy and forbidden studies, misquoting the Bible for your own purposes, reading without guidance, showing independence of thought, studying without permission, at the wrong time, studying forbidden books . . .' the man continued, reading from the list. He looked at Luca: 'Thinking for yourself. That's the worst of it, isn't it? You were sworn into an order with certain established beliefs and then you started thinking for yourself.'

Luca nodded. 'I am sorry.'

'The priesthood does not need men who think for themselves.'

'I know,' Luca said, very low.

'You made a vow of obedience – that is a vow not to think for yourself.'

Luca bowed his head, waiting to hear his sentence.

The flame of the candles bobbed as somewhere outside a door opened and a cold draught blew through the rooms.

'Always thought like this? With numbers?'

Luca nodded.

'Any friends in the monastery? Have you discussed this with anyone?'

He shook his head. 'I didn't discuss this.'

The man looked at his notes. 'You have a companion called Freize?'

Luca smiled for the first time. 'He's just the kitchen boy at the monastery,' he said. 'He took a liking to me as soon as I arrived, when I was just eleven. He was only twelve or thirteen himself. He made up his mind that I was too thin, he said I wouldn't last the winter. He kept bringing me extra food. He's just the spit lad really.'

'You have no brother or sister?'

'I am alone in the world.'

'You miss your parents?'

'I do.'

'You are lonely?' The way he said it sounded like yet another accusation.

'I suppose so. I feel very alone, if that is the same thing.'

The man rested the black feather of the quill against his lips in thought. 'Your parents . . .' He returned to the first question of the interrogation. 'They were quite old when you were born?'

'Yes,' Luca said, surprised. 'Yes.'

'People talked at the time, I understand. That such an old

couple should suddenly give birth to a son, and such a handsome son, who grew to be such an exceptionally clever boy?'

'It's a small village,' Luca said defensively. 'People have nothing to do but gossip.'

'But clearly, you are handsome. Clearly, you are clever. And yet they did not brag about you, or show you off. They kept you quietly at home.'

'We were close,' Luca replied. 'We were a close small family. We troubled nobody else, we lived quietly, the three of us.'

'Then why did they give you to the Church? Was it that they thought you would be safer inside the Church? That you were specially gifted? That you needed the Church's protection?'

Luca, still on his knees, shuffled in discomfort. 'I don't know. I was a child: I was only eleven. I don't know what they were thinking.'

The Inquisitor waited.

'They wanted me to have the education of a priest,' he said eventually. 'My father—' He paused at the thought of his beloved father, of his grey hair and his hard grip, of his tenderness to his funny quirky little son. 'My father was very proud that I learned to read, that I taught myself about numbers. He couldn't write or read himself, he thought it was a great talent. Then, when some gypsies came through the village, I learned their language.'

The man made a note. 'You can speak languages?'

'People remarked that I learned to speak Romany in a day. My father thought that I had a gift, a God-given gift. It's not so uncommon,' he tried to explain. 'Freize, the spit boy, is good with animals, he can do anything with horses, he can ride anything. My father thought that I had a gift like that, only for studying. He wanted me to be more than a farmer. He wanted me to do better.'

The Inquisitor sat back in his chair as if he was weary of listening, as if he had heard more than enough. 'You can get up.'

He looked at the paper with its few black ink notes as Luca scrambled to his feet. 'Now I will answer the questions that will be in your mind. I am the spiritual commander of an Order appointed by the Holy Father, the Pope himself, and I answer to him for our work. You need not know my name nor the name of the Order. We have been commanded by Pope Nicholas V to explore the mysteries, the heresies and the sins, to explain them where possible, and defeat them where we can. We are making a map of the fears of the world, travelling outwards from Rome to the very ends of Christendom to discover what people are saying, what they are fearing, what they are fighting. We have to know where the Devil is walking through the world. The Holy Father knows that we are approaching the end of days.'

'The end of days?'

'When Christ comes again to judge the living, the dead, and the undead. You will have heard that the Ottomans have taken Constantinople, the heart of the Byzantine empire, the centre of the Church in the east?'

Luca crossed himself. The fall of the eastern capital of the Church to an unbeatable army of heretics and infidels was the most terrible thing that could have happened, an unimaginable disaster.

'Next, the forces of darkness will come against Rome, and if Rome falls it will be the end of days – the end of the world. Our task is to defend Christendom, to defend Rome – in this world, and in the unseen world beyond.'

'The unseen world?'

'It is all around us,' the man said flatly. 'I see it, perhaps as clearly as you see numbers. And every year, every day, it presses more closely. People come to me with stories of showers of blood, of a dog that can smell out the plague, of witchcraft, of lights in the sky, of water that is wine. The end of days approaches and there are hundreds of mani-festations of good and evil, miracles and heresies. A young man like you can perhaps tell me which of these are true, and which are false, which are the work of God and which of the Devil.' He rose from his great wooden chair and pushed a fresh sheet of paper across the table to Luca. 'See this?'

Luca looked at the marks on the paper. It was the writing of heretics, the Moors' way of numbering. Luca had been taught as a child that one stroke of the pen meant one: I, two strokes meant two: II, and so on. But these were strange rounded shapes. He had seen them before, but the mer-chants in his village and the almoner at the monastery stubbornly refused to use them, clinging to the old ways.

'This means one: 1, this two: 2, and this three: 3,' the man said, the black feather tip of his quill pointing to the marks. 'Put the 1 here, in this column, it means one, but put it here and this blank beside it and it means ten, or put it here and two blanks beside it, it means one hundred.'

Luca gaped. 'The position of the number shows its value?'

'Just so.' The man pointed the plume of the black feather to the shape of the blank, like an elongated O, which filled the columns. His arm stretched from the sleeve of his robe and Luca looked from the O to the white skin of the man's inner wrist. Tattooed on the inside of his arm, so that it almost appeared engraved on skin, Luca could just make out the head and twisted tail of a dragon, a design in red ink of a dragon coiled around on itself.

'This is not just a blank, it is not just an O, it is what they call a zero. Look at the position of it – that means something. What if it meant something of itself?'

'Does it mean a space?' Luca said, looking at the paper again. 'Does it mean: nothing?'

'It is a number like any other,' the man told him. 'They have made a number from nothing. So they can calculate to nothing, and beyond.'

'Beyond? Beyond nothing?'

The man pointed to another number: –10. 'That is beyond nothing. That is ten places beyond nothing, that is the numbering of absence,' he said.

Luca, with his mind whirling, reached out for the paper. But the man quietly drew it back towards him and placed his broad hand over it, keeping it from Luca like a prize he would have to win. The sleeve fell down over his wrist again, hiding the tattoo. 'You know how they got to that sign, the number zero?' he asked.

Luca shook his head. 'Who got to it?'

'Arabs, Moors, Ottomans, call them what you will. Mussulmen, Muslim-men, infidels, our enemies, our new conquerors. Do you know how they got that sign?'

'No.'

'It is the shape left by a counter in the sand when you have taken the counter away. It is the symbol for nothing, it looks like a nothing. It is what it symbolises. That is how they think. That is what we have to learn from them.'

'I don't understand. What do we have to learn?'

'To look, and look, and look. That is what they do. They look at everything, they think about everything, that is why they have seen stars in the sky that we have never seen. That is why they make physic from plants that we have never noticed.' He pulled his hood closer, so that his face was completely shadowed. 'That is why they will defeat us unless we learn to see like they see, to think like they think, to count like they count. Perhaps a young man like you can learn their language too.'

Luca could not take his eyes from the paper where the man had marked out ten spaces of counting, down to zero and then beyond.

'So, what do you think?' the Inquisitor asked him. 'Do you think ten nothings are beings of the unseen world? Like ten invisible things? Ten ghosts? Ten angels?'

'If you could calculate beyond nothing,' Luca started, 'you could show what you had lost. Say someone was a merchant, and his debt in one country, or on one voyage, was greater than his fortune, you could show exactly how much his debt was. You could show his loss. You could show how much less than nothing he had, how much he would have to earn before he had something again.'

'Yes,' the man said. 'With zero you can measure what is not there. The Ottomans took Constantinople and our empire in the east not only because they had the strongest armies and the best commanders, but because they had a

14

weapon that we did not have: a cannon so massive that it took sixty oxen to pull it into place. They have knowledge of things that we don't understand. The reason that I sent for you, the reason that you were expelled from your monastery but not punished there for disobedience or tortured for heresy, is that I want you to learn these mysteries; I want you to explore them, so that we can know them, and arm ourselves against them.'

'Is zero one of the things I must study? Will I go to the Ottomans and learn from them? Will I learn about their studies?'

The man laughed and pushed the piece of paper with the Arabic numerals towards the novice priest, holding it with one finger on the page. 'I will let you have this,' he promised. 'It can be your reward when you have worked to my satisfaction and set out on your mission. And yes, perhaps you will go to the infidel and live among them and learn their ways. But for now, you have to swear obedience to me and to our Order. I will send you out to be my ears and eyes. I will send you to hunt for mysteries, to find knowledge. I will send you to map fears, to seek darkness in all its shapes and forms. I will send you out to understand things, to be part of our Order that seeks to understand everything.'

He could see Luca's face light up at the thought of a life devoted to inquiry. But then the young man hesitated. 'I won't know what to do,' Luca confessed. 'I wouldn't know where to begin. I understand nothing! How will I know where to go or what to do?'

'I am going to send you to be trained. I will send you to study with masters. They will teach you the law, and what powers you have to convene a court or an inquiry. You will learn what to look for and how to question someone. You will understand when someone must be released to earthly powers – the mayors of towns or the lords of the manor; or when they can be punished by the Church. You will learn when to forgive and when to punish. When you are ready, when you have been trained, I will send you on your first mission.'

Luca nodded.

'You will be trained for some months and then I shall send you out into the world with my orders,' the man said. 'You will go where I command and study what you find there. You will report to me. You may judge and punish where you find wrong-doing. You may exorcise devils and unclean spirits. You may learn. You may question everything, all the time. But you will serve God and me, as I tell you. You will be obedient to me and to the Order. And you will walk in the unseen world and look at unseen things, and question them.'

There was a silence. 'You can go,' the man said, as if he had given the simplest of instructions. Luca started from his silent attention and went to the door. As his hand was on the bronze handle the man said: 'One thing more . . .'

Luca turned.

'They said you were a changeling, didn't they?' The accusation dropped into the room like a sudden shower of ice. 'The people of the village? When they gossiped about you being born, so handsome and so clever, to a woman who had been barren all her life, to a man who could neither read nor write. They said you were a changeling, left on her doorstep by the faeries, didn't they?'

There was a cold silence. Luca's stern young face revealed nothing. 'I have never answered such a question, and I hope that I never do. I don't know what they said about us,' he said harshly. 'They were ignorant fearful country people. My mother said to pay no attention to the things they said. She said that she was my mother and that she loved me above all else. That's all that mattered, not stories about faerie children.'

The man laughed shortly and waved Luca to go, and watched as the door closed beind him. 'Perhaps I am sending out a changeling to map fear itself,' he said to himself, as he tidied the papers together and pushed back his chair. 'What a joke for the worlds seen and unseen! A faerie child in the Order. A faerie child to map fear.'

THE CASTLE OF LUCRETILI,
JUNE 1453

At about the time that Luca was being questioned, a young
woman was seated in a rich chair in the chapel of her family
home, the Castle of Lucretili, about twenty miles north-east
of Rome, her dark blue eyes fixed on the rich crucifix, her
fair hair twisted in a careless plait under a black veil, her
face strained and pale. A candle in a rose crystal bowl flickered on the altar as the priest moved in the shadows. She
knelt, her hands clasped tightly together, praying fervently
for her father, who was fighting for his life in his bed-
chamber, refusing to see her.

The door at the back of the chapel opened and her brother
came in quietly, saw her bowed head and went to kneel
beside her. She looked sideways at him, a handsome young

man, dark-haired, dark-browed, his face stern with grief. 'He's gone, Isolde, he's gone. May he rest in peace.'

Her white face crumpled and she put her hands over her eyes. 'He didn't ask for me? Not even at the end?'

'He didn't want you to see him in pain. He wanted you to remember him as he had been, strong and healthy. But his last words were to send you his blessing, and his last thoughts were of your future.'

She shook her head. 'I can't believe he would not give me his blessing.'

Giorgio turned from her and spoke to the priest, who hurried at once to the back of the chapel. Isolde heard the big bell start to toll; everyone would know that the great crusader, the Lord of Lucretili, was dead.

'I must pray for him,' she said quietly. 'You'll bring his body here?'

He nodded.

'I will share the vigil tonight,' she decided. 'I will sit beside him now that he is dead though he didn't allow it while he lived.' She paused. 'He didn't leave me a letter? Nothing?'

'His will,' her brother said softly. 'He planned for you. At the very end of his life he was thinking of you.'

She nodded, her dark blue eyes filling with tears, then she clasped her hands together, and prayed for her father's soul.

Isolde spent the first long night of her father's death in a silent vigil beside his coffin, which lay in the family chapel. Four of his men-at-arms stood, one at each point of the compass, their heads bowed over their broadswords, the light from the tall wax candles glittering on the holy water that had been sprinkled on the coffin lid. Isolde, dressed in white, knelt before the coffin all night long until dawn when the priest came to say Prime, the first office of prayers of the day. Only then did she rise up and let her ladies-in-waiting help her to her room to sleep, until a message from her brother told her that she must get up and show herself, it was time for dinner and the household would want to see their lady.

She did not hesitate. She had been raised to do her duty by the great household and she had a sense of obligation to the people who lived on the lands of Lucretili. Her father, she knew, had left the castle and the lands to her; these people were in her charge. They would want to see her at the head of the table, they would want to see her enter the great hall. Even if her eyes were red from crying over the loss of a very beloved father, they would expect her to dine with them. Her father himself would have expected it. She would not fail them or him.

There was a sudden hush as she entered the great hall where the servants were sitting at trestle tables, talking quietly, waiting for dinner to be served. More than two hundred men-at-arms, servants and grooms filled the hall, where the smoke from the central fire coiled up to the darkened beams of the high ceiling.

As soon as the men saw Isolde followed by the three women of her household, they rose to their feet and pulled their hats from their heads, and bowed low to honour the daughter of the late Lord of Lucretili, and the heiress to the castle.

Isolde was wearing the deep blue of mourning: a high conical hat draped in indigo lace hiding her fair hair, a priceless belt of Arabic gold worn tightly at the high waist of her gown, the keys to the castle on a gold chain at her side. Behind her came her women companions, firstly Ishraq, her childhood friend, wearing Moorish dress, a long tunic over loose pantaloons with a long veil over her head held lightly across her face so that only her dark eyes were visible as she looked around the hall.

Two other women followed behind her and as the household whispered their blessings on Isolde, the women took their seats at the ladies' table to the side of the raised dais. Isolde went up the shallow stairs to the great table, and recoiled at the sight of her brother in the wooden chair, as grand as a throne, that had been their father's seat. She knew that she should have anticipated he would be there, just as he knew that she would inherit this castle and would take the great chair as soon as the will was read. But she was dull with grief, and she had not thought that from now on she would always see her brother where her father ought to be. She was so new to grief that she had not yet fully realised that she would never see her father again.

Giorgio smiled blandly at her, and gestured that she should take her seat at his right hand, where she used to sit beside her father.

'And you will remember Prince Roberto.' Giorgio indicated a fleshy man with a round sweating face on his left, who rose and came around the table to bow to her. Isolde gave her hand to the prince and looked questioningly at her brother. 'He has come to sympathise with us for our loss.'

The prince kissed her hand and Isolde tried not to flinch from the damp touch of his lips. He looked at her as if he wanted to whisper something, as if they might share a secret. Isolde took back her hand, and bent towards her brother's ear. 'I am surprised you have a guest at dinner when my father died only yesterday.'

'It was good of him to come at once,' Giorgio said, beckoning the servers who came down the hall, their trays held at shoulder height loaded with game, meat, and fish dishes, great loaves of bread and flagons of wine and jugs of ale.

The castle priest sang grace and then the servers banged down the trays of food, the men drew their daggers from their belts and their boots to carve their portions of meat, and heaped slices of thick brown bread with poached fish, and stewed venison.

It was hard for Isolde to eat dinner in the great hall as if nothing had changed, when her dead father lay in his vigil, guarded in the chapel by his men-at-arms, and would be buried the next day. She found that tears kept blurring the sight of the servants coming in, carrying more food for each table, banging down jugs of small ale, and bringing the best dishes and flagons of best red wine to the top table where Giorgio and his guest the prince picked the best and sent

23

the rest down the hall to those men who had served them well during the day. The prince and her brother ate a good dinner and called for more wine. Isolde picked at her food and glanced down to the women's table where Ishraq met her gaze with silent sympathy.

When they had finished, and the sugared fruits and marchpane had been offered to the top table, and taken away, Giorgio touched her hand. 'Don't go to your rooms just yet,' he said. 'I want to talk to you.'

Isolde nodded to dismiss Ishraq and her ladies from their dining table and send them back to the ladies' rooms, then she went through the little door behind the dais to the private room where the Lucretili family sat after dinner. A fire was burning against the wall and there were three chairs drawn up around it. A flagon of wine was set ready for the men, a glass of small ale for Isolde. As she took her seat the two men came in together.

'I want to talk to you about our father's will,' Giorgio said, once they were seated.

Isolde glanced towards Prince Roberto.

'Roberto is concerned in this,' Giorgio explained. 'When Father was dying he said that his greatest hope was to know that you would be safe and happy. He loved you very dearly.'

Isolde pressed her fingers to her cold lips and blinked the tears from her eyes.

'I know,' her brother said gently. 'I know you are grieving. But you have to know that Father made plans for you and gave to me the sacred trust of carrying them out.'

'Why didn't he tell me so himself?' she asked. 'Why would he not talk to me? We always talked of everything together. I know what he planned for me; he said if I chose not to marry then I was to live here, I would inherit this castle and you would have his castle and lands in France. We agreed this. We all three agreed this.'

'We agreed it when he was well,' Giorgio said patiently. 'But when he became sick and fearful, he changed his mind. And then he could not bear for you to see him so very ill and in so much pain. When he thought about you then, with the very jaws of death opening before him, he thought better of his first plan. He wanted to be certain that you would be safe. Then, he planned well for you – he suggested that you marry Prince Roberto here, and agreed that we should take a thousand crowns from the treasury as your dowry.'

It was a tiny payment for a woman who had been raised to think of herself as heiress to this castle, the fertile pastures, the thick woods, the high mountains. Isolde gaped at him. 'Why so little?'

'Because the prince here has done us the honour of indicating that he will accept you just as you are – with no more than a thousand crowns in your pocket.'

'And you shall keep it all,' the man assured her, pressing her hand as it rested on the arm of her chair. 'You shall have it to spend on whatever you want. Pretty things for a pretty princess.'

Isolde looked at her brother, her dark blue eyes narrowing as she understood what this meant. 'A dowry as small as this will mean that no-one else will offer for me,' she said. 'You know that. And yet you did not ask for more? You did not warn Father that this would leave me without any prospects at all? And Father? Did he want to force me to marry the prince?'

The prince put his hand on his fleshy chest and cast his

eyes modestly down. 'Most ladies would not require forcing,' he pointed out.

'I know of no better husband that you might have,' Giorgio said smoothly. His friend smiled and nodded at her. 'And Father thought so too. We agreed this dowry with Prince Roberto and he was so pleased to marry you that he did not specify that you should bring a greater fortune than this. There is no need to accuse anyone of failing to guard your interests. What could be better for you than marriage to a family friend, a prince, and a wealthy man?'

It took her only a moment to decide. 'I cannot think of marriage,' Isolde said flatly. 'Forgive me, Prince Roberto. But it is too soon after my father's death. I cannot bear even to think of it, let alone talk of it.'

'We have to talk of it,' Giorgio insisted. 'The terms of our father's will are that we have to get you settled. He would not allow any delay. Either immediate marriage to my friend here, or . . .' He paused.

'Or what?' Isolde asked, suddenly afraid.

'The abbey,' he said simply. 'Father said that if you would not marry, I was to appoint you as abbess and that you should go there to live.'

'Never!' Isolde exclaimed. 'My father would never have done this to me!'

Giorgio nodded. 'I too was surprised, but he said that it was the future he had planned for you all along. That was why he did not fill the post when the last abbess died. He was thinking even then, a year ago, that you must be kept safe. You can't be exposed to the dangers of the world, left here alone at Lucretili. If you don't want to marry, you must be kept safe in the abbey.'

Prince Roberto smiled slyly at her. 'A nun or a princess,' he suggested. 'I would think you would find it easy to choose.'

Isolde jumped to her feet. 'I cannot believe Father planned this for me,' she said. 'He never suggested anything like this. He was clear he would divide the lands between us. He knew how much I love it here; how I love these lands and know these people. He said he would will this castle and the lands to me, and give you our lands in France.'

Giorgio shook his head as if in gentle regret. 'No, he changed his mind. As the oldest child, the only son, the only true heir, I will have everything, both in France and here, and you, as a woman, will have to leave.'

'Giorgio, my brother, you cannot send me from my home?'

He spread his hands. 'There is nothing I can do. It is our father's last wish and I have it in writing, signed by him. You will either marry – and no-one will have you but Prince Roberto – or you will go to the abbey. It was good of him to give you this choice. Many fathers would simply have left orders.'

'Excuse me,' Isolde said, her voice shaking as she fought to control her anger, 'I shall leave you and go to my rooms and think about this.'

'Don't take too long!' Prince Roberto said with an intimate smile. 'I won't wait too long.'

'I shall give you my answer tomorrow.' She paused in the doorway, and looked back at her brother. 'May I see my father's letter?'

Giorgio nodded and drew it from inside his jacket. 'You can keep this. It is a copy. I have the other in safe-keeping;

there is no doubt as to his wishes. You will have to consider not whether you will obey him, but only how you obey him. He knew that you would obey him.'

'I know,' she said. 'I am his daughter. Of course I will obey him.' She went from the room without looking at the prince, though he rose to his feet and made her a flourishing bow, and then winked at Giorgio as if he thought the matter settled.

Isolde woke in the night to hear a quiet tap on her door. Her pillow was damp beneath her cheek; she had been crying in her sleep. For a moment she wondered why she felt such a pain, as if she were heartbroken – and then she remembered the coffin in the chapel and the silent knights keeping watch. She crossed herself: 'God bless him, and save his soul,' she whispered. 'God comfort me in this sorrow. I don't know that I can bear it.'

The little tap came again, and she put back the richly embroidered covers of her bed and went to the door, the key in her hand. 'Who is it?'

'It is Prince Roberto. I have to speak with you.'

'I can't open the door, I will speak with you tomorrow.'

'I need to speak to you tonight. It is about the will, your father's wishes.'

She hesitated. 'Tomorrow . . .'

'I think I can see a way out for you. I understand how you feel, I think I can help.'

'What way out?'

'I can't shout it through the door. Just open the door a crack so that I can whisper.'

'Just a crack,' she said, and turned the key, keeping her foot pressed against the bottom of the door to ensure that it opened only a little.

As soon as he heard the key turn, the prince banged the door open with such force that it hit Isolde's head and sent her reeling back into the room. He slammed the door behind him and turned the key, locking them in together.

'You thought you would reject me?' he demanded furiously, as she scrambled to her feet. 'You thought you – practically penniless – would reject me? You thought I would beg to speak to you through a closed door?'

'How dare you force your way in here?' Isolde demanded, white-faced and furious. 'My brother would kill you—'

'Your brother allowed it,' he laughed. 'Your brother approves me as your husband. He himself suggested that I come to you. Now get on the bed.'

'My brother?' She could feel her shock turning into horror as she realised that she had been betrayed by her own brother, and that now this stranger was coming towards her, his fat face creased in a confident smile.

'He said I might as well take you now as later,' he said. 'You can fight me if you like. It makes no difference to me. I like a fight. I like a woman of spirit, they are more obedient in the end.'

'You are mad,' she said with certainty.

'Whatever you like. But I consider you my betrothed

29

wife, and we are going to consummate our betrothal right now, so you don't make any mistake tomorrow.'

'You're drunk,' she said, smelling the sour stink of wine on his breath.

'Yes, thank God, and you can get used to that too.'

He came towards her, shrugging his jacket off his fleshy shoulders. She shrank back until she felt the tall wooden pole of the four-poster bed behind her, blocking her retreat. She put her hands behind her back so that he could not grab them, and felt the velvet of the counterpane, and beneath it the handle of the brass warming pan filled with hot embers that had been pushed between the cold sheets.

'Please,' she said. 'This is ridiculous. It is an offence against hospitality. You are our guest, my father's body lies in the chapel. I am without defence, and you are drunk on our wine. Please go to your room and I will speak kindly to you in the morning.'

'No,' he leered. 'I don't think so. I think I shall spend the night here in your bed and I am very sure you will speak kindly to me in the morning.'

Behind her back, Isolde's fingers closed on the handle of the warming pan. As Roberto paused to untie the laces on the front of his breeches, she got a sickening glimpse of grey linen poking out. He reached for her arm. 'This need not hurt you,' he said. 'You might even enjoy it . . .'

With a great swing she brought the warming pan round to clap him on the side of his head. Red-hot embers and ash dashed against his face and tumbled to the floor. He let out of a howl of pain as she drew back and hit him once again, hard, and he dropped down like a fat stunned ox before the slaughter.

She picked up a jug and flung water over the coals smouldering on the rug beneath him and then, cautiously, she kicked him gently with her slippered foot. He did not stir, he was knocked out cold. Isolde went to an inner room and unlocked the door, whispering 'Ishraq!' When the girl came, rubbing sleep from her eyes, Isolde showed her the man crumpled on the ground.

'Is he dead?' the girl asked calmly.

'No. I don't think so. Help me get him out of here.'

The two young women pulled the rug and the limp body of Prince Roberto slid along the floor, leaving a slimy trail of water and ashes. They got him into the gallery outside her room and paused.

'I take it your brother allowed him to come to you?'

Isolde nodded, and Ishraq turned her head and spat contemptuously on the prince's white face. 'Why ever did you open the door?'

'I thought he would help me. He said he had an idea to help me then he pushed his way in.'

'Did he hurt you?' The girl's dark eyes scanned her friend's face. 'Your forehead?'

'He knocked me when he pushed the door.'

'Was he going to rape you?'

Isolde nodded.

'Then let's leave him here,' Ishraq decided. 'He can come to on the floor like the dog that he is, and crawl to his room. If he's still here in the morning then the servants can find him and make him a laughing-stock.' She bent down and felt for his pulses at his throat, his wrists and under the bulging waistband of his breeches. 'He'll live,' she said certainly. 'Though he wouldn't be missed if we quietly cut his throat.'

'Of course we can't do that,' Isolde said shakily.

They left him there, laid out like a beached whale on his back, with his breeches still unlaced.

'Wait here,' Ishraq said and went back to her room.

She returned swiftly, with a small box in her hand. Delicately, using the tips of her fingers and scowling with distaste, she pulled at the prince's breeches so that they were gaping wide open. She lifted his linen shirt so that his limp nakedness was clearly visible. She took the lid from the box and shook the spice onto his bare skin.

'What are you doing?' Isolde whispered.

'It's a dried pepper, very strong. He is going to itch like he has the pox, and his skin is going to blister like he has a rash. He is going to regret this night's work very much. He is going to be itching and scratching and bleeding for a month, and he won't trouble another woman for a while.'

Isolde laughed and put out her hand, as her father would have done, and the two young women clasped forearms, hand to elbow, like knights. Ishraq grinned, and they turned and went back into the bedroom, closing the door on the humbled prince and locking it firmly against him.

In the morning, when Isolde went to chapel, her father's coffin was closed and ready for burial in the deep family vault – and the prince was gone.

'He has withdrawn his offer for your hand,' her brother said coldly as he took his place, kneeling beside her on the chancel steps. 'I take it that something passed between the two of you?'

'He's a villain,' Isolde said simply. 'And if you sent him to my door, as he claimed, then you are a traitor to me.'

He bowed his head. 'Of course I did no such thing. I am sorry, I got drunk like a fool and said that he could plead his case with you. Why ever did you open your door?'

'Because I believed your friend was an honourable man, as you did.'

'You were very wrong to unlock your door,' her brother reproached her. 'Opening your bedroom door to a man, to a drunk man! You don't know how to take care of yourself. Father was right, we have to place you somewhere safe.'

'I was safe! I was in my own room, in my own castle, speaking to my brother's friend. I should not have been at risk,' she said angrily. 'You should not have brought such a man to our dinner table. Father should never have been advised that he would make a good husband for me.'

She rose to her feet and went down the aisle, her brother following after her. 'Well anyway, what did you say to upset him?'

Isolde hid a smile at the thought of the warming pan crashing against the prince's fat head. 'I made my feelings clear. And I will never meet with him again.'

'Well, that's easily achieved,' Giorgio said bluntly. 'Because you will never be able to meet with any man again. If you will not marry Prince Roberto, then you will have to go to the abbey. Our father's will leaves you with no other choice.'

Isolde paused as his words sank in, and put a hesitant

hand on his arm, wondering how she could persuade him to let her go free.

'There's no need to look like that,' he said roughly. 'The terms of the will are clear, I told you last night. It was the prince or the nunnery. Now it is just the nunnery.'

'I will go on a pilgrimage,' she offered. 'Away from here.'

'You will not. How would you survive for one moment? You can't keep yourself safe even at home.'

'I will go and stay with some friends of Father's – anyone. I could go to my godfather's son, the Count of Wallachia, I could go to the Duke of Bradour ...'

His face was grim. 'You can't. You know you can't. You have to do as Father commanded you. I have no choice, Isolde. God knows I would do anything for you, but his will is clear, and I have to obey my father – just as you do.'

'Brother – don't force me to do this.'

He turned to the arched wall of the chapel doorway, and put his forehead to the cold stone, as if she was making his head ache. 'Sister, I can do nothing. Prince Roberto was your only chance to escape the abbey. It is our father's will. I am sworn on his sword, on his own broadsword, to see that his will is done. My sister – I am powerless, as you are.'

'He promised he would leave his broadsword to me.'

'It is mine now. As is everything else.'

Gently she put her hand on his shoulder. 'If I take an oath of celibacy, may I not stay here with you? I will marry no-one. The castle is yours, I see that. In the end he did what every man does and favoured his son over his daughter. In the end he did what all great men do and excluded a woman from wealth and power. But if I will live here, poor and powerless, never seeing a man, obedient to you, can I not stay here?'

He shook his head. 'It is not my will, but his. And it is – as you admit – the way of the world. He brought you up almost as if you had been born a boy, with too much wealth and freedom. But now you must live the life of a noble-woman. You should be glad at least that the abbey is nearby, and so you don't have to go far from these lands that I know you love. You've not been sent into exile – he could have ordered that you go anywhere. But instead you will be in our own property: the abbey. I will come and see you now and then. I will bring you news. Perhaps later you will be able to ride out with me.'

'Can Ishraq come with me?'

'You can take Ishraq, you can take all your ladies if you wish, and if they are willing to go. But they are expecting you at the abbey tomorrow. You will have to go, Isolde. You will have to take your vows as a nun and become their abbess. You have no choice.'

He turned back to her and saw she was trembling like a young mare will tremble when she is being forced into har-ness for the first time. 'It is like being imprisoned,' she whispered. 'And I have done nothing wrong.'

He had tears in his own eyes. 'It is like losing a sister,' he said. 'I am burying a father and losing a sister. I don't know how it will be without you here.'

THE ABBEY OF LUCRETILI,
OCTOBER 1453

A few months later, Luca was on the road from Rome, riding east, wearing a plain working robe and cape of ruddy brown, and newly equipped with a horse of his own.

He was accompanied by his servant Freize, a broad-shouldered, square-faced youth, just out of his teens, who had plucked up his courage when Luca left their monastery, and volunteered to work for the young man, and follow him wherever the quest might take him. The abbot had been doubtful, but Freize had convinced him that his skills as a kitchen lad were so poor, and his love of adventure so strong, that he would serve God better by following a remarkable master on a secret quest ordained by the Pope himself, than by burning the bacon for the long-suffering monks. The abbot, secretly glad to lose the challenging young novice priest, thought the loss of an accident-prone spit lad was a small price to pay.

Freize rode a strong cob and led a donkey laden with their belongings. At the rear of the little procession was a surprise addition to their partnership: a clerk, Brother Peter, who had been ordered to travel with them at the last moment, to keep a record of their work.

'A spy,' Freize muttered out of the side of his mouth to his new master. 'A spy if ever I saw one. Pale-faced, soft hands, trusting brown eyes: the shaved head of a monk and yet the clothes of a gentleman. A spy without a doubt.

'Is he spying on me? No, for I don't do anything and know nothing. Who is he spying on, then? Must be the young master, my little sparrow. For there is no-one else but the horses and they're not heretics, nor pagans. They are the only honest beasts here.'

'He is here to serve as my clerk,' Luca replied irritably. 'And I have to have him whether I need a clerk or no. So hold your tongue.'

'Do I need a clerk?' Freize asked himself as he reined in his horse. 'No. For I do nothing and know nothing and, if I did, I wouldn't write it down – not trusting words on a page. Also, not being able to read or write would likely prevent me.'

'Fool,' the clerk Peter said as he rode by.

'"Fool," he says,' Freize remarked to his horse's ears and to the gently climbing road before them. 'Easy to say: hard to prove. And anyway, I have been called worse.'

They had been riding all day on a track little more than a narrow path for goats, which wound upwards out of the fertile valley, alongside little terraced slopes growing olives and vines, and then higher into the woodland where the huge beech trees were turning gold and bronze. At sunset, when the arching skies above them went rosy pink, the clerk drew a paper from the inner pocket of his jacket. 'I was ordered to give you this at sunset,' he said. 'Forgive me if it is bad news. I don't know what it says.'

'Who gave it you?' Luca asked. The seal on the back of the folded letter was shiny and smooth, unmarked with any crest.

'The lord who hired me, the same lord who commands you,' Peter said. 'This is how your orders will come. He tells me a day and a time, or sometimes a destination, and I give you your orders then and there.'

'Got them tucked away in your pocket all the time?' Freize inquired.

Grandly, the clerk nodded.

'Could always turn him upside down and shake him,' Freize remarked quietly to his master.

'We'll do this as we are ordered to do it,' Luca replied, looping the reins of his horse casually around his shoulder to leave his hands free to break the seal to open the folded paper. 'It's an instruction to go to the abbey of Lucretili,' he said. 'The abbey is set between two houses, a nunnery and a monastery. I am to investigate the nunnery. They are expecting us.' He folded the letter and gave it back to Peter.

'Does it say how to find them?' Freize asked gloomily. 'For otherwise it's bed under the trees and nothing but cold bread for supper. Beechnuts, I suppose. All you could eat of beechnuts. You could go mad with gluttony on them. I suppose I might get lucky and find us a mushroom.'

'The road is just up ahead,' Peter interrupted. 'The abbey is near to the castle. I should think we can claim hospitality at either monastery or nunnery.'

'We'll go to the convent,' Luca ruled. 'It says that they are expecting us.'

It did not look as if the convent was expecting anyone. It was growing dark, but there were no warm welcoming lights showing and no open doors. The shutters were closed at all the windows in the outer wall, and only narrow beams of flickering candlelight shone through the slats. In the darkness they could not tell how big it was; they just had a sense of great walls marching off either side of the wide-arched entrance gateway. A dim horn lantern was hung by the small door set in the great wooden gate, throwing a thin yellow light downward, and when Freize dismounted and hammered on the wooden gate with the handle of his dagger they could hear someone inside protesting at the noise and then opening a little spy hole in the door, to peer out at them.

'I am Luca Vero, with my two servants,' Luca shouted. 'I am expected. Let us in.'

The spy hole slammed shut, then they could hear the slow unbolting of the gate and the lifting of wooden bars and, finally, one side of the gate creaked reluctantly open.

Freize led his horse and the donkey, Luca and Peter rode into the cobbled yard as a sturdy woman-servant pushed the gate shut behind them. The men dismounted and looked around as a wizened old lady in a habit of grey wool, with a tabard of grey tied at her waist by a plain rope, held up the torch she was carrying, to inspect the three of them.

'Are you the man they sent to make inquiry? For if you are not, and it is hospitality that you want, you had better go on to the monastery, our brother house,' she said to Peter, looking at him and his fine horse. 'This house is in troubled times, we don't want guests.'

'No, I am to write the report. I am the clerk to the inquiry. This is Luca Vero, he is here to inquire.'

'A boy!' she exclaimed scornfully. 'A beardless boy?'

Luca flushed in irritation, then swung his leg over the neck of his horse, and jumped down to the ground, throwing the reins to Freize. 'It doesn't matter how many years I have, or if I have a beard or not. I am appointed to make inquiry here, and I will do so tomorrow. In the meantime we are tired and hungry and you should show me to the refectory and to the guest rooms. Please inform the Lady Abbess that I am here and will see her after Prime tomorrow.'

'Rich in nothing,' the old woman remarked, holding up her torch to take another look at Luca's handsome young face, flushed under his dark fringe, his hazel eyes bright with anger.

'Rich in nothing, is it?' Freize questioned the horse as he led him to the stables ahead. 'A virgin so old that she is like a pickled walnut and she calls the little lord a beardless boy? And him a genius and perhaps a changeling?'

'You, take the horses to the stables and the lay sister there will take you to the kitchen,' she snapped with sudden energy at Freize. 'You can eat and sleep in the barn. You—' She took in the measure of Peter the clerk and judged him superior to Freize but still wanting. 'You can dine in the kitchen gallery. You'll find it through that doorway. They'll show you where to sleep in the guesthouse. You—' She turned to Luca. 'You, the inquirer, I will show to the refectory and to your own bedroom. They said you were a priest?'

'I have not yet said my vows,' he said. 'I am in the service of the Church, but I am not ordained.'

'Too handsome by far for the priesthood, and with his tonsure grown out already,' she said to herself. To Luca she said: 'You can sleep in the rooms for the visiting priest, anyway. And in the morning I will tell my Lady Abbess that you are here.'

She was leading the way to the refectory when a lady came through the archway from the inner cloister. Her habit was made of the softest bleached wool, the wimple on her head pushed back to show a pale lovely face with smiling grey eyes. The girdle at her waist was of the finest leather and she had soft leather slippers, not the rough wooden pattens that working women wore to keep their shoes out of the mud.

'I came to greet the inquirer,' she said, holding up the set of wax candles in her hand.

Luca stepped forwards. 'I am the inquirer,' he said.

She smiled, taking in his height, his good looks and his youth in one swift gaze. 'Let me take you to your dinner, you must be weary. Sister Anna here will see that your horses are stabled and your men comfortable.'

He bowed and she turned ahead of him, leaving him to follow her through the stone archway, along a flagged gallery that opened into the arching refectory room. At the far end, near the fire that was banked in for the night, a place had been laid for one person; there was wine in the glass, bread on the plate, a knife and spoon either side of a bowl. Luca sighed with pleasure and sat down in the chair as a maidservant came in with a ewer and bowl to wash his hands, good linen to dry them, and behind her came a kitchen maid with a bowl of stewed chicken and vegetables.

'You have everything that you need?' the lady asked.

'Thank you,' he said awkwardly. He was uncomfortable in her presence; he had not spoken to a woman other than his mother since he had been sworn into the monastery at the age of eleven. 'And you are?'

She smiled at him and he realised in the glow of her smile that she was beautiful. 'I am Sister Ursula, the Lady Almoner, responsible for the management of the abbey. I am glad you have come. I have been very anxious. I hope you can tell us what is happening and save us . . .'

'Save you?'

'This is a long-established and beautiful nunnery,' Sister Ursula said earnestly. 'I joined it when I was just a little girl. I have served God and my sisters here for all my life, I have been here for more than twenty years. I cannot bear the thought that Satan has entered in.'

Luca dipped his bread in the rich thick gravy, and concentrated on the food to hide his consternation. 'Satan?'

She crossed herself, a quick unthinking gesture of devotion. 'Some days I think it really is that bad, other days I think

I am like a foolish girl, frightening myself with shadows.' She gave him a shy, apologetic smile. 'You will be able to judge. You will discover the truth of it all. But if we cannot rid ourselves of the gossip we will be ruined: no family will send their daughters to us, and now the farmers are starting to refuse to trade with us. It is my duty to make sure that the abbey earns its own living, that we sell our goods and farm produce in order to buy what we need. I can't do that if the farmers' wives refuse to speak with us when I send my lay sisters with our goods to market. We can't trade if the people will neither sell to us nor buy from us.' She shook her head. 'Anyway, I will leave you to eat. The kitchen maid will show you to your bedroom in the guesthouse when you have finished eating. Bless you, my brother.'

Luca suddenly realised he had quite forgotten to say grace: she would think he was an ignorant mannerless hedge friar. He had stared at her like a fool and stammered when he spoke to her. He had behaved like a young man who had never seen a beautiful woman before and not at all like a man of some importance, come to head a papal inquiry. What must she think of him? 'Bless you, Lady Almoner,' he said awkwardly.

She bowed, hiding a little smile at his confusion, and walked slowly from the room, and he watched the sway of the hem of her gown as she left.

On the east side of the enclosed abbey, the shutter of the ground-floor window was slightly open so that two pairs of eyes could watch the Lady Almoner's candle illuminate her pale silhouette as she walked gracefully across the yard and then vanished into her house.

'She's greeted him, but she won't have told him anything,' Isolde whispered.

'He will find nothing unless someone helps him,' Ishraq agreed.

The two drew back from the window and noiselessly closed the shutter. 'I wish I could see my way clear,' Isolde said. 'I wish I knew what to do. I wish I had someone who could advise me.'

'What would your father have done?'

Isolde laughed shortly. 'My father would never have let himself be forced in here. He would have laid down his life before he allowed someone to imprison him. Or, if captured, he would have died attempting to escape. He wouldn't just have sat here, like a doll, like a cowardly girl, crying, missing him, and not knowing what to do.'

She turned away and roughly rubbed her eyes. Ishraq put a gentle hand on her shoulder. 'Don't blame yourself,' she said. 'There was nothing we could do when we first came here. And now that the whole abbey is falling apart around us, we can still do nothing until we understand what is going on. But everything is changing even while we wait, powerless. Even if we do nothing; something is going to happen. This is our chance. Perhaps this is the moment when the door swings open. We're going to be ready for our chance.'

Isolde took the hand from her shoulder and held it against her cheek. 'At least I have you.'

'Always.'

Luca slept heavily; not even the church bell tolling the hour in the tower above his head could wake him. But, just when the night was darkest, before three in the morning, a sharp scream cut through his sleep and then he heard the sound of running feet.

Luca was up and out of his bed in a moment, his hand snatching for the dagger under his pillow, peering out of his window at the dark yard. A glint of moonlight shining on the cobblestones showed him a woman in white racing across the yard to scrabble at the beams barring the heavy wooden gate. Three women pursued her, and the old porteress came running out of the gatehouse and grabbed the woman's hands as she clawed like a cat at the timbers.

The other women were quick to catch the girl from behind and Luca heard her sharp wail of despair as they grabbed hold of her, and saw her knees buckle as she went down under their weight. He pulled on his breeches and boots, threw a cape over his naked shoulders, then sprinted from his room, out into the yard, tucking the dagger out of sight in the scabbard in his boot. He stepped back into the shadow of the building, certain they had not noticed him, determined to see their faces in the shadowy light of the moon, so that he would know them, when he saw them again.

The porteress held up her torch as they lifted the girl, two women holding her shoulders, the third supporting her legs. As they carried her past him, Luca shrank back into the concealing darkness of the doorway. They were so close that he could hear their panting breaths, one of them was sobbing quietly.

It was the strangest sight. The girl's hand had swung down as they lifted her; now she was quite unconscious. It seemed that she had fainted when they had pulled her from the barred gate. Her head was rolled back, the little laces from her nightcap brushing the ground as they carried her, her long nightgown trailing in the dust. But it was no normal fainting fit. She was as limp as a corpse, her eyes closed, her young face serene. Then Luca gave a little hiss of horror. The girl's swinging hand was pierced in the palm, the wound oozing blood. They had folded her other hand across her slight body and Luca could see a smudge of blood on her nightgown. She had the hands of a girl crucified. Luca froze where he stood, forcing himself to stay hidden in the shadows, unable to look away from the strange terrible wounds. And then he saw something that seemed even worse.

All three women carrying the sleeping girl wore her expression of rapt serenity. As they shuffled along, carrying their limp bleeding burden, all three were slightly smiling, all three were radiant as if with an inner secret joy.

And their eyes were closed like hers.

Luca waited till they had sleepwalked past him, steady as

pall-bearers, then he went back into the guesthouse room and knelt at the side of his bed, praying fervently for guidance to somehow find the wisdom, despite his self-doubt, to discover what was so very wrong in this holy place, and put it right.

He was still on his knees in prayer when Freize banged open the door with a jug of hot water for washing, just before dawn. 'Thought you'd want to go to Prime.'

'Yes.' Luca rose stiffly, crossed himself, and kissed the cross that always hung around his neck, a gift from his mother on his fourteenth birthday, the last time he had seen her.

'Bad things are happening here,' Freize said portentously, splashing the water into a bowl and putting a clean strip of linen beside it.

Luca sluiced his face and hands with water. 'I know it. God knows, I have seen some of it. What do you hear?'

'Sleepwalking, visions, the nuns fasting on feast days, starving themselves and fainting in the chapel. Some of them are seeing lights in the sky, like the star before the Magi, and then some wanted to set off for Bethlehem and had to be restrained. The people of the village and the servants from the castle say they're all going mad. They say the whole abbey is touched with madness and the women are losing their wits.'

Luca shook his head. 'The saints alone know what is going on here. Did you hear the screams in the night?'

'Lord save us, no. I slept in the kitchen and all I could hear was snoring. But all the cooks say that the Pope should send a bishop to inquire. They say that Satan is walking here. The Pope should set up an inquiry.'

'He has done! That's me,' Luca snapped. 'I shall hold an inquiry. I shall be the judge.'

'Course you will,' Freize encouraged him. 'Doesn't matter how old you are.'

'Actually, it *doesn't* matter how old I am. What matters is that I am appointed to inquire.'

'You'd better start with the new Lady Abbess, then.'

'Why?'

'Because it all started as soon as she got here.'

'I won't listen to kitchen gossip,' Luca declared haughtily, rubbing his face. He tossed the cloth to Freize. 'I shall have a proper inquiry with witnesses and people giving evidence under oath. For I am the inquirer, appointed by the Pope, and it would be better if everyone remembered it. Especially those people who are supposed to be in service to me, who should be supporting my reputation.'

'Course I do! Course you are! Course you will! You're the lord and I never forget it, though still only a little one.' Freize shook out Luca's linen shirt and then handed him his novice's robe, which he wore belted high, out of the way of his long stride. Luca strapped his short sword on his belt and notched it round his waist, dropping the robe over the sword to hide it.

'You speak to me like I was a child,' Luca said irritably. 'And you're no great age yourself.'

'It's affection,' Freize said firmly. 'It's how I show affection. And respect. To me, you'll always be "Sparrow", the skinny novice.'

'"Goose", the kitchen boy,' Luca replied with a grin.

'Got your dagger?' Freize checked.

Luca tapped the cuff of his boot where the dagger was safe in the scabbard.

'They all say that the new Lady Abbess had no vocation, and was not raised to the life,' Freize volunteered, ignoring Luca's ban on gossip. 'Her father's will sent her in here and she took her vows and she'll never get out again. It's the only inheritance her father left her, everything else went to the brother. Bad as being walled up. And, ever since she came, the nuns have started to see things and cry out. Half the village says that Satan came in with the new abbess. Cause she was unwilling.'

'And what do they say the brother is like?' Luca asked, tempted to gossip despite his resolution.

'Nothing but good of him. Good landlord, generous with the abbey. His grandfather built the abbey with a nunnery on one side and a brother house for the monks nearby. The nuns and the monks share the services in the abbey. His father endowed both houses and handed the woods and the high pasture over to the nuns, and gave some farms and fields to the monastery. They run themselves as independent houses, working together for the glory of God, and helping the poor. Now the new lord in his turn supports it. His father was a crusader, famously brave, very hot on religion. The new lord sounds quieter, stays at home, wants a bit of peace. Very keen that this is kept quiet, that you make your inquiry, take your decision, report the guilty, exorcise whatever is going on, and everything gets back to normal.'

Above their heads the bell tolled for Prime, the dawn prayer.

'Come on,' Luca said, and led the way from the visiting priest's rooms towards the cloisters and the beautiful church.

They could hear the music as they crossed the yard, their way lit by a procession of white-gowned nuns, carrying torches and singing as they went like a choir of angels gliding through the pearly light of the morning. Luca stepped back, and even Freize fell silent at the beauty of the voices rising faultlessly into the dawn sky. Then the two men, joined by Brother Peter, followed the choir into the church and took their seats in an alcove at the back. Two hundred nuns, veiled with white wimples, filled the stalls of the choir either side of the screened altar, and stood in rows facing it.

The service was a sung Mass; the voice of the serving priest at the altar rang out the sacred Latin words in a steady baritone, and the sweet high voices of the women answered. Luca gazed at the vaulting ceiling, the beautiful columns carved with stone fruit and flowers, and above them, stars and moons of silver-painted stone, all the while listening to the purity of the responses and wondering what could be tormenting such holy women every night, and how they could wake every dawn and sing like this to God.

At the end of the service, the three visiting men remained seated on the stone bench at the back of the chapel as the nuns filed out past them, their eyes modestly down. Luca scanned their faces, looking for the young woman he had seen in such a frenzy last night, but one pale young face veiled in white was identical to another. He tried to see their palms, for the telltale sign of scabs, but all the women kept their hands clasped together, hidden in their long sleeves. As they filed out, their sandals pattering quietly on the stone floor, the priest followed them, and stopped before the young men to say pleasantly, 'I'll break my fast with you and then I have to go back to my side of the abbey.'

'Are you not a resident priest?' Luca asked, first shaking the man's hand and then kneeling for his blessing.

'We have a monastery just the other side of the great house,' the priest explained. 'The first Lord of Lucretili chose to found two religious houses: one for men and one for women. We priests come over daily to take the services. Alas, this house is of the order of Augustine nuns. We men are of the Dominican order.' He leaned towards Luca. 'As you'd understand, I think it would be better for everyone if the nunnery were put under the discipline of the Dominican order. They could be supervised from our monastery and enjoy the discipline of our order. Under the Augustinian order these women have been allowed to simply do as they please. And now you see what happens.'

'They observe the services,' Luca protested. 'They're not running wild.'

'Only because they choose to do so. If they wanted to stop or to change, then they could. They have no rule, unlike us Dominicans, for whom everything is set down. Under the Augustinian order every house can live as they please. They serve God as they think best and as a result—'

He broke off as the Lady Almoner came up, treading quietly on the beautiful marble floor of the church. 'Well, here is my Lady Almoner come to bid us to breakfast, I am sure.'

'You can take breakfast in my parlour,' she said. 'There is a fire lit there. Please, Father, show our guests the way.'

'I will, I will,' he said pleasantly and, as she left them, he turned to Luca. 'She holds this place together,' he said. 'A remarkable woman. Manages the farmlands, maintains the buildings, buys the goods, sells the produce. She could have been the lady of any castle in Italy, a natural Magistra: a teacher, a leader, a natural lady of any great house.' He beamed. 'And, I have to say, her parlour is the most comfortable room in this place and her cook second to none.'

He led the way out of the church across the cloister through the entrance yard to the house that formed the eastern side of the courtyard. The wooden front door stood open, and they went into the parlour, where a table was already laid for the three of them. Luca and Peter took their seats. Freize stood at the doorway to serve the men as one of the lay-woman cooks passed him dishes to set on the table. They had three sorts of roasted meats: ham, lamb and beef; and two types of bread: white manchet and dark rye. There were local cheeses, and jams, a basket of hard-boiled eggs, and a bowl of plums with a taste so strong that Luca sliced them on a slice of wheat bread to eat like sweet jam.

'Does the Lady Almoner always eat privately and not dine with her sisters in the refectory?' Luca asked curiously.

'Wouldn't you, if you had a cook like this?' the priest asked. 'High days and holy days, I don't doubt that she sits with her sisters. But she likes things done just so; and one of the privileges of her office is that she has things as she likes them, in her own house. She doesn't sleep in a dormitory nor eat in the refectory. The Lady Abbess is the same in her own house next door.

'Now,' he said with a broad smile. 'I have a drop of brandy in my saddlebag. I'll pour us a measure. It settles the belly after a good breakfast.' He went out of the room and Peter got to his feet and looked out of the window at the entry courtyard where the priest's mule was waiting.

Idly, Luca glanced round the room as Freize cleared their plates. The chimney breast was a beautifully carved wall of polished wood. When Luca had been a little boy his grand-father, a carpenter, had made just such a carved chimney breast for the hall of their farmhouse. Then, it had been an innovation and the envy of the village. Behind one of the carvings had been a secret cupboard where his father had kept sugared plums, which he gave to Luca on a Sunday, if he had been good all the week. On a whim, Luca turned the five bosses along the front of the carved chimney breast one after the other. One yielded under his hand and, to his sur-prise, a hidden door swung open, just like the one he'd known as a child. Behind it was a glass jar holding not sug-ared plums but some sort of spice: dried black seeds. Beside it was a cobbler's awl – a little tool for piercing lace holes in leather.

Luca shut the cupboard door. 'My father always used to hide sugared plums in the chimney cupboard,' he remarked.

'We didn't have anything like this,' Peter the clerk replied. 'We all lived in the kitchen, and my mother turned her roast meats on the spit in the fireplace and smoked all her hams in the chimney. When it was morning and the fire was out and we children were really hungry, we'd put our heads up into the soot and nibble at the fatty edges of the hams. She used to tell my father it was mice, God bless her.'

'How did you get your learning in such a poor house?' Luca asked.

Peter shrugged. 'The priest saw that I was a bright boy, so my parents sent me to the monastery.'

'And then?'

'Milord asked me if I would serve him, serve the order. Of course I said yes.'

The door opened and the priest returned, a small bottle discreetly tucked into the sleeve of his robe. 'Just a drop helps me on my way,' he said. Luca took a splash of the strong liquor in his earthenware cup, Peter refused, and the priest took a hearty swig from the mouth of the bottle. Freize looked longingly from the doorway, but decided against saying anything.

'Now I'll take you to the Lady Abbess,' the priest said, carefully stoppering the cork. 'And you'll bear in mind, if she asks you for advice, that she could put this nunnery under the care of her brother monastery, we would run it for her, and all her troubles would be over.'

'I'll remember,' Luca said, without committing himself to one view or the other.

The abbess's house was next door, built on the outer wall of the nunnery, facing inwards onto the cloister and outwards to the forest and the high mountains beyond. The windows that looked to the outer world were heavily leaded, and shielded with thick metal grilles.

'This place is built like a square within a square,' the priest told them. 'The inner square is made up of the church, with the cloister and the nuns' cells around it. This house extends from the cloister to the outer courtyard. The Lady Almoner's half of the house faces the courtyard and the main gate, so she can see all the comings and goings, and the south wall is the hospital for the poor.'

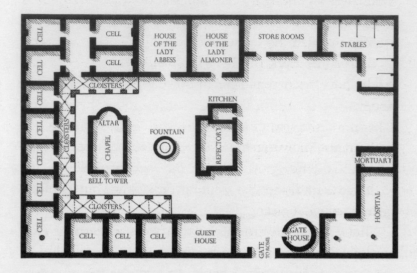

The priest gestured towards the door. 'The Lady Abbess said for you to go in.' He stood back, and Luca and Peter went in, Freize behind them. They found themselves in a small room furnished with two wooden benches and two very plain chairs. A strong wrought-iron grille in the wall on the far side blocked the opening into the next room, veiled by a curtain of white wool. As they stood waiting, the curtain was silently drawn back and on the other side they could just make out a white robe, a wimple headdress, and a pale face through the obscuring mesh of the metal.

'God bless you and keep you,' a clear voice said. 'I welcome you to this abbey. I am the Lady Abbess here.'

'I am Luca Vero.' Luca stepped up to the grille, but he could see only the silhouette of a woman through the richly wrought ironwork of grapes, fruit, leaves and flowers. There was a faint light perfume, like rosewater. Behind the lady, he could just make out the shadowy outline of another woman in a dark robe.

'This is my clerk Brother Peter, and my servant Freize. And I have been sent here to make an inquiry into your abbey.'

'I know,' she said quietly.

'I did not know that you were enclosed,' Luca said, careful not to offend.

'It is the tradition that visitors speak to the ladies of our order through a grille.'

'But I shall need to speak with them for my inquiry. I shall need them to come to report to me.'

He could sense her reluctance through the bars.

'Very well,' she said. 'Since we have agreed to your inquiry.'

Luca knew perfectly well, that this cool Lady Abbess had not agreed to the inquiry: she had been offered no choice in the matter. His inquiry had been sent to her house by the lord of the Order, and he would interrogate her sisters with or without her consent.

'I shall need a room for my private use, and the nuns will have to come and report to me, under oath, what has been happening here,' Luca said more confidently. At his side the priest nodded his approval.

'I have ordered them to prepare a room for you next door to this one,' she said. 'I think it better that you should hear evidence in my house, in the house of the Lady Abbess.

They will know then that I am co-operating with your inquiry, that they come here to speak to you under my blessing.'

'It would be better somewhere else altogether,' the priest said quietly to Luca. 'You should come to the monastery and order them to attend in our house, under our supervision. The rule of men, you know ... the logic of men ... always a powerful thing to invoke. This needs a man's mind on it, not a woman's fleeting whimsy.'

'Thank you, but I will meet them here,' Luca said to the priest. To the Lady Abbess he said, 'I thank you for your assistance. I am happy to meet with the nuns in your house.'

'But I do wonder why,' Freize prompted under his breath to a fat bee bumbling against the small leaded window pane.

'But I do wonder why,' Luca repeated out loud.

Freize opened the little window and released the bee out into the sunshine.

'There has been much scandal talked, and some of it directed against me,' the Lady Abbess said frankly. 'I have been accused personally. It is better that the house sees that the inquiry is under my control, is under my blessing. I hope that you will clear my name, as well as discovering any wrong-doing and rooting it out.'

'We will have to interview you, as well as all the members of the order,' Luca pointed out.

He could see through the grille that the white figure had moved, and realised she had bowed her head as if he had shamed her.

'I am ordered from Rome to help you to discover the truth,' he insisted.

She did not reply but merely turned her head and spoke

58

to someone out of his sight and then the door to the room opened and the elderly nun, the porteress Sister Anna who had greeted them on their first night, said abruptly, 'The Lady Abbess says I am to show you the room for your inquiry.'

It appeared that their interview with the Lady Abbess was over, and they had not even seen her face.

It was a plain room, looking out over the woods behind the abbey, in the back of the house so that they could not see the cloister, the nuns' cells, or the comings and goings of the courtyard before the church. But, equally, the community could not see who came to give evidence.

'Discreet,' Peter the clerk remarked.

'Secretive,' Freize said cheerfully. 'Am I to stand outside and make sure no-one interrupts or eavesdrops?'

'Yes.' Luca pulled up a chair to the empty table and waited while Brother Peter produced papers, a black quill pen and a pot of ink, then seated himself at the end of the table, and looked at Luca expectantly. The three young men paused. Luca, overwhelmed with the task that lay before him, looked blankly back at the other two. Freize grinned at him, and made an encouraging gesture like someone waving a flag. 'Onward!' he said. 'Things are so bad here, that we can't make them worse.'

Luca choked on a boyish laugh. 'I suppose so,' he said, taking his seat, and turned to Brother Peter. 'We'll start with the Lady Almoner,' he said, trying to speak decisively. 'At least we know her name.'

Freize nodded and went to the door. 'Fetch the Lady Almoner,' he said to Sister Anna.

She came straight away, and took a seat opposite Luca. He tried not to look at the serene beauty of her face, her grey knowing eyes that seemed to smile at him with some private knowledge.

Formally, he took her name, her age – twenty-four – the name of her parents, and the duration of her stay in the abbey. She had been behind the abbey walls for twenty years, since her earliest childhood.

'What do you think is happening here?' Luca asked her, emboldened by his position as the inquirer, by his sense of his own self-importance, and by the trappings of his work: Freize at the door, and Brother Peter with his black quill pen.

She looked down at the plain wooden table. 'I don't know. There are strange occurrences, and my sisters are very troubled.'

'What sort of occurrences?'

'Some of my sisters have started to have visions, and two of them have been rising up in their sleep – getting out of their beds and walking though their eyes are still closed. One cannot eat the food that is served in the refectory, she is starving herself and cannot be persuaded to eat. And there are other things. Other manifestations.'

'When did it start?' Luca asked her.

She nodded wearily, as if she expected such a question. 'It was about three months ago.'

'Was that when the new Lady Abbess came?'

A breath of a sigh. 'Yes. But I am convinced that she has nothing to do with it. I would not want to give evidence to an inquiry that was used against her. Our troubles started then – but you must remember she has no authority with the nuns, being so new, so inexperienced, having declared herself unwilling. A nunnery needs strong leadership, supervision, a woman who loves the life here. The new Lady Abbess lived a very sheltered life before she came to us, she was the favoured child of a great lord, the indulged daughter of a great house; she is not accustomed to command a religious house. She was not raised here. It is not surprising that she does not know how to command.'

'Could the nuns be commanded to stop seeing visions? Is it within their choice? Has she failed them through her inability to command?'

Peter the clerk made a note of the question.

The Lady Almoner smiled. 'Not if they are true visions from God,' she said easily. 'If they are true visions, then nothing would stop them. But if they are errors and folly, if they are women frightening themselves and allowing their fears to rule them ... If they are women dreaming and making up stories ... Forgive me for being so blunt, Brother Luca, but I have lived in this community for twenty years and I know that two hundred women living together can whip up a storm over nothing if they are allowed to do so.'

Luca raised his eyebrows. 'They can invoke sleepwalking? They can invoke running out at night and trying to get out of the gates?'

She sighed. 'You saw?'

'Last night,' he confirmed.

'I am sure that there are one or two who are truly sleep-walkers. I am sure that one, perhaps two, have truly seen visions. But now I have dozens of young women who are hearing angels, and seeing the movement of stars, who are waking in the night and are shrieking out in pain. You must understand, Brother, not all of our novices are here because they have a calling. Very many are sent here by families who have too many children at home, or because the girl is too scholarly, or because she has lost her betrothed or cannot be married for some other reason. Sometimes they send us girls who are disobedient. Of course, they bring their troubles here, at first. Not everyone has a vocation, not everyone wants to be here. And once one young woman leaves her cell at night, against the rules, and runs around the cloisters, there is always someone who is going to join her.' She paused. 'And then another, and another.'

'And the stigmata? The sign of the cross on her palms?'

He could see the shock in her face. 'Who told you about that?'

'I saw the girl myself, last night, and the other women who ran after her.'

She bowed her head and clasped her hands together; he thought for a moment that she was praying for guidance as to what she should say next. 'Perhaps it is a miracle,' she said quietly. 'The stigmata. We cannot know for sure. Perhaps not. Perhaps – Our Lady defend us from evil – it is something worse.'

Luca leaned across the table to hear her. 'Worse? What d'you mean?'

'Sometimes a devout young woman will mark herself

with the five wounds of Christ. Mark herself as an act of devotion. Sometimes young women will go too far.' She took a nervous shuddering breath. 'That is why we need strong discipline in the house. The nuns need to feel that they can be cared for, as a daughter is cared for by her father. They need to know that there are strict limits to their behaviour. They need to be carefully ruled.'

'You fear that the women are harming themselves?' Luca asked, shocked.

'They are young women,' the Lady Almoner repeated. 'And they have no leadership. They become passionate, stirred up. It is not unknown for them to cut themselves, or each other.'

Brother Peter and Luca exchanged a horrified glance, Brother Peter ducked down his head and made a note.

'The abbey is wealthy,' Luca observed, speaking at random, to divert himself from his shock.

She shook her head. 'No, we have a vow of poverty, each and every one of us. Poverty, obedience and chastity. We can own nothing, we cannot follow our own will, and we cannot love a man. We have all taken these vows; there is no escaping them. We have all taken them. We have all willingly consented.'

'Except the Lady Abbess,' Luca suggested. 'I understand that she protested. She did not want to come. She was ordered to enter the abbey. She did not choose to be obedient, poor, and without the love of a man.'

'You would have to ask her,' the Lady Almoner said with quiet dignity. 'She went through the service. She gave up her rich gowns from the great chests of clothes that she brought in with her. Out of respect for her position in the world she was allowed to change her gown in private. Her own servant shaved her head and helped her dress in coarse linen, and a wool robe of our order, with a wimple around her head and a veil on top of that. When she was ready she came into the chapel and lay alone on the stone floor before the altar, her arms spread out, her face to the cold floor, and she gave herself to God. Only she can know if she took the vows in her heart. Her mind is hidden from us, her sisters.'

She hesitated. 'But her servant, of course, did not take the vows. She lives among us as an outsider. Her servant, as far as I know, follows no rules at all. I don't know if she even obeys the Lady Abbess, or if their relationship is more . . .'

'More what?' Luca asked, horrified.

'More unusual,' she said.

'Her servant? Is she a lay sister?'

'I don't know quite what you would call her. She was the Lady Abbess's personal servant from childhood, and when the Lady Abbess joined us, the slave came too; she just accompanied her when she came, like a dog follows his master. She lives in the house of the Lady Abbess. She used to sleep in the storeroom next door to the Lady Abbess's room, she wouldn't sleep in the nun's cells, then she started to sleep on the threshold of her room, like a slave. Recently she has taken to sleeping in the bed with her.' She paused. 'Like a bedmate.' She hesitated. 'I am not suggesting anything else,' she said.

Brother Peter's pen was suspended, his mouth open; but he said nothing.

'She attends the church, following the Lady Abbess like her shadow; but she doesn't say the prayers, nor confess, nor take Mass. I assume she is an infidel. I really don't know. She is an exception to our rule. We don't call her Sister, we call her Ishraq.'

'Ishraq?' Luca repeated the strange name.

'She was born an Ottoman,' the Lady Almoner said, her voice carefully controlled. 'You will notice her around the abbey. She wears a dark robe like a Moorish woman, sometimes she holds a veil across her face. Her skin is the colour of caramel sugar, it is the same colour: all over. Naked, she is golden, like a woman made of toffee. The last lord brought her back with him as a baby from Jerusalem when he returned from the crusades. Perhaps he owned her as a trophy, perhaps as a pet. He did not change her name nor did he have her baptised; but had her brought up with his daughter as her personal slave.'

'Do you think she could have had anything to do with the disturbances? Since they started when she came into the abbey? Since she came in with the Lady Abbess, at the same time?'

She shrugged. 'Some of the nuns were afraid of her when they first saw her. She is a heretic, of course, and fierce-looking. She is always in the shadow of the Lady Abbess. They found her . . .' She paused. 'Disturbing,' she said, then nodded at the word she had chosen. 'She is disturbing. We would all say that: disturbing.'

'What does she do?'

'She does nothing for God,' the Lady Almoner said with sudden passion. 'For sure, she does nothing for the abbey. Wherever the Lady Abbess goes, she goes too. She never leaves her side.'

'Surely she goes out? She is not enclosed?'

'She never leaves the Lady Abbess's side,' she contradicted him. 'And the Lady Abbess never goes out. The slave haunts the place. She walks in shadows, she stands in dark corners, she watches everything, and she speaks to none of us. It is as if we have trapped a strange animal. I feel as if I am keeping a tawny lioness, encaged.'

'Are you afraid of her, yourself?' Luca asked bluntly.

She raised her head and looked at him with her clear grey gaze. 'I trust that God will protect me from all evil,' she said. 'But if I were not certain sure that I am under the hand of God she would be an utter terror to me.'

There was silence in the little room, as if a whisper of evil had passed among them. Luca felt the hairs on his neck prickle, while beneath the table Brother Peter felt for the crucifix that he wore at his belt.

'Which of the nuns should I speak to first?' Luca asked, breaking the silence. 'Write down for me the names of those who have been walking in their sleep, showing stigmata, seeing visions, fasting.'

He pushed the paper and the quill before her and, without haste or hesitation, she wrote six names clearly, and returned the paper to him.

'And you?' he asked. 'Have you seen visions, or walked in your sleep?'

Her smile at the younger man was almost alluring. 'I wake in the night for the church services, and I go to my prayers,' she said. 'You won't find me anywhere but warm in my bed.'

As Luca blinked that vision from his mind, she rose from the table and left the room.

'Impressive woman,' Peter said quietly, as the door shut

behind her. 'Think of her being in a nunnery from the age of four! If she'd been in the outside world, what might she have done?'

'Silk petticoats,' Freize remarked, inserting his broad head around the door from the hall outside. 'Unusual.'

'What? What?' Luca demanded, furious for no reason, feeling his heart pound at the thought of the Lady Almoner sleeping in her chaste bed.

'Unusual to find a nun in silk petticoats. Hair shirt, yes – that's extreme perhaps, but traditional. Silk petticoats, no.'

'How the Devil do you know that she wears silk petticoats?' Peter demanded irritably. 'And how dare you speak so, and of such a lady?'

'Saw them drying in the laundry, wondered who they belonged to. Seemed an odd sort of garment for a nunnery vowed to poverty. Started to listen. I may be a fool but I can listen. Heard them whisper as she walked by me. She didn't know I was listening, she walked by me as if I was a stone, a tree. Silk gives a little *hss hss hss* sound.' He nodded smugly at Peter. 'More than one way to make inquiry. Don't have to be able to write to be able to think. Sometimes it helps to just listen.'

Brother Peter ignored him completely. 'Who next?' he asked Luca.

'The Lady Abbess,' Luca ruled. 'Then her servant, Ishraq.'

'Why not see Ishraq first, and then we can hold her next door while the Lady Abbess speaks,' Peter suggested. 'That way we can make sure they don't collude.'

'Collude in what?' Luca demanded, impatiently.

'That's the whole thing,' Peter said. 'We don't know what they're doing.'

'Collude.' Freize carefully repeated the strange word. 'Col-lude. Funny how some words just sound guilty.'

'Just fetch the slave,' Luca commanded. 'You're not the inquirer, you are supposed to be serving me as your lord. And make sure she doesn't talk to anyone as she comes to us.'

Freize walked round to the Lady Abbess's kitchen door and asked for the servant, Ishraq. She came veiled like a desert-dweller, dressed in a tunic and pantaloons of black, a shawl over her head pinned across her face, hiding her mouth. All he could see of her were her bare brown feet – a silver ring on one toe – and her dark inscrutable eyes above her veil. Freize smiled reassuringly at her; but she responded not at all, and they walked in silence to the room. She seated herself before Luca and Brother Peter without uttering one word.

'Your name is Ishraq?' Luca asked her.

'I don't speak Italian,' she said in perfect Italian.

'You are speaking it now.'

She shook her head and said again: 'I don't speak Italian.'

'Your name is Ishraq.' He tried again in French.

'I don't speak French,' she replied in perfectly accented French.

'Your name is Ishraq,' he said in Latin.

'It is,' she conceded in Latin. 'But I don't speak Latin.'

'What language do you speak?'

'I don't speak.'

Luca recognised a stalemate and leaned forwards, drawing on as much authority as he could. 'Listen, woman: I am commanded by the Holy Father himself to make inquiry into the events in this nunnery and to send him my report. You had better answer me, or face not just my displeasure, but his.'

She shrugged. 'I am dumb,' she said simply, in Latin. 'And of course, he may be your Holy Father, but he is not mine.'

'Clearly you can speak,' Brother Peter intervened. 'Clearly you can speak several languages.'

She turned her insolent eyes to him, and shook her head.

'You speak to the Lady Abbess.'

Silence.

'We have powers to make you speak,' Brother Peter warned her.

At once she looked down, her dark eyelashes veiling her gaze. When she looked up Luca saw that her dark brown eyes were crinkled at the edges, and she was fighting her desire to laugh out loud at Brother Peter. 'I don't speak,' was all she said. 'And I don't think you have any powers over me.'

Luca flushed scarlet with the quick temper of a young man who has been mocked by a woman. 'Just go,' Luca said shortly.

To Freize, who put his long face around the door, he snapped: 'Send for the Lady Abbess. And hold this dumb woman next door, alone.'

Isolde stood in the inner doorway, her hood pulled so far forwards that it cast a deep shadow over her face, her hands hidden in her deep sleeves, only her lithe white feet showing below her robe, in their plain sandals. Irrelevantly Luca noticed that her toes were rosy with cold and her insteps arched high. 'Come in,' Luca said, trying to recover his temper. 'Please take a seat.'

She sat; but she did not put back her hood, so Luca found he was forced to bend his head to peer under it to try to see her. In the shadow of the hood he could make out only a heart-shaped jaw line with a determined mouth. The rest of her remained a mystery.

'Will you put back your hood, Lady Abbess?'

'I would rather not.'

'The Lady Almoner faced us without a hood.'

'I was made to swear to avoid the company of men,' she said coldly. 'I was commanded to swear to remain inside this order and not meet or speak with men except for the fewest words and the briefest meeting. I am obeying the vows I was forced to take. It was not my choice, it was laid upon me by the Church. You, from the Church, should be pleased at my obedience.'

Brother Peter tucked his papers together and waited, pen poised.

'Would you tell us of the circumstances of your coming to the nunnery?' Luca asked.

'They are well-enough known,' she said. 'My father died three and a half months ago and left his castle and his lands entirely to my brother, the new lord, as is right and proper. My mother was dead, and to me he left nothing but the choice of a suitor in marriage or a place in the abbey. My brother, the new Lord Lucretili, accepted my decision not to marry and did me the great favour of putting me in charge of this nunnery, and I came in, took my vows, and started my service as their Lady Abbess.'

'How old are you?'

'I am seventeen,' she told him.

'Isn't that very young to be a Lady Abbess?'

The half-hidden mouth showed a wry smile. 'Not if your grandfather founded the abbey and your brother is its only patron, of course. The Lord of Lucretili can appoint who he chooses.'

'You had a vocation?'

'Alas, I did not. I came here in obedience to my brother's wish and my father's will. Not because I feel I have a calling.'

'Did you not want to rebel against your brother's wish and your father's will?'

There was a moment of silence. She raised her head and from the depth of her hood he saw her regard him thoughtfully, as if she were considering him as a man who might understand her.

'Of course, I was tempted by the sin of disobedience,' she said levelly. 'I did not understand why my father would treat me so. He had never spoken to me of the abbey nor suggested that he wanted a life of holiness for me. On the contrary, he spoke to me of the outside world, of being a woman of honour and power in the world, of managing my lands and supporting the Church as it comes under attack both here and in the Holy Land. But my brother was with my father on his deathbed, heard his last words, and afterwards he showed me his will. It was clearly my father's last wish that I come here. I loved my father, I love him still. I obey him in death as I obeyed him in life.' Her voice shook slightly as she spoke of her father. 'I am a good daughter to him; now as then.'

'They say that you brought your slave with you, a Moorish girl named Ishraq, and that she is neither a lay sister nor has she taken her vows.'

'She is not my slave; she is a free woman. She may do as she pleases.'

'So what is she doing here?'

'Whatever she wishes.'

Luca was sure that he saw in her shadowed eyes the same gleam of defiance that the slave had shown. 'Lady Abbess,' he said sternly. 'You should have no companions but the sisters of your order.'

She looked at him with an untameable confidence. 'I don't think so,' she said. 'I don't think you have the authority to tell me so. And I don't think that I would listen to you, even if you said that you had the authority. As far as I know there is no law that says a woman, an infidel, may not enter a nunnery and serve alongside the nuns. There is no tradition that excludes her. We are of the Augustine order, and as Lady Abbess I can manage this house as I see fit. Nobody can tell me how to do it. If you make me Lady Abbess then you give me the right to decide how this house shall be run. Having forced me to take the power, you can be sure that I shall rule.' The words were defiant, but her voice was very calm.

'They say she has not left your side since you came to the abbey?'

'This is true.'

'She has never gone out of the gates?'

'Neither have I.'

'She is with you night and day?'

'Yes.'

'They say that she sleeps in your bed?' Luca said boldly.

'Who says?' the Lady Abbess asked him evenly.

Luca looked down at his notes, and Brother Peter shuffled the papers.

She shrugged, as if she were filled with disdain for them and for their gossipy inquiry. 'I suppose you have to ask everybody, everything that they imagine,' she said dismissively. 'You will have to chatter like a clattering of choughs. You will hear the wildest of talk from the most fearful and imaginative people. You will ask silly girls to tell you tales.'

'Where does she sleep?' Luca persisted, feeling a fool.

'Since the abbey became so disturbed she has chosen to sleep in my bed, as she did when we were children. This way she can protect me.'

'Against what?'

She sighed as if she were weary of his curiosity. 'Of course, I don't know. I don't know what she fears for me. I don't know what I fear for myself. In truth, I think no-one knows what is happening here. Isn't this what you are here to find out?'

'Things seem to have gone very badly wrong since you came here.'

She bowed her head in silence for a moment. 'Now that is true,' she conceded. 'But it is nothing that I have deliberately done. I don't know what is happening here. I regret it very much. It causes me, me personally, great pain. I am puzzled. I am . . . lost.'

'Lost?' Luca repeated the word that seemed freighted with loneliness.

'Lost,' she confirmed.

'You don't know how to rule the abbey?'

Her head bowed down as if she were praying again. Then a small silent nod of her head admitted the truth of it: that she did not know how to command the abbey. 'Not like this,' she whispered. 'Not when they say they are possessed, not when they behave like madwomen.'

'You have no vocation,' Luca said very quietly to her. 'Do you wish yourself on the outside of these walls, even now?'

She breathed out a tiny sigh of longing. Luca could almost feel her desire to be free, her sense that she should be free. Absurdly, he thought of the bee that Freize had released to fly out into the sunshine, he thought that every form of life, even the smallest bee, longs to be free.

'How can this abbey hope to thrive with a Lady Abbess who wishes herself free?' he asked her sternly. 'You know that we have to serve where we have sworn to be.'

'You don't.' She rounded on him almost as if she were angry. 'For you were sworn to be a priest in a small country monastery; but here you are – free as a bird. Riding around the country on the best horses that the Church can give you, followed by a squire and a clerk. Going where you want and questioning anyone. Free to question me – even authorised to question me, who lives here and serves here and prays here, and does nothing but sometimes secretly wish . . .'

'It is not for you to pass comment on us,' Brother Peter intervened. 'The Pope himself has authorised us. It is not for you to ask questions.'

Luca let it go, secretly relieved that he did not have to admit to the Lady Abbess his joy at being released from his monastery, his delight in his horse, his unending insatiable curiosity.

She tossed her head at Brother Peter's ruling. 'I would expect you to defend him,' she remarked dismissively. 'I would expect you to stick together, as men do, as men always do.'

She turned to Luca. 'Of course, I have thought that I am utterly unsuited to be a Lady Abbess. But what am I to do? My father's wishes were clear, my brother orders everything now. My father wished me to be Lady Abbess and my brother has ordered that I am. So here I am. It may be against my wishes, it may be against the wishes of the community. But it is the command of my brother and my father. I will do what I can. I have taken my vows. I am bound here till death.'

'You swore fully?'

'I did.'

'You shaved your head and renounced your wealth?'

A tiny gesture of the veiled head warned him that he had caught her in some small deception. 'I cut my hair, and I put away my mother's jewels,' she said cautiously. 'I will never be bare-headed again, I will never wear her sapphires.'

'Do you think that these manifestations of distress and trouble are caused by you?' he asked bluntly.

Her little gasp revealed her distress at the charge. Almost, she recoiled from what he was saying, then gathered her courage and leaned towards him. He caught a glimpse of intense dark blue eyes. 'Perhaps. It is possible. You would be the one to discover such a thing. You have been appointed to discover such things, after all. Certainly I don't wish things as they are. I don't understand them, and they hurt me too. It is not just the sisters, I too am—'

'You are?'

'Touched,' she said quietly.

Luca, his head spinning, looked to Brother Peter, whose pen was suspended in midair over the page, his mouth agape.

'Touched?' Luca repeated wondering wildly if she meant that she was going insane.

'Wounded,' she amended.

'In what way?'

She shook her head as if she would not fully reply. 'Deeply,' was all she said.

There was a long silence in the sunlit room. Freize outside, hearing the voices cease their conversation, opened the door, looked in, and received such a black scowl from Luca that he quickly withdrew. 'Sorry,' he said as the door shut.

'Should not the nunnery be put into the charge of your brother house, the Dominicans?' Peter asked bluntly. 'You could be released from your vows and the head of the monastery could rule both communities. The nuns could come under the discipline of the Lord Abbot, the business affairs of the nunnery could be passed to the castle. You would be free to leave.'

'Put men to rule women?' She looked up as if she would laugh at him. 'Is that all you can suggest – the three of you? Going to the trouble to come all the way from Rome on your fine horses, a clerk, an inquirer and a servant, and the best idea you have is that a nunnery shall give up its independence and be ruled by men? You would break up our

76

old and traditional order, you would destroy us who are made in the image of Our Lady Mary, and put us under the rule of men?'

'God gave men the rule over everything,' Luca pointed out. 'At the creation of the world.'

Her flash of laughing defiance deserted her as soon as it had come. 'Oh, perhaps,' she said, suddenly weary. 'If you say so. I don't know. I wasn't raised to think so. But I know that is what some of the sisters want, I know it is what the brothers say should happen. I don't know if it is the will of God. I don't know that God particularly wants men to rule over women. My father never suggested such a thing to me and he was a crusader who had gone to the Holy Land himself and prayed at the very birthplace of Jesus. He raised me to think of myself as a child of God and a woman of the world. He never told me that God had set men over women. He said God had created them together, to be helpers and lovers to each other. But I don't know. Certainly God – if He ever stoops to speak to a woman – does not speak to me.'

'And what is your own will?' Luca asked her. 'You, who are here, though you say you don't want to be here? With a servant who speaks three languages but claims to be dumb? Praying to a God who does not speak to you? You, who say you are hurt? You, who say you are touched? What is your will?'

'I have no will,' she said simply. 'It's too soon for me. My father died only fourteen weeks ago. Can you imagine what that is like for his daughter? I loved him deeply, he was my only parent, the hero of my childhood. He commanded everything, he was the very sun of my world. I wake every morning and have to remind myself that he is dead. I came into the nunnery only days after his death, in the first week of mourning. Can you imagine that? The troubles started to happen almost at once. My father is dead and everyone around me is either feigning madness, or they are going mad.

'So if you ask me what I want, I will tell you. All I want to do is to cry and sleep. All I want to do is to wish that none of this had ever happened. In my worse moments, I want to tie the rope of the bell in the bell tower around my throat and let it sweep me off my feet and break my neck as it tolls.'

The violence of her words clanged like a tolling bell itself into the quiet room. 'Self-harm is blasphemy,' Luca said quickly. 'Even thinking of it is a sin. You will have to confess such a wish to a priest, accept the penance he sets you, and never think of it again.'

'I know,' she replied. 'I know. And that is why I only wish it, and don't do it.'

'You are a troubled woman.' He had no idea what he should say to comfort her. 'A troubled girl.'

She raised her head and, from the darkness of her hood, he thought he saw the ghost of a smile. 'I don't need an inquirer to come all the way from Rome to tell me that. But would you help me?'

'If I could,' he said. 'If I can, I will.'

They were silent. Luca felt that he had somehow pledged himself to her. Slowly, she pushed back her hood, just a little, so that he could see the blaze of her honest blue eyes. Then Brother Peter noisily dipped his pen in the bottle of ink, and Luca recollected himself.

'I saw a nun last night run across the courtyard, chased

by three others,' he said. 'This woman got to the outer gate and hammered on it with her fists, screaming like a vixen, a terrible sound, the cry of the damned. They caught her and carried her back to the cloister. I assume they put her back in her cell?'

'They did,' she said coldly.

'I saw her hands,' he told her; and now he felt as if he were not making an inquiry, but an accusation. He felt as if he were accusing her. 'She was marked on the palms of her hand, with the sign of the crucifixion, as if she was showing, or faking, the stigmata.'

'She is no fake,' the Lady Abbess told him with quiet dignity. 'This is a pain to her, not a source of pride.'

'You know this?'

'I know it for certain.'

'Then I will see her this afternoon. You will send her to me.'

'I will not.'

Her calm refusal threw Luca. 'You have to!'

'I will not send her this afternoon. The whole community is watching the door to my house. You have arrived with enough fanfare, the whole abbey, brothers and sisters, know that you are here and that you are taking evidence. I will not have her further shamed. It is bad enough for her with everyone knowing that she is showing these signs and dreaming these dreams. You can meet her; but at a time of my choosing, when no-one is watching.'

'I have an order from the Pope himself to interview the wrong-doers.'

'Is that what you think of me? That I am a wrong-doer?' she suddenly asked.

'No. I should have said I have an order from the Pope to hold an inquiry.'

'Then do so,' she said impertinently. 'But you will not see that young woman until it is safe for her to come to you.'

'When will that be?'

'Soon. When I judge it is right.'

Luca realised he would get no further with the Lady Abbess. To his surprise, he was not angry. He found that he admired her; he liked her bright sense of honour, and he shared her own bewilderment at what was happening in the nunnery. But more than anything else, he pitied her loss. Luca knew what it was to miss a parent, to be without someone who would care for you, love you and protect you. He knew what it was to face the world alone and feel yourself to be an orphan.

He found he was smiling at her, though he could not see if she was smiling back. 'Lady Abbess, you are not an easy woman to interrogate.'

'Brother Luca, you are not an easy man to refuse,' she replied, and she rose from the table without permission, and left the room.

For the rest of the day Luca and Brother Peter interviewed one nun after another, taking each one's history, and her hopes, and fears. They ate alone in the Lady Almoner's parlour, served by Freize. In the afternoon, Luca remarked that he could not stand another white-faced girl telling him that she had bad dreams and that she was troubled by her conscience, and swore that he had to take a break from the worries and fears of women.

They saddled their horses and the three men rode out into the great beech forest where the massive trees arched high above them, shedding copper-coloured leaves and beech mast in a constant whisper. The horses were almost silent as their hooves were muffled by the thickness of the forest floor and Luca rode ahead, on his own, weary of the many plaintive voices of the day, wondering if he would be able to make any sense of all he had heard, fearful that all he was doing was listening to meaningless dreams and being frightened by fantasies.

The track led them higher and higher until they emerged above the woodland, looking down the way they had come. Above them, the track went on, narrower and more stony, up to the high mountains that stood, bleak and lovely, all around them.

'This is better.' Freize patted his horse's neck as they paused for a moment. Down below them they could see the little village of Lucretili, the grey slate roof of the abbey, the two religious houses placed on either side of it, and the dominating castle where the new lord's standard fluttered in the wind over the round gatehouse tower.

The air was cold. Above them a solitary eagle wheeled away. Brother Peter tightened his cloak around his shoulders and looked at Luca, to remind him that they must not stay out too long.

Together they turned the horses and rode along the crest

of the hill, keeping the woodland to their right, and then, at the first woodcutter's trail, dropped down towards the valley again, falling silent as the trees closed around them.

The trail wound through the forest. Once they heard the trickle of water, and then the drilling noise of a woodpecker. Just when they thought they had overshot the village they came out into a clearing and saw a wide track heading to the castle of Lucretili which stood, like a grey stone guard post, dominating the road.

'He does all right for himself,' Freize observed, looking at the high castle walls, the drawbridge and the rippling standards. From the lord's stables they could hear the howling of his pack of deerhounds. 'Not a bad life. The wealth to enjoy it all, hunting your own deer, living off your own game, enough money to take a ride into Rome to see the sights when you feel like it, and a cellar full of your own wine.'

'Saints save her, how she must miss her home,' Luca remarked, looking at the tall towers of the beautiful castle, the rides which led deep into the forest and beyond to lakes, hills, and streams. 'From all this wealth and freedom to four square walls and a life enclosed till death! How could a father who loved his daughter bring her up to be free here, and then have her locked up on his death?'

'Better that than a bad husband who would beat her as soon as her brother's back was turned, better that than die in childbirth,' Brother Peter pointed out. 'Better that than being swept off her feet by some fortune-hunter, and all the family wealth and good name destroyed in a year.'

'Depends on the fortune-hunter,' Freize volunteered. 'A lusty man with a bit of charm about him might have brought a flush to her cheek, given her something pleasant to dream about.'

'Enough,' Luca ruled. 'You may not talk about her like that.'

'Seems we mustn't think of her like a pretty lass,' Freize remarked to his horse.

'Enough,' Luca repeated. 'And you don't know what she looks like, any more than I do.'

'Ha, but I can tell by her walk,' Freize said quietly to his horse. 'You can always tell a pretty girl by the way she walks. A pretty girl walks like she owns the world.'

Isolde and Ishraq were at the window as the young men came back through the gate. 'Can't you just smell the open air on their clothes?' the first one whispered. 'When he leaned forwards I could just smell the forest, and the fresh air, and the wind that comes off the mountain.'

'We could go out, Isolde.'

'You know I cannot.'

'We could go out in secret,' the other replied. 'At night, through the little postern gate. We could just walk in the woods in the starlight. If you long for the outside, we don't have to be prisoners here.'

'You know that I took vows that I would never leave here . . .'

'When so many vows are being broken?' the other urged. 'When we have turned the abbey upside down and brought hell in here with us? What would one more sin matter? How does it matter what we do now?'

The gaze that Isolde turned on her friend was dark with guilt. 'I can't give up,' she whispered. 'Whatever people think I have done or say I have done, whatever I have done – I won't give up on myself. I'll keep my word.'

The three men attended Compline, the last service before the nuns went to bed for the night. Freize looked longingly at the Lady Almoner's stores as the three men walked out of the cloister and separated to go to their rooms. 'What I wouldn't give for a glass of sweet wine as a nightcap,' he said. 'Or two. Or three.'

'You really are a hopeless servant for a religious man,' Peter remarked. 'Wouldn't you have done better in an ale house?'

'And how would the little lord manage without me?' Freize demanded indignantly. 'Who watched over him in the monastery and kept him safe? Who fed him when he was nothing more than a long-legged sparrow? Who follows him now wherever he goes? Who keeps the door for him?'

'Did he watch over you in the monastery?' Peter asked, turning in surprise to Luca.

Luca laughed. 'He watched over my dinner and ate everything I left,' he said. 'He drank my wine allowance. In that sense he watched me very closely.'

At Freize's protest, Luca thumped him on the shoulder. 'Ah, all right! All right!' To Peter he said: 'When I first entered the monastery he watched out for me so that I wasn't beaten by the older boys. When I was charged with heresy he gave witness for me, though he couldn't make head nor tail of what they said I had done. He has been loyal to me, always, from the moment of our first meeting when I was a scared novice and he was a lazy kitchen boy. And when I was given this mission he asked to be released to go with me.'

'There you are!' Freize said triumphantly.

'But why does he call you "little lord"?' Peter pursued.

Luca shook his head. 'Who knows? I don't.'

'Because he was no ordinary boy,' Freize explained eagerly. 'So clever and, when he was a child, quite beautiful like an angel. And then everyone said he was not of earthly making . . .'

'Enough of that!' Luca said shortly. 'He calls me "little lord" to serve his own vanity. He would pretend he was in service to a prince if he thought he could get away with it.'

'You'll see,' Freize said, nodding solemnly to Brother Peter. 'He's not an ordinary young man.'

'I look forward to witnessing exceptional abilities,' Brother Peter said drily. 'Sooner rather than later, if possible. Now, I'm for my bed.'

Luca raised his hand in goodnight to the two of them and turned into the priest house. He closed the door behind him and pulled off his boots, putting his concealed dagger carefully under the pillow. He laid out the paper about the number zero on one side of the table, and the statements that Peter had written down on the other. He planned to study the statements and then reward himself with looking at the manuscript about zero, working through the night. Then he would attend the service of Lauds.

At about two in the morning, a tiny knock at the door made him move swiftly from the table to take up the dagger from under his pillow. 'Who's there?'

'A sister.'

Luca tucked the knife into his belt, at his back, and opened the door a crack. A woman, a veil of thick lace completely obscuring her face, stood silently in his doorway. He glanced quickly up and down the deserted gallery and stepped back to indicate that she could come inside. In the back of his mind he thought he was taking a risk letting her come to him without witnesses, without Brother Peter to take a note of all that was said. But she too was taking a risk, and breaking her vows, to be alone with a man. She must be driven by something very powerful to step into a man's bedroom, alone.

He saw that she held her hands cupped, as if she were hiding something small in her palms.

'You wanted to see me,' she said quietly. Her voice was low and sweet. 'You wanted to see this.'

She held out her hands to him. Luca flinched in horror as he saw that in the centre of both was a neat shallow hole, and each palm was filled with blood. 'Jesu save us!'

'Amen,' she said instantly.

Luca reached for the linen washcloth and tore a strip roughly off the side. He splashed water onto it from the ewer, and gently patted each wound. She flinched a little as he touched her. 'I am sorry, I am sorry.'

'They don't hurt much, they're not deep.'

Luca dabbed away the blood and saw that both wounds had stopped bleeding and were beginning to form small scabs. 'When did this happen?'

'I woke just now, and they were like this.'

'Has it happened before?'

'Last night. I had a terrible dream, and when I woke I was in my cell, in my bed, but my feet were muddy and my hands were filled with blood.'

'I think that it was you that I saw,' he said. 'In the entrance yard? Do you remember nothing?'

She shook her head and the lace veil moved but did not reveal her face. 'I just woke and my hands were like this, newly marked. It has happened before. Sometimes I have woken in the morning and found them wounded but they have already stopped bleeding, as if they came earlier in the night, without even waking me. They are not deep, you see, they heal within days.'

'Do you have a vision?'

'A vision of horror!' she suddenly broke out. 'I cannot believe it is the work of God to wake me with bleeding hands. I have no sense of holiness, I feel nothing but terror. This cannot be God stabbing me. These must be blasphe-mous wounds.'

'God might be working through you, mysteriously ...' Luca tried.

87

She shook her head. 'It feels more like punishment. For being here, for following the services, and yet being cursed with a rebellious heart.'

'How many of you are here unwillingly?'

'Who knows? Who knows what people think when they go through each day in silence, praying as they are commanded to do, singing as they are ordered? We are not allowed to speak to one another during the day except to repeat our orders or say our prayers. Who knows what anyone is thinking? Who knows what we are all privately thinking?'

She spoke so powerfully to Luca's own sense that the nunnery was full of secrets that he could not bring himself to ask her anything more, but chose to act instead. He took a sheet of clean paper. 'Put your palms down on this,' he commanded. 'First the right and then the left.'

She looked as if she would like to refuse but did as he ordered, and they both looked, in horror, at the two neat triangular prints that her blood left on the whiteness of the manuscript and the haze of her bloody palm print around them.

'Brother Peter has to see your hands,' Luca decided. 'You will have to make a statement.'

He expected her to protest; but she did not. She bowed her head in obedience to him.

'Come to my inquiry room tomorrow, first thing,' he said. 'Straight after Prime.'

'Very well,' she said easily. She opened the door and slipped through.

'And what is your name, Sister?' Luca asked, but she was already gone. It was only then that he realised that she would not come to the inquiry room and testify, and that he did not know her name.

Luca waited impatiently after Prime, but the nun did not come. He was too irritated with himself to explain to Freize and Brother Peter why he would see no-one else, but sat in the room, the door open, the papers on the table before them.

In the end, he declared that he had to ride out to clear his head, and went to the stables. One of the lay sisters was hauling muck out of the stable yard, and she brought his horse and saddled it for him. It was odd to Luca, who had lived for so long in a world without women, to see all the hard labouring work done by women, all the religious services observed by women, living completely self-sufficiently, in a world without men except for the visiting priest. It added to his sense of unease and displacement. These women lived in a community as if men did not exist, as if God had not created men to be their masters. They were complete to themselves and ruled by a girl. It was against everything he had observed and everything he had been taught and it seemed to him no wonder at all that everything had gone wrong.

As Luca was waiting for his horse to be led out, he saw Freize appear in the archway with his skewbald cob tacked up, and watched him haul himself into the saddle.

'I ride alone,' Luca said sharply.

'You can. I'll ride alone too,' Freize said equably.

'I don't want you with me.'

'I won't be with you.'

'Ride in the other direction then.'

'Just as you say.'

Freize paused, tightened his girth, and went through the gate, bowing with elaborate courtesy to the old porteress who scowled at him, and then he waited outside the gate for Luca to come trotting through.

'I told you, I don't want you riding with me.'

'Which is why I waited,' Freize explained patiently. 'To see what direction you were going in, so that I could make sure I took the opposite one. But of course, there may be wolves, or thieves, highwaymen or brigands, so I don't mind your company for the first hour or so.'

'Just shut up and let me think,' Luca said ungraciously.

'Not a word,' Freize remarked to his horse, who flickered a brown ear at him. 'Silent as the grave.'

He actually managed to keep his silence for several hours as they rode north, at a hard pace away from the abbey, from Castle Lucretili, and the little village that sheltered beneath its walls. They took a broad smooth track with matted grass growing down the middle and Luca put his horse in a canter, hardly seeing the odd farmhouse, the scattering flock of sheep, the carefully tended vines. But then, as it grew hotter towards midday, Luca drew up his horse, suddenly realising that they were some way from the abbey, and said, 'I suppose we should be heading back.'

'Maybe you'd like a drop of small ale and a speck of bread and ham first?' Freize offered invitingly.

'Do you have that?'

'In my pack. Just in case we got to this very point and thought we might like a drop of small ale and a bite to eat.'

Luca grinned. 'Thank you,' he said. 'Thank you for bringing food, and thank you for coming with me.'

Freize nodded smugly, and led the way off the road into a small copse where they would be sheltered from the sun. He dismounted from his cob and slung the reins loosely over the saddle. The horse immediately dropped its head and started to graze the thin grass of the forest floor. Freize spread his cape for Luca to sit, and unpacked a stone jug of small ale, and two loaves of bread. The two men ate in silence, then Freize produced, with a flourish, a half bottle of exquisitely good red wine.

'This is excellent,' Luca observed.

'Best in the house,' Freize answered, draining the very dregs.

Luca rose, brushed off the crumbs, and took up the reins of his horse, which he had looped over a bush.

'Horses could do with watering before we go back,' Freize remarked.

The two young men led the horses back along the track, and then mounted up to head for home. They rode for some time until they heard the noise of a stream, off to their left, deeper in the forest. They broke off from the track and, guided by the noise of running water, first found their way to a broad stream, and then followed it downhill to where it formed a wide deep pool. The bank was muddy and well-trodden, as if many people came here for water, an odd sight in the deserted forest. Luca could see the marks in the mud of the wooden pattens that the nuns wore over their shoes when they were working in the abbey gardens and fields.

Freize slipped, nearly losing his footing, and exclaimed as he saw that he had stepped in a dark green puddle of goose-shit. 'Look at that! Damned bird. I would snare and eat him, I would.'

Luca took both horses' reins and let them drink from the water as Freize bent to wipe his boot with a dock leaf.

'Well, I'll be . . . !'

'What is it?'

Wordlessly, Freize held out the leaf with the dirt on it.

'What?' asked Luca, leaning away from the offering.

'Look closer. People always say that there's money where muck is – and here it is. Look closer, for I think I have made my fortune!'

Luca looked closer. Speckled among the dark green of the goose-shit were tiny grains of sand, shining brightly. 'What is it?'

'It's gold, little lord!' Freize was bubbling with delight. 'See it? Goose feeds on the reeds in the river, the river water is carrying tiny grains of gold washed out of a seam some-where in the mountain, probably nobody knows where. Goose eats it up, passes it out, I find it on my boot. All I need to do now is to find out who owns the lands around the stream, buy it off them for pennies, pan for gold, and I am a lord myself and shall ride a handsome horse and own my own hounds!'

'If the landlord will sell,' Luca cautioned him. 'And I think we are still on the lands of the Lord of Lucretili. Perhaps he would like to pan for his own gold.'

'I'll buy it from him without telling him,' Freize exulted.

'I'll tell him I want to live by the stream. I'll tell him I have a vocation, like that poor lass, his sister. I'll tell him I have a calling, I want to be a holy hermit and live by the pool and pray all day.'

Luca laughed aloud at the thought of Freize's vocation for solitary prayer but suddenly Freize held up his hand. 'Someone's coming,' he warned. 'Hush, let's get ourselves out of the way.'

'Why should we hide? We're doing no harm.'

'You never know,' Freize whispered. 'And I'd rather not be found by a gold-bearing stream.'

The two of them backed their horses deeper into the forest, off the path, and waited. Luca threw his cape over his horse's head so that it would make no noise, and Freize reached up to his cob's ear and whispered one word to it. The horse bent his head and stood quietly. The two men watched through the trees as half a dozen nuns wearing their dark brown working robes wound their way along the path, their wooden pattens squelching in the mud. Freize gently gripped the nose of his horse so that it did not whinny.

The last two nuns were leading a little donkey, its back piled high with dirty fleeces from the nunnery flock. As Freize and Luca watched through the sheltering bushes, the women pegged the fleeces down in the stream, for the waters to rinse them clean, and then turned the donkey round and went back the way they had come. Obedient to their vows, they worked in silence, but as they led the little donkey away they struck up a psalm and the two young men could hear them singing:

'The Lord is my Shepherd, I'll not want . . .'

'I'll not want,' Freize muttered, as the two emerged from hiding. 'Damn. Damn "I'll not want" indeed! Because I will want. I do want. And I will go on wanting, wanting and dreaming and always disappointed.'

'Why?' Luca asked. 'They're just washing the fleeces. You can still buy your stream and pan for gold.'

'Not them,' Freize said. 'Not them, the cunning little vixens. They're not washing the fleeces. Why come all this way just to wash fleeces, when there are half a dozen streams between here and the abbey? No, they're panning for gold in the old way. They put the fleeces in the stream – see how they've pegged them out all across the stream so the water flows through? The staple of the wool catches the grains of gold, catches even the smallest dust. In a week or so, they'll come back and pull out their harvest: wet fleeces, heavy with gold. They'll take them back to the abbey, dry them, brush out the gold dust and there they are with a fortune on the floor! Little thieves!'

'How much would it be worth?' Luca demanded. 'How much gold would a fleece of wool hold?'

'And why has no-one mentioned this little business of theirs?' Freize demanded. 'I wonder if the Lord of Lucretili knows? It'd be a good joke on him if he put his sister in the nunnery only for her to steal his fortune from under his nose, using the very nuns he gave her to rule.'

Luca looked blankly at Freize. 'What?'

'I was jesting . . .'

'No, it might not be a joke. What if she came here and found the gold, just like you did, and set the nuns to work. And then thought that she would make out that the nunnery had fallen into sin, so that no-one came to visit any more, so that no-one would trust the word of the nuns . . .'

'Then she wouldn't be caught in her little enterprise and, though she'd still be a Lady Abbess, she could live like a lady once more,' Freize finished. 'Happy all the day long, rolling in gold dust.'

'I'll be damned,' Luca said heavily. He and Freize stood in silence for a long moment, and then Luca turned without another word, mounted his horse and kicked it into a canter. He realised as he rode that he was not just shocked by the massive crime that the whole nunnery was undertaking, but personally offended by the Lady Abbess – as if he thought he could have done anything to help her! As if his promise to help her had meant anything to her! As if she had wanted anything from him but his naïve trust, and his faith in her story. 'Damn!' he said again.

They rode in silence, Freize shaking his head over the loss of his imaginary fortune, Luca raging at being played as a fool. As they drew near to the nunnery, Luca tightened his reins and pulled his horse up until Freize drew level. 'You truly think it is her? Because she struck me as a most unhappy woman, a grieving daughter – she was sincere in her grief for her father, I am sure of that. And yet to face me and lie to me about everything else . . . do you think she is capable of such dishonesty? I can't see it.'

'They might be doing it behind her back,' Freize conceded. 'Though the madness in the nunnery is a good way of keeping strangers away. But I suppose she might be in ignorance of it all. We'd have to know who takes the gold to be sold. That's how you'd know who was taking the fortune. And we'd have to know if it was going on before she got here.'

Luca nodded. 'Say nothing to Brother Peter.'

'The spy,' supplemented Freize cheerfully.

'But tonight we will break into the storeroom and see if we can find any evidence: any drying fleeces, any gold.'

'No need to break in, I have the key.'

'How did you get that?'

'How did you think you got such superb wine after dinner?'

Luca shook his head at his servant, and then said quietly, 'We'll meet at two of the clock.'

The two young men rode on together and, behind them, making no more sound than the trees that sighed in the wind, the slave Ishraq watched them go.

Isolde was in her bed, tied like a prisoner to the four posts, her feet strapped at the bottom, her two hands lashed to the two upper posts of the headboard. Ishraq pulled the covers up under her chin and smoothed them flat. 'I hate to see you like this. It is beyond bearing. For your own God's sake tell me that we can leave this place. I cannot tie you to your bed like some madwoman.'

'I know,' Isolde replied, 'but I can't risk walking in my sleep. I can't bear it. I will not have this madness descend on me. Ishraq, I won't walk in the night, scream out in dreams. If I go mad, if I really go mad, you will have to kill me. I cannot bear it.'

Ishraq leaned down and put her brown cheek to the other girl's pale face. 'I never would. I never could. We will fight this, and we will defeat them.'

'What about the inquirer?'

'He is talking to all of the sisters, he is learning far too much. His report will destroy this abbey, will ruin your good name. Everything they tell him blames us, names you, dates the start of the troubles to the time when we arrived. We have to get hold of him. We have to stop him.'

'Stop him?' she asked.

Ishraq nodded, her face grim. 'We have to stop him, one way or another. We have to do whatever it takes to stop him.'

The moon was up, but it was a half moon hidden behind scudding clouds and shedding little light as Luca went quietly across the cobbled yard. He saw a shadowy figure step out of the darkness: Freize. In his hand he had the key ready, oiled to make no sound, and slid it quietly in the lock. The door creaked as Luca pushed it open and both men froze at the sound, but no-one stirred. All the narrow windows that faced over the courtyard were dark, apart from the window of the Lady Abbess's house, where a candle burned, but other than that flickering light, there was no sign that she was awake.

The two young men slipped into the storeroom and closed the door quietly behind them. Freize struck a spark from a flint, blew a flame, lit a tallow candle taken from his pocket, and they looked around.

'Wine is over there.' Freize gestured to a sturdy grille. 'Key's hidden up high on the wall, any fool could find it – practically an invitation. They make their own wine. Small ale over there, home-brewed too. Foods are over there.' He pointed to the sacks of wheat, rye and rice. Smoked hams in their linen sleeves hung above them, and on the cold inner wall were racks of round cheeses.

Luca was looking around; there was no sign of the fleeces. They ducked through an archway to a room at the back. Here there were piles of cloth of all different sorts of quality, all in the unbleached cream that the nuns wore. A pile of brown hessian cloth for their working robes was heaped in another corner. Leather for making their own shoes, satchels, and even saddlery, was sorted in tidy piles according to the grade. A rickety wooden ladder led up to the half-floor above.

'Nothing down here,' Freize observed.

'Next we'll search the Lady Abbess's house,' Luca ruled. 'But first, I'll check upstairs.' He took the candle and started up the ladder. 'You wait down here.'

'Not without a light,' pleaded Freize.

'Just stand still.'

Freize watched the wavering flame go upwards and then stood, nervously, in pitch darkness. From above he heard a sudden strangled exclamation. 'What is it?' he hissed into the darkness. 'Are you all right?'

Just then a cloth was flung over his head, blinding him,

and as he ducked down he heard the whistle of a heavy blow in the air above him. He flung himself to the ground and rolled sideways, shouting a muffled warning as something thudded against the side of his head. He heard Luca coming quickly down the ladder and then a splintering sound as the ladder was heaved away from the wall. Freize struggled against the pain and the darkness, took a wickedly placed kick in the belly, heard Luca's whooping shout as he fell, and then the terrible thud as he hit the stone floor. Freize, gasping for breath, called out for his master, but there was nothing but silence.

Both young men lay still for long frightening moments in the darkness, then Freize sat up, pulled the hood from his head, and patted himself all over. His hand came away wet from his face; he was bleeding from forehead to chin. 'Are you there, Sparrow?' he asked hoarsely.

He was answered by silence. 'Dearest saints, don't say she has killed him,' he moaned. 'Not the little lord, not the changeling boy!'

He got to his hands and knees and crawled his way around, feeling across the floor, bumping into the heaped piles of cloth, as he quartered the room. It took him painful stumbling minutes to be sure: Luca was not in the storeroom at all.

Luca was gone.

'Fool that I am, why did I not lock the door behind me?' Freize muttered remorsefully to himself. He staggered to his feet and felt his way round the wall, past the broken stair, to the opening. There was a little light in the front storeroom, for the door was wide open and the waning moon shone in. As Freize stumbled towards it, he saw the iron grille to the wine and ale cellar stood wide open. He rubbed his bleeding head, leaned for a moment on the trestle table, and went on towards the light. As he reached the doorway, the abbey bell rang for Lauds and he realised he had been unconscious for perhaps half an hour.

He was setting out for the chapel to raise the alarm for Luca when he saw a light at the hospital window. He turned towards it, just as the Lady Almoner came hastily out into the yard. 'Freize! Is that you?'

He stumbled towards her, and saw her recoil as she saw his bloodstained face. 'Saints save us! What has happened to you?'

'Somebody hit me,' Freize said shortly. 'I have lost the little lord! Raise the alarm, he can't be far.'

'I have him! I have him! He is in a stupor,' she said. 'What happened to him?'

'Praise God you have him. Where was he?'

'I found him staggering in the yard just now on my way to Lauds. When I got him into the infirmary he fainted. I was coming to wake you and Brother Peter.'

'Take me to him.'

She turned, and Freize staggered after her into the long low room. There were about ten beds arranged on both sides of the room, poor pallet beds of straw with unbleached sacking thrown over them. Only one was occupied. It was Luca – deathly pale, eyes shut, breathing lightly.

'Dearest saints!' Freize murmured, in an agony of anxiety. 'Little lord, speak to me!'

Slowly Luca opened his hazel eyes. 'Is that you?'

'Praise God, it is. Thank Our Lady that it is, as ever it was.'

'I heard you shout and then I fell down the stairs,' he said, his speech muffled by the bruise on his mouth.

'I heard you come down like a sack of potatoes,' confirmed Freize. 'Dearest saints, when I heard you hit the floor! And someone hit me . . .'

'I feel like the damned in hell.'

'Me too.'

'Sleep then, we'll talk in the morning.'

Luca closed his eyes. The Lady Almoner approached. 'Let me bathe your wounds.' She was holding a bowl with a white linen cloth, and there was a scent of lavender and crushed leaves of arnica. Freize allowed himself to be persuaded onto another bed.

'Were you attacked in your beds?' she asked him. 'How did this happen?'

'I don't know,' Freize said, too stunned by the blow to make anything up. Besides, she could see the open door to the storeroom as well as he, and she had found Luca in the yard. 'I can't remember anything,' he said lamely and, as she dabbed and exclaimed at the bruises and scratches on his face, he stretched out under the luxury of a woman's care, and fell fast asleep.

Freize woke to a very grey cold dawn. Luca was snoring slightly on the opposite bed, a little snuffle followed by a long relaxed whistle. Freize lay listening to the penetrating noise for some time before he opened his eyes, and then he blinked and raised himself up onto his arm. He could not believe what he saw. The bed next to him was now occupied by a nun, laid on her back, her face as white as her hood, which was pushed back exposing her clammy shaven head. Her fingers, enfolded in a position of prayer on her completely still breast, were blue, the fingernails rimmed as if with ink. But worst of all were her eyes, which were horribly open, the pupils dilated black in black. She was completely still. She was clearly – even to Freize's inexperienced frightened stare – dead.

A praying nun knelt at her feet, endlessly murmuring the rosary. Another knelt by her head, muttering the same prayers. The narrow bed was ringed with candles, which illuminated the scene like a tableau of martyrdom. Freize sat up, certain that he was dreaming, hoping that he was dreaming, pinched himself in the hope of waking, and put his feet on the floor, silently cursing the thudding in his head, not daring to stand yet. 'Sister, God bless you. What happened to the poor girl?'

The nun at the head of the bed did not speak until she

finished the prayer but looked at him with eyes that were dark with unshed tears. 'She died in her sleep,' she said eventually. 'We don't know why.'

'Who is she?' Freize crossed himself with a sudden superstitious fear that it was one of the nuns who had come to give evidence to their inquiry. 'Bless her soul and keep her.'

'Sister Augusta,' she said, a name he did not know.

He stole a quick glance at the white cold face and recoiled from the blackness of her dead gaze.

'Saint's sake! Why have you not closed her eyes and weighted them?'

'They won't close,' the nun at the foot of the bed said, trembling. 'We have tried and tried. They won't close.'

'They must do! Why would they not?'

She spoke in a low monotone: 'Her eyes are black because she was dreaming of Death again. She was always dreaming of Death. And now He has come for her. Her dark eyes are filled with that last vision, of Him coming for her. That's why they won't close, that's why they are as black as jet. If you look deeply into her terrible black eyes you will see Death himself reflected in them like a mirror. You will see the face of Death looking out at you.'

The first nun let out a little wail, a cold keening noise. 'He will come for us all,' she whispered.

They both crossed themselves and returned to their muttered prayers as Freize shuddered and bowed his head in a prayer for the dead. Gingerly, he got up and, gritting his teeth against his swimming head, walked cautiously around the nuns to the bed where Luca still snored. He shook his shoulder: 'Little lord, wake up.'

'I wish you wouldn't call me that,' said Luca groggily.

'Wake up, wake up. One of the nuns is dead.'

Luca sat up abruptly then held his head and swayed. 'Was she attacked?'

Freize nodded at the praying nuns. 'They say she died in her sleep.'

'Can you see?' Luca whispered.

Freize shook his head. 'She has no head wound, I can't see anything else.'

'What do they say?' Luca's nod indicated the praying nuns who had returned to their devotions. To his surprise, he saw Freize shiver as if a cold wind had touched him.

'They don't make any sense,' Freize said, denying the thought that Death was coming for them all.

Just then, the door opened and the Lady Almoner came in, leading four lay sisters. The nuns at the head and foot of the corpse rose up and stood aside as the women in brown robes carefully lifted the lifeless body onto a rough stretcher, and took it through an arched stone doorway into the neighbouring room.

'They will dress her and prepare her for burial tomorrow,' the Lady Almoner said in reply to Luca's questioning glance. She was white with strain and fatigue. The nuns took their candles and went to keep their vigil in the cold outer room. Luca saw their shadows jump huge on the stone walls, black as big monsters, as they set down their lights and knelt to pray, then someone closed the door on them.

'What happened to her?' he asked quietly.

'She died in her sleep,' the Lady Almoner said. 'God alone knows what is happening here. When they went to wake her early, for she was to serve at Prime, she was gone. She was cold and stiff and her eyes were fixed open. Who knows what she saw or dreamed, or what came to torment her?' Quickly she crossed herself and put her hand to the small gold cross that hung from a gold chain on her belt.

She came closer to Luca and looked into his eyes. 'And you? Are you dizzy? Or faint?'

'I'll live,' he said wryly.

'I'm faint,' Freize volunteered hopefully.

'I'll get you some small ale,' she said, and poured some from a pitcher. She handed them both a cup. 'Did you see your assassin?'

'Assassin.' Freize repeated the word, strange to him, which usually meant a hired Arab killer.

'Whoever it was who tried to kill you,' she amended. 'And anyway, what were you doing in the storeroom?'

'I was searching for something,' Luca said evasively. 'Will you take me there now?'

'We should wait for sunrise,' she replied.

'You have the keys?'

'I don't know . . .'

'Then Freize will let us in with his key.'

The look she gave Freize was very cold. 'You have a key to my storeroom?'

Freize nodded, his face a picture of guilt. 'Just for essential supplies. So as not to be a nuisance.'

'I don't think you are well enough to walk over there,' she said to Luca.

'Yes I am,' he said. 'We have to go.'

'The stair is broken.'

'Then we'll get a ladder.'

She realised that he would insist. 'I'm afraid. To be honest, I am afraid to go.'

'I understand,' Luca said with a quick smile. 'Of course you are. Terrible things happened last night. But you have to be brave. You will be with us and we won't be caught like fools again. Take courage, come on.'

'Can we not go after sunrise, when it is fully light?'

'No,' he said gently. 'It has to be now.'

She bit her lip. 'Very well,' she said. 'Very well.'

She lifted a torch from the sconce in the wall and led the way across the courtyard to the storerooms. Someone had closed the door and she opened it, and stood back to let them go in. The wooden ladder was still on the floor, where it had been thrown down. Freize lifted it back into place, and shook it to make sure that it was firm. 'This time, I'll lock the door behind us,' he remarked, and turned the key and locked them in.

'Oh, she can get through a locked door,' the Lady Almoner said with a frightened little laugh. 'I think she can go through walls. I think she can go anywhere she wishes.'

'Who can?' Luca demanded.

She shrugged. 'Go on up, I will tell you everything. I will keep no more secrets. A nun has died under this roof, in our care. The time has come for you to know everything that has been done here. And you must stop it. You must stop her. I have been driven far beyond defending this nunnery, far beyond defending this Lady Abbess. I will tell you everything now. But first you shall see what she has done.'

Luca went carefully up the steps, the Lady Almoner following, holding her robe out of the way as she climbed. Freize stood at the bottom with the torch, lighting their way.

It was dark in the loft, but the Lady Almoner crossed to the far wall and threw open the half-door, for the dawn light. The beams from the rising sun poured into the loft through the opening and shone on glistening fleeces of gold, hanging up to dry, as the gold dust sifted through the wool to fall onto the linen sheets spread on the floor below. The room was like a treasure chamber, with gold dust underfoot and golden fleeces hanging like priceless washing on the bowed lines.

'Good God,' Luca whispered. 'It is so. The gold ...' He looked around as if he could not believe what he was seeing. 'So much! So bright!'

She sighed. 'It is. Have you seen enough?'

He bent and took a pinch of the dust. Here and there were little nuggets of gold, like grit. 'How much? How much is this worth?'

'She harvests a couple of fleeces a month,' the Lady Almoner said. 'If she is allowed to continue it will add up to a fortune.'

'How long has this been going on?'

She closed the half-door to shut out the sunlight, and barred it. 'Ever since the Lady Abbess came. She knows the land, being brought up here; she knows it better than her brother, for he was sent away for his education while she stayed at home with their father. The stream belongs to our abbey, it is in our woods. Her slave, being a Moor, knew how her people pan for gold and she taught the sisters to peg out the fleeces in the stream, telling them it would clean the wool. They have no idea what they are doing, she plays them for fools – she told them that the stream has special purifying qualities for the wool, and they know no better.

They peg out the fleeces in the stream and bring them back here to dry; they never see them drying out and the gold pattering down on the linen sheets. The slave comes in secretly to sweep up the gold dust, takes it to sell, and the sisters come in when the gold is gone and the loft is empty, and take the fleeces away to card and spin.' She laughed bitterly. 'Sometimes they remark how soft the wool is. They are fools for her. She has made fools of us all.'

'The slave brings the money to you? For the abbey?'

The Lady Almoner turned to go down the ladder. 'What do you think? Does this look like an abbey that is rich in its own gold? Have you seen my infirmary? Have you seen any costly medicines? You have seen my storeroom, I know. Do we seem wealthy to you?'

'Where does she sell it? How does she sell the gold?'

The Lady Almoner shrugged. 'I don't know. Rome, I suppose. I know nothing about it. She sends the slave in secret.'

Luca hesitated, briefly, as if there were something more he would ask, but then he turned and went down after her, ignoring the bruise on his shoulder and the pain in his neck. 'You are saying that the Lady Abbess uses the nuns to pan for gold and keeps the money for herself?'

She nodded. 'You have seen it for yourself now. And I think she hopes to close the nunnery altogether. I believe that she plans to open a gold mine here, on our fields. I think she is deliberately leading the nunnery into disgrace so that you recommend it should be closed down. When it is abolished as a nunnery she will say she is free from her father's will. She will renounce her vows, she will claim it as her inheritance from her father, she will continue to live here, and she and the slave will be left here alone.'

'Why didn't you tell me this before?' Luca demanded. 'When I opened the inquiry? Why keep this back?'

'Because this place is my life,' she said fiercely. 'It has been a beacon on the hill, a refuge for women and a place to serve God. I hoped that the Lady Abbess would learn to live here in peace. I thought God would call her, that her vocation would grow. Then I hoped that she would be satisfied with making a fortune here. I thought she might be an evil woman, but that we might contain her. But since a nun has died in our care—' She choked on a sob. 'Sister Augusta, one of the most innocent and simple women who has been here for years—' She broke off.

'Well, now it is all over,' she said with dignity. 'I can't hide what she is doing. She is using this place of God to hide her fortune-hunting, and I believe that her slave is practising witchcraft on the nuns. They dream, they sleepwalk, they show strange signs, and now one has died in her sleep. Before God, I believe that the Lady Abbess and her slave are driving us all mad so that they can get at the gold.'

Her hand sought the cross at her waist and Luca saw her hold it tightly, as if it were a talisman.

'I understand,' he said, as calmly as he could, though his own throat was dry with superstitious fear. 'I have been sent here to end these heresies, these sins. I am authorised by the Pope himself to inquire and judge. There is nothing that I will not see with my own eyes. There is nothing I will not question. Later this morning I will speak to the Lady Abbess again and, if she cannot explain herself, I will see that she is dismissed from her post.'

'Sent away from here?'

He nodded.

'And the gold? You will let the abbey keep the gold so that we can feed the poor and establish a library? Be a beacon on the hill for the benighted?'

'Yes,' he said. 'The abbey should have its fortune.'

He saw her face light up with joy. 'Nothing matters more than the abbey,' she assured him. 'You will let my sisters stay here and live their former lives, their holy lives? You will put them under the discipline of a good woman, a new Lady Abbess who can command them and guide them?'

'I will put it under the charge of the Dominican brothers,' Luca decided. 'And they will harvest the gold from the stream and endow the abbey. This is no longer a house in the service of God, as it has been suborned. I will put it under the control of men, there will be no Lady Abbess. The gold shall be restored to God, the abbey to the brothers.'

She gave a shuddering sigh and hid her face in her hands. Luca stretched his hand towards her to comfort her and only a warning glance from Freize reminded him that she was still in holy orders and he should not touch her.

'What will you do?' Luca asked quietly.

'I don't know. My whole life has been here. I will serve as Lady Almoner until we come under the command of the Brothers. They will need me for the first months, no-one but me knows how this place is run. Then perhaps I will ask if I may go to another order. I would like an order that was more enclosed, more at peace. These have been terrible days. I want to go to an order where the vows are kept more strictly.'

'Poverty?' Freize asked at random. 'You want to be poor?'

She nodded. 'An order that respects the commands, an order with more simplicity. Knowing that we were storing a fortune of gold in our own loft ... not knowing what the Lady Abbess was doing or what she intended, fearing she was serving the Devil himself ... it has been heavy on my conscience.'

The bell tolled the call to chapel, echoing in the morning air. 'Prime,' she said. 'I have to go to church. The sisters need to see me there.'

'We'll come too,' Luca said.

They closed the door to the storeroom and locked it behind them. While Luca watched, she turned to Freize and held out her hand for his key. Luca smiled at her simple dignity as she stood still while Freize patted his pockets in a pantomime of searching, and then, reluctantly, handed over the key. 'Thank you,' she said. 'If you want anything from the abbey stores you may come to me.'

Freize gave a funny little mock bow, as if to recognise her authority. She turned to Luca. 'I could be the new Lady Abbess,' she said quietly. 'You could recommend me for the post. The abbey would be safe in my keeping.'

Before he could answer she looked beyond him at the windows of the hospital, suddenly paused, and put her hand on Luca's sleeve. At once he froze, acutely aware of her touch. Freize behind him stopped still. She held her finger to her lips for silence and then slowly pointed ahead. She was indicating the mortuary beside the hospital, where a little light gleamed from the slatted shutters, and they could see someone moving.

'What is it?' Luca whispered. 'Who is in there?'

'The lights should be shielded, and the nuns should be still and silent in their vigil,' she breathed. 'But someone is moving in there.'

'The sisters, washing her?' Luca asked.

'They should have finished their work.'

Quietly, the three of them moved across the yard and looked in the open door to the hospital. The door leading from the hospital ward through to the mortuary was firmly closed. The Lady Almoner stepped back, as if she were too afraid to go further.

'Is there another way in?'

'They take the pauper coffins out through a back door, to the stables,' she whispered. 'That door may be unbolted.'

Quickly, they crossed the stable yard to the double door to the mortuary, big enough for a cart and a horse, barred by a thick beam of wood. The two young men silently lifted the beam from its sockets and the door stood closed, held shut only by its own weight. Freize lifted a useful pitchfork from the nearby wall, and Luca bent and took his dagger from the scabbard in his boot.

'When I give the word, open it quickly,' he said to the Lady Almoner. She nodded, her face as white as her veil.

'Now!'

The Lady Almoner flung the door open, the two young men rushed into the room, weapons at the ready – then fell back in horror.

Before them was a nightmare scene, like a butcher's shop, with the butcher and his lad working over a fresh carcass. But it was worse by far than that. It was not a butcher, and it was no animal on the slab. The Lady Abbess was in a brown working gown, her head tied in a scarf, and Ishraq was in her usual black robe covered with a white apron. The two girls had their sleeves rolled up, and were bloodstained to the elbows, standing over the dead body of Sister Augusta, Ishraq wielding a bloodied knife in her hand, disembowelling the dead girl. The nuns keeping vigil were nowhere to be seen. As the men burst in, the two young women looked up and froze, the knife poised above the open belly of the dead nun, blood on their aprons, blood on the bed, blood on their hands.

'Step back,' Luca ordered, his voice ice-cold with shock. He pointed his dagger at Ishraq, who looked to the Lady Abbess for her command. Freize raised his pitchfork as if he would spear her on the tines.

'Step back from that body, and no-one will be hurt,' Luca said. 'Leave this – whatever it is that you are doing.' He could not bear to look, he could not find the words to name it. 'Leave it, and step against the wall.'

He heard the Lady Almoner come in behind him and her gasp of horror at the butchery before them. 'Merciful God!' She staggered and he heard her lean against the wall, then retch.

'Get a rope,' Freize said, without turning his head to her. 'Get two ropes. And fetch Brother Peter.'

She choked back her nausea. 'What in the name of God are you doing? Lady Abbess, answer me! What are you doing to her?'

'Go,' said Luca. 'Go at once.'

They heard her running feet cross the cobbles of the stable yard as the Lady Abbess raised her eyes to Luca. 'I can explain this,' she said.

He nodded, gripping the dagger. Clearly, nothing could explain this scene: her sleeves rolled to her elbows, her hands stained red with the blood of a dead nun.

'I believe that this woman has been poisoned,' she said. 'My friend is a physician—'

'Can't be,' Freize said quietly.

'She is,' the Lady Abbess insisted. 'We . . . we decided to cut open her belly and see what she had been fed.'

'They were eating her.' The Lady Almoner's voice trembled from the doorway. She came back into the room, Brother Peter white-faced behind her. 'The two of them were eating her in a Satanic Mass. They were eating the body of Sister Augusta. Look at the blood on their hands. They were drinking her blood. The Lady Abbess has gone over to Satan and she and her heretic slave are holding a Devil's Mass on this, our sanctified ground.'

Luca shuddered and crossed himself. Brother Peter stepped towards the slave with a rope held out before him. 'Put down the knife and put out your hands,' he said. 'Give yourself up. In the name of God, I command you, demon or woman or fallen angel, to surrender.'

Holding Freize's gaze, Ishraq put down the knife on the bed beside the dead nun, then suddenly darted for the doorway that led into the empty hospital. She flung it open and was through it, followed in a moment by the Lady Abbess. As Luca and Freize raced after the two young women, she led the way, running across the yard to the main gate.

Luca bellowed to the porteress, 'Bar the gate! Stop thief!' and flung himself on the Lady Abbess as she sprinted ahead of him, bringing her down to the ground in a heavy tackle and knocking the air out of her. As they went down, her veil fell from her head and a tumble of blonde hair swept over his face with the haunting scent of rosewater.

The Moorish slave was half way up the outer gate now, springing from hinge to beam like a lithe animal, as Freize grabbed at her bare feet and missed, and then leaped up and snatched a handful of her robe and tore her off the gate, bringing her tumbling down to fall backwards on the stone cobbles with a cry of pain.

Freize gripped her arms to her sides so tightly that she could barely breathe, while Brother Peter tied her hands behind her back, roped her feet together, and then turned to the Lady Abbess, still pinned down by Luca. As Luca dragged her to her feet, holding her wrists, her thick golden-blonde hair tumbled down over her shoulders, hiding her face.

'Shame!' the Lady Almoner exclaimed. 'Her hair!'

Luca could not drag his eyes from this girl who had veiled her face from him, and hooded her hair so that he should never know what she looked like. In the golden light of the rising sun he stared at her, seeing her for the first time, her dark blue eyes under brown up-swinging brows, a straight perfect nose, and a warm tempting mouth. Then Brother Peter came towards them and he saw her blood-stained hands as the clerk bound them with a rope, and Luca realised that she was a thing of horror, a beautiful thing of horror, the worst thing between heaven and hell: a fallen angel.

'The lay sisters will be coming into the yards to work, the nuns will be coming from church, we must tidy up,' the Lady Almoner ruled. 'They cannot see this. It will distress them beyond anything . . . it will break their hearts. I must shield them from this evil. They cannot see Sister Augusta so abused. They cannot see these . . . these . . .' She could not find the words for the Lady Abbess and her slave. 'These devils. These missionaries from hell.'

'Do you have a secure room for them?' Brother Peter asked. 'They will have to stand trial. We'll have to send for Lord Lucretili. He is the lord of these lands. This is outside our jurisdiction now. This is a criminal matter, this is a hanging offence, a burning offence; he will have to judge.'

'The cellar of the gatehouse,' the Lady Almoner replied promptly. 'The only way in or out is a hatch in the floor.'

Freize had the Moorish girl slung like a sack over his shoulder. Brother Peter took the tied hands of the Lady Abbess and led her to the gatehouse. Luca was left alone with the Lady Almoner.

'What will you do with the body?'

'I will ask the village midwives to put her into her coffin. Poor child, I cannot let her sisters see her. And I will send for the priest to bless what is left of her poor body. She can lie in the church for now and then I will ask Lord Lucretili if she can lie in his chapel. I won't leave her in the mortuary, I won't have her in our chapel. As soon as they have cleaned her up and dressed her again she shall go to sanctified ground away from here.'

She shuddered and swayed, almost as if she might faint. Luca put his hand around her waist to support her and she leaned towards him for a moment, resting her head on his shoulder.

'You were very brave,' he said to her. 'This has been a terrible ordeal.'

She looked up at him, and then, as if she had suddenly realised that his arm was around her, and that she was leaning against him, he felt her heart flutter like a captured bird and she stepped away. 'Forgive me,' she said. 'I am not allowed . . .'

'I know,' he said quickly. 'It is for you to forgive me. I should not have touched you.'

'It has been so shocking . . .' There was a tremble in her voice that she could not conceal.

Luca put his hands behind his back so that he would not reach for her again. 'You must rest,' he said helplessly. 'This has been too much for any woman.'

'I can't rest,' she said brokenly. 'I must put things to rights here. I cannot let my sisters see this terrible sight, or find out what has been done here. I will fetch the women to clean up. I must make everything right again. I will command them, I will lead them, out of error into the ways of righteousness; out of darkness into light.' She smoothed her robe and shook it out. Luca heard the seductive whisper of her silk shift, and then she turned away from him to go to her work.

At the door of the hospital she paused and glanced back. She saw that he was looking after her. 'Thank you,' she said, with a tiny smile. 'No man has ever held me, not in all my life before. I am glad to know a man's kindness. I will live here all my life, I will live here inside this order, perhaps as the Lady Abbess, and yet I will always remember this.'

He almost stepped towards her as she held his gaze for just a moment and then was gone.

Freize and Brother Peter joined Luca in the cobbled yard. 'Are they secure?' Luca asked.

'Regular gaol they have there,' Freize remarked. 'There

were chains fixed on the wall, handcuffs, manacles. He insisted that we put everything on them, and I hammered them on as if they were both slaves.'

'Just till the Lord Lucretili gets here,' Brother Peter replied defensively. 'And if we had left them in ropes and they had got themselves free, what would we have done?'

'Caught them again when we opened the hatch?' Freize suggested. To Luca he said, 'They're in a round cave, no way in or out except a hatch in the roof and they can't reach that until it is opened and a wooden ladder lowered in. They aren't even stone walls, the cellar is dug down into solid rock. They're secure as a pair of mice in a trap. But he had to put them in irons as if they were pirates.'

Luca looked at his new clerk and saw that the man was deeply afraid of the mystery and the terrible nature of the two women. 'You were right to be cautious,' he said, reassuringly. 'We don't know what powers they have.'

'Good God, when I saw them with blood up to the elbows, and they looked at us, their faces as innocent as scholars at a desk! What were they doing? What Satan's work were they doing? Was it a Mass? Were they really eating her flesh and drinking her blood in a Satanic Mass?'

'I don't know,' Luca said. He put his hand to his head. 'I can't think . . .'

'Now look at you!' Freize exclaimed. 'You should still be in bed, and the Lord knows I feel badly myself. I'll take you back to the hospital and you can rest.'

Luca recoiled. 'Not there,' he said. 'I'm not going back in there. Take me to my room at the priest house and I will sleep till Lord Lucretili gets here. Wake me as soon as he comes.'

In the cellar, the two young women were shrouded in darkness as if they were already in their grave. It was like being buried alive. They blinked and strained their eyes but they were blind.

'I can't see you,' Isolde said, her voice catching on a sob.

'I can see you.' The reply came steadily out of the pitch blackness. 'And anyway, I always know when you are near.'

'We have to get word to the inquirer. We have to find some way to speak with him.'

'I know.'

'They will be fetching my brother. He will put us on trial.'

There was a silence from Ishraq.

'Ishraq, I should be certain that my brother will hear me, that he will believe what I say, that he will free me – but more and more do I think that he has betrayed me. He encouraged the prince to come to my room, he left me no choice but to come here as Lady Abbess. What if he has been trying to drive me away from my home all along? What if he has been trying to destroy me?'

'I think so,' the other girl said steadily. 'I do think so.'

There was a silence while Isolde absorbed the thought. 'How could he be so false? How could he be so wicked?'

The chains clinked as Ishraq shrugged.

'What shall we do?' Isolde asked hopelessly.

'Hush.'

'Hush? Why? What are you doing?'

'I am wishing . . .'

'Ishraq – we need a plan, wishing won't save us.'

'Let me wish. This is deep wishing. And it might save us.'

Luca had thought he would toss and turn with the pain in his neck and shoulder, but as soon as his boots were off and his head was on the pillow he slipped into a deep sleep. Almost at once he started to dream.

He dreamed that he was running after the Lady Abbess again, and she was outpacing him easily. The ground beneath his feet changed from the cobbles of the yard to the floor of the forest, and all the leaves were crisp like autumn, and then he saw they had been dipped in gold and he was running through a forest of gold. Still she kept ahead of him, weaving in and out of golden tree trunks, passing bushes crusted with gold, until he managed a sudden burst of speed, far faster than before, and he leaped towards her, like a mountain lion will leap on a deer, and caught her around the waist to bring her down. But as she fell, she turned in his arms and he saw her smiling as if with desire, as if she had all along wanted him to catch her, to hold her, to lie foot to foot, leg against leg, his hard young body against her lithe slimness, looking into her eyes, their faces close enough to kiss. Her thick mane of blonde hair swirled around him and he smelt the heady scent of rosewater again. Her eyes were dark, so dark; he had thought they were blue so he looked again, but the blue of her eyes was only a tiny rim around the darkness of the pupil. Her eyes were so dilated they were not blue but black. In his head he heard the words 'beautiful lady' and he thought, 'Yes, she is a beautiful lady.'

'*Bella donna*.' He heard the words in Latin and it was the voice of the slave to the Lady Abbess with her odd foreign accent as she repeated, with a strange urgency: '*Bella donna! Luca, listen! Bella donna!*'

The door to the guest room opened, as Luca lurched out of his dream and held his aching head.

'Only me,' Freize said, slopping warmed small ale out of a jug as he banged into the room with a tray of bread, meat, cheese and a mug.

'Saints, Freize, I am glad that you waked me. I have had the strangest of dreams.'

'Me too,' Freize said. 'All night long I dreamed that I was gathering berries in the hedgerow, like a gipsy.'

'I dreamed of a beautiful woman, and the words *bella donna*.'

At once Freize burst into song:
'Bella donna, give me your love –
Bella donna, bright stars above . . .'

'What?' Luca sat himself at the table and let his servant put the food before him.

'It's a song, a popular song. Did you never hear it in the monastery?'

'We only ever sang hymns and psalms in the church,'

Luca reminded him. 'Not love songs in the kitchen like you.'

'Anyway, everyone was singing it last summer. Bella donna: beautiful lady.'

Luca cut himself a slice of meat from the joint, chewed thoughtfully, and drank three deep gulps of small ale. 'There's another meaning of the words *bella donna*,' he said. 'It doesn't just mean beautiful lady. It's a plant, a hedgerow plant.'

Freize slapped his head. 'It's the plant in my dream! I dreamed I was in the hedgerow, looking for berries, black berries; but though I wanted blackberries or sloe berries or even elderberries, all I could find was deadly nightshade ... the black berries of deadly nightshade.'

Luca got to his feet, taking a hunk of the bread in his hand. 'It's a poison,' he said. 'The Lady Abbess said that they believed the nun was poisoned. She said they were cutting her open to see what she had eaten, what she had in her belly.'

'It's a drug,' Freize said. 'They use it in the torture rooms, to make people speak out, to drive them mad. It gives the wildest dreams, it could make—' He broke off.

'It could make a whole nunnery of women go mad,' Luca finished for him. 'It could make them have visions, and sleepwalk – it could make them dream and imagine things. And, if you were given too much ... it would kill you.'

Without another word the two young men went to the guesthouse door and walked quickly to the hospital. In the centre of the entrance yard the lay sisters were making two massive piles of wood, as if they were preparing for a bonfire. Freize paused there, but Luca went past them without a second glance, completely focused on the hospital where he could see through the open windows, the nursing nuns moving about setting things to rights. Luca went through the open doors, and looked around him in surprise.

It was all as clean and as tidy as if there had never been anything wrong. The door to the mortuary was open and the body of the dead nun was gone, the candles and censers taken away. Half a dozen beds were made ready with clean plain sheets, a cross hung centrally on the lime washed walls. As Luca stood there, baffled, a nun came in with a jug of water in her hand from the pump outside, poured it into a bowl and went down on her knees to scrub the floor.

'Where is the body of the sister who died?' Luca asked. His voice sounded too loud in the empty silent room. The nun sat back on her heels and answered him. 'She is lying in the chapel. The Lady Almoner closed the coffin herself, nailed it down and ordered a vigil to be kept in the chapel. Shall I take you to pray?'

He nodded. There was something uncanny about the complete restoration of the room. He could hardly believe that he had burst through that door, chased the Lady Abbess and her slave, knocked her to the ground and sent them chained into a windowless cellar; that he had seen them, bloodstained to their elbows, hacking into the body of the dead nun.

'The Lady Almoner said that she is to lie on sacred ground in the Lucretili chapel,' the nun remarked, leading the way out of the hospital. 'Both for her vigil and her burial. The Lord Lucretili is to bring the special coffin carriage and take her to lie for a night in the castle chapel. Then she'll be buried in our graveyard. God bless her soul.'

As they went past the piles of wood, Freize fell into step beside Luca. 'Pyres,' he said out of the corner of his mouth. 'Two pyres for two witches. Lord Lucretili is on his way to sit in judgement, but it looks like they have already decided what the verdict will be and are preparing for the sentence already. These are the stakes and firewood for burning the witches.'

Luca reeled around, in shock. 'No!'

Freize nodded, his face grim. 'Why not? We saw ourselves what they were doing. There's no doubt they were engaged in witchcraft, a Satanic Mass, or cutting up the body. Either way it's a crime punishable by death. But I will say that your Lady Almoner doesn't waste much time in preparation. Here she is with two bonfires ready before the trial has even started.'

The waiting nun tapped her foot. Luca turned back to her. 'What are these wood piles for?'

'I think we are selling the firewood,' she said. 'The Lady Almoner ordered the lay sisters to make two piles like this. May I show you to the chapel now? I have to get back to the hospital and wash the floor.'

'Yes, I am sorry to have delayed you.'

Luca and Freize followed her past the refectory, through the cloisters to the chapel. As soon as the nun pushed open the heavy wooden door they could hear the low musical chanting of nuns keeping vigil over the body. Blinking, as their eyes were blinded by the darkness, they went slowly up the aisle until they could see that the space before the altar was covered with a snowy white cloth, and on the cloth lay a newly made simple wooden coffin with the lid nailed firmly shut.

Luca grimaced at the sight. 'We have to see the body,' he whispered. 'It's the only way we can know if she was poisoned.'

'Rather you than me,' Freize said bluntly. 'I wouldn't want to tell the Lady Almoner that I'm opening a sanctified coffin because I had a funny dream.'

'We have to know.'

'She won't want anyone seeing the body,' Freize whispered to Luca. 'She was horribly cut up. And if those witches ate her flesh, then the poor girl will bleed when she is resurrected, God help her. The Lady Almoner won't want the nuns to know that.'

'We'll have to get permission from the priest,' Luca decided. 'We'd better ask him, not the Lady Almoner – we'll give him a request in writing. Peter can write it.'

They stepped back and watched the priest. He had a heavy silver censer that blew incense smoke all around the coffin. When the air was chokingly thick with the heavy perfume, he handed it to one of the nuns and then took the holy water from another and doused the coffin. Then he went to the altar and, turning his back on them all, he lifted his hands in prayer for their departed sister.

The two men bowed to the altar, crossed themselves, and went quietly out of the church. At once they could hear a commotion from the stable yard, the sound of many horses arriving, and the great gates being thrown open.

'Lord Lucretili,' Luca guessed, and strode back to the yard.

The lord, and patron of the abbey, was mounted on a big black warhorse, which pawed the ground, its iron horseshoes throwing sparks from the cobbles. As Luca watched he threw his red leather reins to his pageboy and jumped easily from the saddle. The Lady Almoner went up to him, curtseyed, and then stood quietly, her hands hidden inside her long sleeves, her head bowed, her hood modestly shielding her face.

Following Lord Lucretili into the courtyard came half a dozen men wearing the lord's livery of an olive bough overlaid with a sword, signifying the peaceful descendant of a crusader knight. Three or four grave-looking clerks came in on horseback, then the Lord Abbot of Lucretili with his own retinue of priests.

As the men dismounted, Luca stepped forwards.

'You must be Luca Vero. I am glad you are here,' Lord Lucretili said pleasantly. 'I am Giorgio, Lord Lucretili. This is my Lord Abbot. He will sit in judgement with me. I understand you are in the middle of your investigation here?'

'I am,' Luca said. 'Forgive me, but I have to go to the visitors' house. I am looking for my clerk.'

The Lord Lucretili intervened. 'Fetch the inquirer's clerk,' he said to his pageboy, who set off to the visitors' house at a run. The lord turned back to Luca. 'They tell me that it was you who arrested the Lady Abbess, and her slave?'

'His own sister,' Freize breathed from behind. 'Though I might remark that he doesn't seem very upset.'

'Myself, my clerk Brother Peter, and my servant Freize, together with the Lady Almoner,' Luca confirmed. 'Brother Peter and my servant put the two women in the cellar below the gatehouse.'

'We'll hold our trial in the first-floor room of the gatehouse,' Lord Lucretili decided. 'That way they can be brought up the ladder, and we'll keep it all out of the way of the nunnery.'

'I would prefer that,' the Lady Almoner said. 'The fewer people who see them, and know of this, the better.'

The lord nodded. 'It shames us all,' he said. 'God alone knows what my father would have made of it. So let's get it over and done with.'

Two black-plumed horses pulled a cart into the yard, and stood waiting. 'For the coffin,' the lord explained to Luca. To the Lady Almoner he said: 'You'll see it's loaded up and my men will take it to my chapel?'

The Lady Almoner nodded, then turned from the men and led the way to the gatehouse room, where she watched the clerks set a long table and chairs for the Lord Lucretili, the Lord Abbot, Luca and Brother Peter. While they were preparing the room, Luca went to Lord Lucretili. 'I think we need to have the coffin opened before Sister Augusta is buried,' he said quietly. 'I am sorry to say that I suspect the sister was poisoned.'

'Poisoned?'

Luca nodded.

The lord shook his head in shock. 'God save her soul and forgive my sister her sins. But anyway, we can't open the coffin here. The nuns would be far too distressed. Come to my castle this evening and we'll do it privately at my chapel. In the meantime, we'll question the Lady Abbess and her slave.'

'They won't answer,' Luca said certainly. 'The slave swore she was dumb in three languages when I questioned her before.'

The lord laughed shortly. 'I think they can be made to answer. You are an inquirer for the Church, you have the right to use the rack, the press, you can bleed them. They are only young women, vain and frail as all women are. You will see that they will answer your questions rather than have their joints pulled from the sockets. They will speak rather than have boulders placed on their chests. I can promise you that my sister will say anything rather than have leeches on her face.'

Luca went white. 'That's not how I make an inquiry. I have never . . .' he started. 'I would never . . .'

The older man put a gentle hand on his shoulder. 'I will do it for you,' he said. 'You shall wrestle with them for their souls until their evil pride has been broken and they are crying to confess. I have seen it done, it is easily done. You can trust me to make them ready for their confession.'

'I could not allow . . .' Luca choked.

'The room is ready for your lordship.' The Lady Almoner came out from the gatehouse and stood aside as the lord went in without another word. He seated himself behind the table where the great chair, like a throne, was placed ready for him, the Lord Abbot to his left. Luca was on his right, with a clerk at one end of the table and Brother Peter at the other. When everyone was seated, the lord ordered the door to the yard closed, and Luca saw Freize's anxious face peering in, as the Lord Lucretili said, 'My Lord Abbot, will you bless the work that we are doing today?'

The abbot half-closed his eyes and folded his hands over his curved stomach. 'Heavenly Father, bless the work that is done here today. May this abbey be purified and cleansed of sin and returned to the discipline of God and man. May these women understand their sins and cleanse their hearts with penitence, and may we, their judges, be just and righteous in our wrath. May we offer you a willing brand for the burning, Lord, always remembering that vengeance is not ours; but only yours. Amen.'

'Amen,' Lord Lucretili confirmed. He gestured to the two priests who were standing guard at the outer door. 'Get them up.'

Brother Peter rose to his feet. 'Freize has the key to the chains,' he said. He opened the door to get the ring of keys from Freize, who was hovering on the threshold. The men inside the courtroom could see the stable yard filled with curious faces. Brother Peter closed the door on the crowd outside, stepped forwards and opened the trap-door set in the wooden floorboards. Everyone went silent as Brother Peter looked down into the dark cellar. Leaning against the wall of the gatehouse room was a rough wooden ladder. One of the priests lifted it and lowered it into the darkness of the hole. Everyone hesitated. There was something very forbidding about the deep blackness below, almost as if it were a well, and the women far below had been drowned in the inky waters. Brother Peter handed the keys to Luca, and everyone looked at him. Clearly they were all expecting him to go down into the darkness and fetch the women up.

Luca found that he was chilled, perhaps by a blast of cold air from the windowless deep room below. He thought of the two young women down there, chained to the damp walls, waiting for judgement, their eyes wide and glassy in the darkness. He remembered the black glazed look of the dead nun and thought that perhaps the Lady Abbess and her Moorish slave would be drugged into hallucinations too. At the thought of their dark eyes, shining in the darkness like waiting rats, he got to his feet, determined to delay. 'I'll get a torch,' he said and went out into the entrance yard.

Outside, in the clean air, he sent one of the lord's servants running for a light. The man returned with one of the sconces from the refectory burning brightly. Luca took it in his hand and went back into the gatehouse, feeling as if he were about to go deep into an ancient cave to face a monster.

He held the torch up high as he stepped on the first rung of the ladder. He had to go backwards, and he could not help looking over his shoulder and down between his feet, trying to see what was there waiting for him in the darkness.

'Take care!' Brother Peter said, his voice sharp with warning.

'What of?' Luca asked impatiently, hiding his own fear. Two more rungs of the ladder and he could see the walls were black and shiny with damp. The women would be chilled, chained down here in the darkness. Two steps more and he could see a little pool of light at the foot of the ladder and his own leaping shadow on the wall and the shadow of the ladder like a black hatched line going downwards into nothingness. He was at the bottom rung now. He kept one hand on the rough wood for safety, as he turned and looked around.

Nothing.

There was nothing there.

There was nobody there.

He swung the pool of light ahead of him; the stone floor was empty of anything, and the dark wall just six paces away from him on all sides was blank stone, black stone. The cellar was empty. They were not there.

Luca exclaimed and held the torch higher, looking all around. For a moment he had a terror of them making a sudden rush at him out of the darkness, the two women freed and dashing at him like dark devils in hell; but there was no-one there. His eye caught a glint of metal on the floor.

'What is it?' Brother Peter peered down from the floor above. 'What's the matter?'

Luca raised the torch high, so that the beams of light raked the darkness of the circular room all around him. Now, he could see the handcuffs and leg-cuffs lying on the ground, still safely locked, still firmly chained to the wall, intact and undamaged. But of the Lady Abbess and the Moorish girl there was no sign at all.

'Witchcraft!' Lord Lucretili hissed, his face as white as a sheet, looking down at Luca from the floor above. 'God save us from them.' He crossed himself, kissed his thumbnail, and crossed himself again. 'The manacles are not broken?'

'No.' Luca gave them a kick and they rattled but did not spring open.

'I locked them myself, I made no mistake,' Brother Peter said, scrambling down the ladder and shaking as he tested the chains on the wall.

Luca thrust the torch at Peter and swarmed his way up the ladder to the light, obeying a panic-stricken sense that he did not want to be trapped in the dark cellar from which the women had, so mysteriously, disappeared. Lord Lucretili took his hand and heaved him up the last steps and then stayed hand clasped with him. Luca, feeling his own hands were icy in the lord's warm grip, had a sense of relief at a human touch.

'Be of good heart, Inquirer,' the lord said. 'For these are dark and terrible days. It must be witchcraft. It must be so. My sister is a witch. I have lost her to Satan.'

'Where could they have gone?' Luca asked the older man.

'Anywhere they choose, since they got out of locked chains and a closed cellar. They could be anywhere in this world or the next.'

Brother Peter came up from the darkness, carrying the torch. It was as if he came out of a well and the dark water closed behind him. He shut the door of the hatch, and stamped the bolt into place as if he were afraid of the very darkness beneath their feet. 'What shall we do now?' he asked Luca.

Luca hesitated, unsure. He glanced towards Lord Lucretili who smoothly took command. 'We'll set a hue and cry for them, naming them as witches, but I don't expect them to be found,' the lord ruled. 'In her absence I shall declare my sister dead.' He turned his head, to hide his grief. 'I can't even have Masses said for her soul ... A sainted father and a cursed sister both gone within four months. He will never even meet her in heaven.'

Luca gave him a moment to recover. 'Admit the Lady Almoner,' he said to Brother Peter.

She was waiting outside the door. Luca caught a glimpse of Freize's grimace of curiosity as she came quietly in and closed the door behind her. She observed the closed hatch, and looked to Luca for an explanation. Carefully, she did not address the Lord Lucretili. Luca assumed that her vows forbade anything but the briefest of contact with men who were not already ordained in the priesthood. 'What has happened, my brother?' she asked him quietly.

'The accused women are missing.'

Her head jolted up to exchange one swift glance with Lord Lucretili. 'How is it possible?' she demanded.

'These are mysteries,' Luca said shortly. 'My question, though, is this: now that we have no suspects, now their guilt is strongly shown by their disappearance, and the way they have got away – what is to be done? Should I continue my inquiry? Or is it closed? You are the Lady Almoner, and in the absence of the Lady Abbess you are the senior lady of the abbey. What is your opinion?'

He could see her flush with pleasure that he had consulted her, that he had named her as the most senior woman of the abbey. 'I think you have completed your inquiry,' she said quietly to him. 'I think you have done everything that anyone could ask of you. You found the very cause of the troubles here, you proved what she was doing, you arrested her and her heretic slave and named them as witches, and they are now gone. Their escape proves their guilt. Your inquiry is closed and – if God is merciful – this abbey is cleansed of their presence. We can get back to normal here.'

Luca nodded. 'You will appoint a new Lady Abbess?' he asked Lord Lucretili.

The Lady Almoner folded her hands inside her sleeves and looked down, modestly, at the floor.

'I would.' He paused, still very shaken. 'If there was anyone I could trust to take the place of such a false sister!

When I think of the damage that she might have done!'

'What she did!' the Lady Almoner reminded him. 'The house destroyed and distracted, one nun dead—'

'Is that all she has done?' Luca inquired limpidly.

'All?' the lord exclaimed. 'Escaping her chains and practising witchcraft, keeping a Moorish slave, heretical practices and murder?'

'Give me a moment,' Luca said thoughtfully. He went to the door and said a quiet word to Freize, then came back to them. 'I am sorry. I knew he would wait there all day until he had a word from me. I have told him to pack our things, so we can leave this afternoon. You are ready to send your report, Brother Peter?'

Luca looked towards Brother Peter but sensed, out of the corner of his eye, a second quick exchange of glances between the Lord Lucretili and the Lady Almoner.

'Oh, of course.' Luca turned to her. 'Lady Almoner, you will be wondering what I recommend for the future of the abbey?'

'It is a great concern to me,' she said, her eyes lowered once more. 'It is my life here, you understand. I am in your hands. We are, all of us, in your hands.'

Luca paused for a moment. 'I can think of no-one who would make a better Lady Abbess. If the nunnery were not handed over to the monastery but were to remain a sister house, an independent sister house for women, would you undertake the duty of being the Lady Abbess?'

She bowed. 'I am very sure that our holy brothers could run this order very well, but if I were called to serve . . .'

'But if I were to recommend that it remain under the rule of women?' For a moment only he remembered the bright pride of the Lady Abbess when she told him that she had never learned that women should be under the rule of men. Almost, he smiled at the memory.

'I could only be appointed by the lord himself,' the Lady Almoner said deferentially, recalling him to the present.

'What do you think?' Luca said, turning to the lord.

'If the place were to be thoroughly exorcised by the priests, if my Lady Almoner were to accept the duty, if you recommend it, I can think of no-one better to guide the souls of these poor young women.'

'I agree,' said Luca. He paused as if a thought had suddenly struck him. 'But doesn't this overset your father's will? Was the abbey not left entirely to your sister? The abbey and the lands around it? The woods and the streams? Were they not to be in your sister's keeping and she to be Lady Abbess till death?'

'As a murderer and a witch, then she is a dead woman in law,' the lord said. 'She is disinherited by her sins; it will be as if she had never been born. She will be an outlaw, with no home anywhere in Christendom. The declaration of her guilt will mean that no-one can offer her shelter, she will have nowhere to lay her false head. She will be dead to the law, a ghost to the people. The Lady Almoner can become the new Lady Abbess and command the lands and the abbey and all.' He put his hand up to shield his eyes. 'Forgive me, I can't help but grieve for my sister!'

'Very well,' Luca said.

'I'll draw up the finding of guilt and the writ for her arrest,' Brother Peter said, unfurling his papers. 'You can sign it at once.'

'And then you will leave, and we will never meet again,' the Lady Almoner said quietly to Luca. Her voice was filled with regret.

'I have to,' he said for her ears alone. 'I have my duty and my vows too.'

'And I have to stay here,' she replied. 'To serve my sisters as well as I can. Our paths will never cross again – but I won't forget you. I won't ever forget you.'

He stepped close so that his mouth was almost against her veil. He could smell a hint of perfume on the linen. 'What of the gold?'

She shook her head. 'I shall leave it where it lies in the waters of the stream,' she promised him. 'It has cost us too dear. I shall lead my sisters to renew their vows of poverty. I won't even tell Lord Lucretili about it. It shall be our secret: yours and mine. Will you keep the secret with me? Shall it be the last thing that we share together?'

Luca bowed his head so that she could not see the bitter twist of his mouth. 'So at the end of my inquiry, you are Lady Abbess, the gold runs quietly in the stream, and the Lady Isolde is as a dead woman.'

Something in his tone alerted her keen senses. 'This is justice!' she said quickly. 'This is how it should be.'

'Certainly, I am beginning to see that this is how some people think it should be,' Luca said drily.

'Here is the writ of arrest and the finding of guilt for the Lady Isolde, formerly known as Lady Abbess of the abbey of Lucretili,' Brother Peter said, pushing the document across the table, the ink still wet. 'And here is the letter approving the Lady Almoner as the new Lady Abbess.'

'Very efficient,' Luca remarked. 'Quick.'

Brother Peter looked startled at the coldness of his tone. 'I thought we had all agreed?'

'There is just one thing remaining,' Luca said. He opened the door and Freize was standing there, holding a leather sack. Luca took it without a word, and put it on the table, then untied the string. He unpacked the objects in order. 'A shoemaker's awl, from the Lady Almoner's secret cupboard in the carved chimney breast of her parlour ...' He heard her sharp gasp and whisper of denial. He reached into his jacket pocket and took out the piece of paper. Slowly, in the silently attentive room, he unfolded it and showed them the print of the bloodstained palm of the nun who had come to him in the night and shown him the stigmata. He put the sharp triangular point of the shoemaker's awl over the bloodstained print: it fitted exactly.

Luca gritted his teeth, facing the fact that his suspicions were true, though he had hoped so much that this hunch, this late awareness, would prove false. He felt like a man gambling with blank-faced dice; now he did not even know what he was betting on. 'There is only one thing that I think certain,' he said tightly. 'There is only one thing that I can be sure of. I think it most unlikely that Our Lord's sacred wounds would be exactly the shape and size of a common shoemaker's awl. These wounds, which I saw and recorded on the palm of a nun of this abbey, were made by human hands, with a cobbler's tools, with this tool in particular.'

'They were hurting themselves,' the Lady Almoner said quickly. 'Hysterical women will do that. I warned you of it.'

'Using the awl from your cupboard?' He took out the little glass jar of seeds, and showed them to the Lady Almoner. 'I take it that these are belladonna seeds?'

Lord Lucretili interrupted. 'I don't know what you are suggesting?'

'Don't you?' Luca asked, as if he were interested. 'Does anyone? Do you know what I am suggesting, my Lady Almoner?'

Her face was as white as the wimple that framed it. She shook her head, her grey eyes wordlessly begging him to say nothing more. Luca looked at her, his young face grim. 'I have to go on,' he said, as if in answer to her unspoken question. 'I was sent here to inquire and I have to go on. Besides, I have to know. I always have to know.'

'There is no need . . .' she whispered. 'The wicked Lady Abbess is gone, whatever she did with the awl, with belladonna . . .'

'I need to know,' he repeated. The last object he brought out was the book of the abbey's accounts that Freize had taken from her room.

'There's nothing wrong with the list of work,' she said, suddenly confident. 'You cannot say that there is anything missing from the goods listed and the market takings. I have been a good steward to this abbey. I have cared for it as if it were my own house. I have worked for it as if I were the lady of the house, I have been the Magistra, I have been in command here.'

'There is no doubt that you have been a good steward,' Luca assured her. 'But there is one thing missing.' He turned to the clerk. 'Brother Peter, look at these and tell me, do you see a fortune in gold mentioned anywhere?'

Peter took the leather-bound book and flipped the pages quickly. 'Eggs,' he volunteered. 'Vegetables, some sewing work, some laundry work, some copying work – no fortune. Certainly no fortune in gold.'

'You know I didn't take the gold,' the Lady Almoner said, turning to Luca, putting a pleading hand on his arm. 'I stole nothing. It was all the Lady Abbess, she that is a witch. She set the nuns to soak the fleeces in the river, she stole the gold dust and sent it out for sale to the gold merchants. As I told you, as you saw for yourself. It was not me. Nobody will say it was me. It was done by her.'

'Gold?' Lord Lucretili demanded in a stagey shout of surprise. 'What gold?'

'The Lady Abbess and her slave have been panning for gold in the abbey stream, and selling it,' the Lady Almoner told him quickly. 'I learned of it by chance when they first came. The inquirer discovered this only yesterday.'

'And where is the gold now?' Luca asked.

'Sold to the merchants on Via Portico d'Ottavia, I suppose,' she flared at him. 'And the profit taken by the witches. We will never get it back. We will never know for sure.'

'Who sold it?' Luca asked, as if genuinely curious.

'The slave, the heretic slave, she must have gone to the Jews, to the gold merchants,' she said quickly. 'She would know what to do, she would trade with them. She would speak their language, she would know how to haggle with them. She is a heretic like them, greedy like them, allowed to profiteer like they are. As bad as them … worse.'

Luca shook his head at her, almost as if he was sorry as his trap closed on her. 'You told me yourself that she never left the nunnery,' he said slowly. He nodded at Brother Peter. 'You took a note of what the Lady Almoner said, that first day, when she was so charming and so helpful.'

Brother Peter turned to the page in his collection of papers, riffling the manuscript pages. 'She said: "She never leaves the Lady Abbess's side. And the Lady Abbess never goes out. The slave haunts the place."'

Luca turned back to the Lady Almoner whose grey eyes flicked – just once – to the lord, as if asking for his help, and then back to Luca.

'You told me yourself she was the Lady Abbess's shadow,' Luca said steadily. 'She never left the nunnery: the gold has never left the nunnery. You have it hidden here.'

Her white face blanched yet more pale but she seemed to draw courage from somewhere. 'Search for it!' she defied him. 'You can tear my storeroom apart and you will not find it. Search my room, search my house, I have no hidden gold here! You can prove nothing against me!'

'Enough of this. My damned sister was a sinner, a heretic, a witch, and now a thief,' Lord Lucretili suddenly intervened. He signed the contract for her arrest without hesitation, and handed it back to Brother Peter. 'Get this published at once. Announce a hue and cry for her. If we take her and her heretic familiar, I shall burn them without further trial. I shall burn them without allowing them to open their mouths.' He reached towards Luca. 'Give me your hand,' he said. 'I thank you, for all you have done here. You have pursued an inquiry and completed it. It's over, thank God. It's done. Let's make an end to it now, like men. Let's finish it here.'

'No, it's not quite over,' Luca said, detaching himself

from the lord's grip. He opened the gatehouse door and led all of them out to the yard where they were loading the coffin of the dead nun onto the black-draped cart.

'What's this?' the lord said irritably, following Luca outside. 'You can't interfere with the coffin. We agreed. I am taking it to a vigil in my chapel. You cannot touch it. You must show respect. Hasn't she suffered enough?'

The lay sisters heaved at the coffin, sweating with effort. There were eight of them hauling it onto the low cart. Luca observed, grimly, that it was a heavy load.

The lord took Luca firmly by the arm. 'Come tonight to the castle,' he whispered. 'We can open it there if you insist. I will help you, as I promised I would.'

Luca was watching Freize, who had gone to help the lay sisters slide the coffin onto the cart. First he shouldered the coffin with them, and then nimbly climbed up into the cart, standing alongside the coffin, a crowbar in his hand.

'Don't you dare touch it!' The Lady Almoner was on the cart, beside him, in a moment, her hands on his forearm. 'This coffin is sanctified, blessed by the priest himself. Don't you dare touch her coffin, she has been censed and blessed with sanctified water, let her rest in peace!'

There was a murmur from the lay sisters and one of them, seeing Freize's determined face as he gently put the Lady Almoner aside, slipped away to the chapel where the nuns were praying for their departed sister's soul.

'Get down,' the Lady Almoner commanded Freize, holding on to his arm. 'I order it. You shall not abuse her in death! You shall not see her poor sainted face!'

'Tell your man to get down,' Lord Lucretili said quietly to Luca, as one man to another. 'Whatever you suspect, it won't help if there is a scandal now, and these women have borne too much already. We have all gone through too much today. We can sort this out later in my chapel. Let the nuns say farewell to their sister and get the coffin away.'

The nuns were pouring out of the chapel towards the yard, their faces white and furious. When they saw Freize on the cart, they started to run.

'Freize!' Luca shouted a warning, as the women fell onto the cart like a sea of white, keening high notes, like a mad choir turning on an enemy. 'Freize, leave it!'

He was too late. Freize had got his crowbar beneath the lid and heaved it up as the first nuns reached the cart and started to grab at him. With a terrible creak the nails yielded on one side and the lid lifted up. Dourly triumphant, Freize fended off one slight woman, and nodded down at Luca. 'As you thought,' he said.

The first of the nuns recoiled at the sight of the open coffin and whispered to the others what they had seen. The others, running up, checked and stopped, as someone at the back let out a bewildered sob. 'What is it now? What in the name of Our Lady is it now?'

Luca climbed up beside Freize, and the sight of the coffin blazed at him. He saw that the dead nun had been packed in bags of gold and one of them had split, showering her with treasure so that she appeared like a glorious pharaoh. Gold dust filled her coffin, gilded her face, enamelled the coins on her staring eyes, glittered in her wimple and turned her gown to treasure. She was a golden icon, a Byzantine glory, not a corpse.

'The witches did this! It's their work,' the Lady Almoner

shouted. 'They put their stolen treasure in with their victim.'

Luca shook his head, at this, her last attempt, and turned to the Lady Almoner and to Lord Lucretili, his young face grave. 'I charge you, Lady Almoner, with the murder of this young woman, Sister Augusta, by feeding her belladonna to cause dreams and hallucinations to disturb the peace and serenity of this nunnery, to shame the Lady Abbess and drive her from her place. I charge you, Lord Lucretili, of conspiring with the Lady Almoner to drive the Lady Abbess from her home, which was her inheritance under the terms of her father's will, and setting the Lady Almoner to steal the gold from the abbey. I charge you both with attempting to smuggle this gold, the Lady Abbess's property, from the abbey in this coffin, and of falsely accusing the Lady Abbess and her slave of witchcraft and conspiring to cause their deaths.'

The lord tried to laugh. 'You're dreaming too. They've driven you mad too!' he started. 'You're wandering in your wits!'

Luca shook his head. 'No, I am not.'

'But the evidence?' Brother Peter muttered to him. 'Evidence?'

'The slave never sold the gold, she never left the abbey – the Lady Almoner told us so. So neither she nor the Lady Abbess ever profited from the gold-panning. But the Lady Almoner accused them, even naming the street in Rome where the gold merchants trade. The only people who tried to get this month's gold out of the abbey were the Lady Almoner and the Lord Lucretili – right now in this coffin. The only woman who showed any signs of wealth was the Lady Almoner, in her silk petticoats and her fine leather slippers. She plotted with the lord to drive his sister from the abbey so that she could become Lady Abbess and they would share the gold together.'

Lord Lucretili looked at Brother Peter, Freize and Luca, and then at his own men-at-arms, the clerks and priests. Then he turned to the blank-faced nuns who were swaying like a field of white lilies and whispering, 'What is he saying? What is the stranger saying? Is he saying bad things? Is he accusing us? Who is he? I don't like him. Did he kill Sister Augusta? Is he the figure of Death that she saw?'

'Whatever you believe, whatever you say, I think you are outnumbered,' Lord Lucretili said in quiet triumph. 'You can leave now safely, or you can face these madwomen. Just as you like. But I warn you, I think they are so crazed that they will tear you apart.'

The crowd of young women, more than two hundred of them, gathered closer to the coffin cart, one after the other, to see the icon that had been made of their innocent sister, and their sibilant whispers were like a thousand hissing snakes as they saw her lying there in her opened coffin, bathed in gold, and Freize standing above her like an abusing man – an emblem of all the wickedness of the world – with a crowbar in his hands.

'This man is our enemy,' the Lady Almoner told them, stepping away from him to put herself at the head of the women. 'He is defending the false Lady Abbess, who killed our sister. He has broken into our sister's consecrated coffin.'

The nuns' faces turned towards her, their expressions blank, as if they were beyond words; and still the sibilant whispers went on.

'They will do what is right,' Luca gambled. He turned to the white-faced women, and tried to capture their attention. 'Sisters, listen to me. Your Lady Abbess has been driven from her home and you have been driven half-mad by belladonna fed to you in bread from this woman's table. Are you still so sick with the drug that you will be obedient to her? Or will you find your own way? Will you think for yourselves? Can you think for yourselves?'

There was a terrible silence. Luca could see the haunted faces of all the women staring blankly at him and for a moment he thought that they were indeed so sick from the drug that they would take him and Freize and Brother Peter and tear them to pieces. He took hold of the side of the cart with one hand, so that no-one could see it shaking, and he pointed his other hand at the Lady Almoner. 'Get down from the cart,' he said. 'I am taking you to Rome to answer for your crimes against your sisters, against the Lady Abbess, and against God.'

She stayed where she was, high above him, and she looked at the nuns, whose faces turned obediently towards her. She said three short terrible words. 'Sisters! Kill him!'

Luca whirled around, pulling his dagger from his boot, and Freize jumped down to stand alongside him. Brother Peter moved towards them, but in a second the three men were surrounded. The nuns, pale and dull-faced, formed themselves into an unbreakable circle, like a wall of coldness, took one step towards the three men, and then took another step closer.

'St James the Greater protect me,' Freize swore. He raised his crowbar, but the nuns neither flinched nor stopped their steady onward pace.

The first nun put her hand to her head, took hold of her wimple, and threw it down on the ground. Horridly, her shaven head made her look like neither man nor woman, but a strange being, some kind of hairless animal. Beside her the next nun did the same, then they all threw their wimples down showing their heads, some cropped, some shaven quite bald.

'God help us!' Luca whispered to his comrades on either side of him. 'What are they doing?'

'I think—' Brother Peter began.

'Traitor!' the nuns whispered together, like a choir.

Luca looked desperately around, but there was no way to break out of the circle of women.

'Traitor!' they said again, more loudly. But now they were not looking at the men, they were looking over the men's heads, upwards, to the Lady Almoner high on the hearse.

'Traitor!' they breathed again.

'Not me!' she said, her voice cracked with sudden fear. 'These men are your enemies, and the witches who are fled.'

They shook their bald heads in one terrible movement, and now they closed on the cart and their grasping hands reached past the men, as if they were nothing, reached up to pull the Lady Almoner down. She looked from one sister to another, then at the locked gate and the porteress who stood before it, arms folded. 'Traitor!' they said and now they had hold of her robe, of her silk petticoats beneath her robe, and were pawing at her, shaking her gown, pulling at her, grasping hold of the fine leather belt of her rosary, gripping the gold chain of keys, bringing her to her knees.

She tore herself from their grip and jumped over the side

of the cart to Luca, clinging to his arm. 'Arrest me!' she said with sudden urgency. 'Arrest me and take me now. I confess. I am your prisoner. Protect me!'

'I have this woman under arrest!' Luca said clearly to the nuns. 'She is my prisoner, in my charge. I will see that justice is done.'

'Traitor!' They were closing in steadily and fast; nothing could stop them.

'Save me!' she screamed in his ear.

Luca put his arm in front of her but the nuns were pressing forwards. 'Freize! Get her out of here!'

Freize was pinned to the cart by a solid wall of women.

'Giorgio!' she called to Lord Lucretili. 'Giorgio! Save me!'

He shook his head convulsively, like a man in a fit, flinching back from the mob of nuns.

'I did it for you!' she cried to him. 'I did it all for you!'

He turned a hard face to Luca. 'I don't know what she's saying, I don't know what she means.'

The blank-faced women came closer, pressing against the men. Luca tried to gently push them away but it was like pushing against an avalanche of snow. They reached for the Lady Almoner with pinching hands.

'No!' Luca shouted. 'I forbid it! She is under arrest. Let justice be done!'

The lord suddenly tore himself away from the scene, strode past them all to the stables, and came out at once on his red-leather caparisoned horse with his men-at-arms closed up around him. 'Open the gate,' he ordered the porteress. 'Open the gate or I will ride you down.'

Mutely she swung it open. The nuns did not even turn

their heads as his cavalcade flung themselves through the gate and away down the road to his castle.

Luca could feel the weight of the women pressing against him. 'I command . . .' he started again, but they were like a wall bearing down on him, and he was being suffocated by their robes, by their remorseless thrusting against him as if they would stifle him with their numbers. He tried to push himself away from the side of the cart; but then he lost his footing and went down. He kicked and rolled in a spasm of terror at the thought that they would trample him, unknowingly, that he would die beneath their sandalled feet. The Lady Almoner would have clung to him but they dragged her off him. Half a dozen women held Luca down as others forced the Lady Almoner to the pyre that she herself had ordered them to build. Freize was shouting now, thrashing about as a dozen women pinned him to the floor. Brother Peter was frozen in shock, white-robed nuns crushing him into silence, against the side of the cart.

She had ordered them to make two high pyres of dry wood, each built around a central pole, set strongly in the ground. They carried her to the nearest, though she kicked and struggled and screamed for help, and they lashed her to the pole, wrapping the ropes tight around her writhing body.

'Save me!' she screamed to Luca. 'For the love of God, save me!'

He had a wimple over his face so he could not see, he was suffocating on the ground under the fabric, but he shouted to them to stop, even as they took the torch from the gate-house porteress, who gave it silently to them, even as they held it to the tarred wood at the foot of the pile, even as she disappeared from view in a cloud of dark smoke, even as he heard her piercing scream of agony as her expensive silk petticoats and her fine woollen gown blazed up in a plume of yellow flames.

The three young men rode away from the abbey in silence, sickened by the violence, glad to escape without a lynching themselves. Every now and then Luca would shudder and violently brush smuts from the sleeves of his jacket, and Freize would pass his broad hand over his bewildered face and say, 'Sweet saints . . .'

They rode all the day on the high land above the forest, the autumn sun hard in their eyes, the stony ground hard underfoot, and when they saw the swinging bough of holly outside a house that marked it as an inn they turned their horses into the stable yard in silence. 'Does Lord Lucretili own this land?' Freize asked the stable lad, before they had even dismounted.

'He does not, you are out of his lordship's lands now. This inn belongs to Lord Piccante.'

'Then we'll stay,' Luca decided. His voice was hoarse; he hawked and spat out the smell of the smoke. 'Saints alive, I can hardly believe we are away from it all.'

Brother Peter shook his head, still lost for words.

Freize took the horses to the stables as the other two went

into the taproom, shouting for the rough red wine of the region to take the taste of wood smoke and tallow from their mouths. They ordered their food in silence and prayed over it when it came.

'I need to go to confession,' Luca said, after they had eaten. 'Our Lady intercede for me, I feel filthy with sin.'

'I need to write a report,' Brother Peter said.

They looked at one another, sharing their sense of horror. 'Who would ever believe what we have seen?' Luca wondered. 'You can write what you like: who would ever believe it?'

'He will,' Brother Peter said. It was the first time he had owned his fealty to the lord and the Order. 'He will understand. The lord of the Order. He has seen all this, and worse. He is studying the end of days. Nothing surprises him. He will read it, and understand it, and keep it under his hand, and wait for our next report.'

'Our next report? We have to go on?' Luca asked disbelievingly.

'I have our next destination under his own seal,' the clerk said.

'Surely this inquiry was such a failure that we will be recalled?'

'Oh no, he will see this as a success,' Brother Peter said grimly. 'You were sent to inquire after madness and manifestations of evil at the abbey and you have done so. You know how it was caused: the Lady Almoner giving the nuns belladonna so that they would run mad. You know why she did it: her desire to win the place of the Lady Abbess for herself and grow rich. You know that Lord Lucretili encouraged her to do it so that he could murder his sister under the pretence that she was a witch and so gain her inheritance of the abbey and the gold. It was your first investigation, and – though I may have had my doubts as to your methods – I will tell my lord that you have completed it successfully.'

'An innocent woman died, a guilty woman was burned by a mob of madwomen, and two women who may be innocent of theft but who are undoubtedly guilty of witchcraft have disappeared into thin air, and you call that a success?'

Brother Peter allowed himself a thin smile. 'I have seen worse investigations with worse outcomes.'

'You must have been to the jaws of hell itself, then!'

He nodded, utterly serious. 'I have.'

Luca paused. 'With other investigators?'

'There are many of you.'

'Young men like me?'

'Some like you, with gifts and a curiosity like you. Some quite unlike you. I don't think I have ever met one with faerie blood before.'

Luca made a quick gesture of denial. 'That's nonsense.'

'The master of the Order picks out the inquirers himself, sends them out, sees what they discover. You are his private army against sin and the coming of the end of days. He has been preparing for this, for years.'

Luca pushed back his chair from the table. 'I'm going to bed. I hope to heaven that I don't dream.'

'You won't dream,' Brother Peter assured him. 'He chose well with you. You have the nerves to bear it, and the courage to undertake it. Soon you will learn the wisdom to judge more carefully.'

'And then?'

'And then he will send you to the frontier of Christendom,

where the heretics and the devils muster to wage war against us and there are no good people at all.'

The women rode side by side, with their horses shoulder to shoulder. Now and then Isolde would give a shuddering sob, and Ishraq would put out a hand to touch her fists, clenched tightly on the reins.

'What do you think will become of the abbey?' Isolde asked. 'I have abandoned them. I have betrayed them.'

The other girl shrugged her shoulders. 'We had no choice. Your brother was determined to get it back into his keeping, the Lady Almoner was determined to take your place. Either she would have poisoned us, or he would have had us burned as witches.'

'How could she do such a thing – the poisoning, and driving us all mad?'

Ishraq shrugged. 'She wanted the abbey for herself. She had worked her way up, she was determined to be Lady Abbess. She was always against you, for all that she seemed so pleasant and so kind when we first got there. And only she knows how long she was plotting with your brother. Perhaps he promised her the abbey long ago.'

'And the inquirer – she misled him completely. The man is a fool.'

'She talked to him, she confided in him when you would

not. Of course he learned her side of the story. But where shall we go now?'

Isolde turned a pale face to her friend. 'I don't know. Now we are truly lost. I have lost my inheritance and my place in the world, and we have both been named as witches. I am so sorry, Ishraq. I should never have brought you into the abbey, I should have let you return to your homeland. You should go now.'

'I go with you,' the girl said simply. 'We go together, wherever that is.'

'I should order you to leave me,' Isolde said with a wry smile. 'But I can't.'

'Your father, my beloved lord, raised us together and said that we should be together always. Let us obey him in that, since we have failed him in so much else.'

Isolde nodded. 'And anyway, I can't imagine living without you.'

The girl smiled at her friend. 'So where to? We can't stay on Lucretili lands.'

Isolde thought for a moment. 'We should go to my father's friends. Anyone who served with him on crusade would be a friend to us. We should go to them, and tell them of this attack on me, we should tell them about my brother, and what he has done to the abbey. We should clear my name. Perhaps one of them will restore me to my home. Perhaps one will help me accuse my brother and win the castle back from him.'

Ishraq nodded. 'Count Wladislaw was your father's dearest friend. His son would owe you friendship. But I don't see how we'd get to him, he lives miles away, in Wallachia, at the very frontier of Christendom.'

'But he'd help me,' Isolde said. 'His father and mine swore eternal brotherhood. He'd help me.'

'We'll have to get money from somewhere,' Ishraq warned. 'If we're going to attempt such a journey we'll have to hire guards, we can't travel alone. The roads are too dangerous.'

'You still have my mother's jewels safe?'

'I never take off the purse. They're in my hidden belt. I'll sell one at the next town.' Ishraq glanced at Lady Isolde's downturned face, her plain brown gown, the poor horse she was riding and her shabby boots. 'This is not what your father wanted for you.'

The young woman bowed her head and rubbed her eyes with the back of her hand. 'I know it,' she said. 'But who knows what he wanted for me? Why would he send me into the abbey if he wanted me to be the woman that he raised me to be? But somewhere, perhaps in heaven, he will be watching over me and praying that I find my way in this hard world without him.'

Ishraq was about to reply when she suddenly pulled up her horse. 'Isolde!' she cried warningly, but she was too late. A rope that had been tied across the road to a strong tree was suddenly snatched tight by someone hidden in the bushes, catching the front legs of Isolde's horse. At once the animal reared up and, tangled in the rope, staggered and went down on its front knees, so that Isolde was flung heavily to the ground.

Ishraq did not hesitate for a moment. Holding her own reins tightly she jumped from the horse and hauled her friend to her feet. 'Ambush!' she cried. 'Get on my horse!'

Four men came tumbling out of the woods on either side of the road, two holding daggers, two holding cudgels. One grabbed Isolde's horse, and threw the reins over a bush, while the other three came on.

'Now, little ladies, put your hands in the air and then throw down your purses and nobody will get hurt,' the first man said. 'Travelling on your own? That was foolish, my little ladies.'

Ishraq was holding a long thin dagger out before her, her other hand clenched in a fist, standing like a fighter, well-balanced on both feet, swaying slightly as she eyed the three men, wondering which would come first. 'Come any closer and you are a dead man,' she said briefly.

He lunged towards them and Ishraq feinted with the knife and spun round, slashed at the arm of another man, and turned back her fist flying out to crunch against the first man's face. But she was outnumbered. The third man raised the cudgel and smashed it against the side of her head, she went down with a groan, and Isolde at once stepped over her to protect her, and faced the three men. 'You can have my purse,' she said. 'But leave us alone.'

The wounded man clapped his hand over his arm and cursed as the blood flowed between his fingers. 'She-dog,' he said shortly.

The other man gingerly touched his bruised face. 'Give us the purse,' he said angrily.

Isolde untied the purse that hung at her belt and tossed it to him. There was nothing in it but a few pennies. She knew that Ishraq had her mother's sapphires safe in a belt tied inside the bodice of her tunic. 'That's all we have,' she said. 'We're poor girls. That's all we have in the world.'

'Show me your hands,' said the man with the cudgel.

Isolde held out her hands.

'Palms up,' he said.

She turned her hands upwards and at once he stepped forwards, twisted her arms behind her back, and she felt the other man rope her tightly.

'Lady's hands,' he jeered. 'Soft white hands. You've never done a stroke of work in your life. You'll have a wealthy family or friends somewhere who will pay a ransom for you, won't you?'

'I swear to you that no-one will pay for me.' Isolde tried to turn but the ropes bit tight into her arms. 'I swear it. I am alone in the world, my father just dead. My friend is alone too. Let me ...'

'Well, we'll see,' the man said.

On the ground Ishraq stirred and tried to get to her feet. 'Let me help her,' Isolde said. 'She's hurt.'

'Tie them up together,' the man said to his fellows. 'In the morning we'll see if anyone is missing two pretty girls. If they aren't, then we'll see if anyone wants two pretty girls. If they don't, we'll sell them to the Turks.' The men laughed and the one with the bruised face patted Isolde's cheek.

The chief hit his hand away. 'No spoiling the goods,' he said. 'Not till we know who they are.' He heaved Ishraq to her feet and held her as she too was roped. 'I'm sorry,' she mumbled to Isolde.

'Give me water for her,' Isolde commanded the man. 'And let me bathe her head.'

'Come on,' was all he said to the others and led the way off the track to their hidden camp.

Luca and his two companions were quiet the following morning when they started at dawn. Freize was nursing a headache from what he said was the worst ale in Christendom, Brother Peter seemed thoughtful, and Luca was reviewing all that had been said and done at the abbey, certain that he could have done better, sure that he had failed, and – more than anything else – puzzling over the disappearance of the Lady Abbess and her strange companion, out of chains, out of a stone cellar, into thin air.

They left the inn just as the sky was turning from darkness to grey, hours before sunrise, and they wrapped their cloaks tightly around them against the morning chill. Brother Peter said that they were to ride north, until he opened their next orders.

'Because we like nothing more than when he breaks that seal, unfolds that paper, and tells us that some danger is opening up under our feet and we are to ride straight into it.' Freize addressed the ground. 'Mad nuns one day, what's for today? We don't even know.'

'Hush,' Luca said quietly. 'We don't know, nobody knows; that's the very point of it.'

'We know it won't be kindly,' Freize remarked to his horse, who rolled an ear back towards him and seemed to sympathise.

They went on in silence for a little while, following a

dusty track that climbed higher and higher between bare rocks. The trees were fewer here, an odd twisted olive tree, a desiccated pine tree. Above they could see an eagle soaring and the sun was bright in their faces though the wind from the north was cold. As they reached the top of the plateau there was a little forested area, to the right of the road. The horses dropped their heads and plodded, the riders slumped in their saddles, when Luca's eye was caught by something that looked like a long black snake lying in the dust of the road before them. He raised his hand for a halt and, when Freize started to speak, he turned in the saddle and scowled at him, so the man was silent.

'What is it?' Brother Peter mouthed at him.

Luca pointed in reply. In the road in front of them, scuffed over with dust and hidden with carefully placed leaves, was a rope, tied to a tree on one side, disappearing into the woods on the right.

'Ambush,' Freize said quietly. 'You wait here; act like I've gone for a piss. ... Saints save us! That damned ale!' he said more clearly. He hitched his trousers, slid off his horse and went, cursing the ale, to the side of the road. A swift glance in each direction and he was stepping delicately and quietly into the trees, circling the likely destination of the rope into the bushes. There was a brief silence and then a low whistle like a bird call told the others that they could come. They pushed their way through the little trees and scrubby bushes to find Freize seated like a boulder on the chest of a man frozen with fear. Freize's big hand was over his mouth, his large horn-handled dagger blade at the man's throat. The captive's eyes rolled towards Luca and Brother Peter as they came through the bushes, but he lay quite still.

'Sentry,' Freize said quietly. 'Fast asleep. So a pretty poor sentry. But there'll be some band of brigands within earshot.' He leaned forwards to the man, who was gulping for air underneath his weight. 'Where is everyone else?'

The man rolled his eyes to the woods on their right.

'And how many?' Freize asked. 'Blink when I say. Ten? No? Eight? No? Five, then?' He looked towards Luca. 'Five men. Why don't we just leave them to do their business? No point looking for trouble.'

'What is their business?' Luca asked.

'Robbery,' Brother Peter said quietly. 'And sometimes they kidnap people and sell them to the Ottomans for the galleys.'

'Not necessarily,' Freize interrupted quickly. He scowled at Brother Peter to warn him to say no more. 'Might just be poaching a bit of game. Poachers and thieves. Not doing a great deal of harm. No need for us to get involved.'

'Kidnap?' Luca repeated icily.

'Not necessarily so . . .' Freize repeated. 'Probably nothing more than poachers.'

It was too late. Luca was determined to save anyone from the galleys of the Ottoman pirates. 'Gag him, and tie him up,' he ordered. 'We'll see if they are holding anyone.' He looked around the clearing; a little path, scarcely more than a goat's track, led deeper into the woods. He waited till the man was gagged and bound to a tree, and then led the way, sword in one hand, dagger in the other, Freize behind him and Brother Peter bringing up the rear.

'Or we could just ride on,' Freize suggested in an urgent whisper.

'Why are we doing this?' Brother Peter breathed.

'His parents.' Freize nodded towards Luca's back. 'Kidnapped and enslaved into the Ottoman galleys. Probably dead. It's personal for him. I hoped for a moment, that you might have taken my hint, and kept your mouth shut – but no ...'

The slight scent of a damped-down fire warned them that they were near a camp and Luca halted and peered through the trees. Five men lay sleeping around a doused fire, snoring heavily. A couple of empty wineskins and the charred bones of a stolen sheep showed that they had eaten and drunk well before falling asleep. To the side of them, tied back to back, were two figures, hooded and cloaked.

Gambling that the roaring snores would cover any noise that they made, Luca whispered to Freize and sent him towards the horses. Quiet as a cat, Freize moved along the line of tied animals, picked out the two very best and took their reins, and untied the rest. 'Gently,' he said softly to them. 'Wait for my word.'

Brother Peter tiptoed his way back to the road. Their own three horses and the donkey were tied to a tree. He mounted his horse and held the reins of the others, ready for a quick escape. The brightness of the morning sun threw the shadows darkly on the road. Brother Peter prayed briefly but fervently that Luca would save the captives – or whatever he was planning to do – and come away. Bandits were a constant menace on these country roads and it was not their mission to challenge each and every one. The lord of the Order would not thank him if Luca was killed in a brawl when he was showing such early talent as an inquirer for the Order.

Back in the clearing, Luca watched Freize take control of

the horses, then slid his sword into the scabbard and wormed his way through the bushes to where the captives were tied to each other, and roped to a tree. He cut the rope to the tree and both hooded heads came up at once. Luca put his finger to his lips to warn them to be quiet. Quickly, in silence, they squirmed towards him, bending away from their bonds so that he could cut the rope around their wrists. They rubbed their wrists and their hands, without saying a word, as Luca bent to their boots and cut the ropes around their feet. He leaned to the nearest captive and whispered, 'Can you stand? Can you walk?'

There was something that snagged his memory, as sharp as a tap on the shoulder, the minute he leaned towards the captive, and then he realised that this was no stranger. There was a scent of rosewater as she put back her hood and the sea of golden hair tumbled over her shoulders and the former Lady Abbess smiled up at him and whispered, 'Yes, Brother, I can; but please help Ishraq, she's hurt.'

He pulled Isolde to her feet, and then bent to help the other woman. At once he could see that she had taken a blow to the side of her head. There was blood on her face, her beautiful dark skin was bruised like a plum, and her legs buckled beneath her when he tried to get her up.

'You go to the horses,' he whispered to Isolde. 'Quiet as you can. I'll bring her.'

She nodded and went silent as a doe through the trees skirting the clearing to reach Freize, who helped her up into the saddle of the best horse. Luca came behind her carrying Ishraq and bundled her onto a second horse. Tapping the horses' chests, urging them with whispers to back away from where they had been tethered, the two men led the animals with the girls on their backs down a little track to where Brother Peter waited on the road.

'Oh no,' Brother Peter said flatly when he saw the white face and the thick blonde hair of the Lady Abbess. At once she pulled her brown hood up over her hair to hide her face, and lowered her eyes. Peter turned to Freize. 'You let him risk his life for this? You let him risk us? His sacred mission?'

Freize shrugged. 'Better go,' was all he said. 'And maybe we'll get away with it.'

Freize mounted his own cob, and then cocked an ear to the woods behind them. In the clearing, one of the sleeping men grunted, and turned over in his sleep, and another one cursed and raised himself onto one elbow. The horses left untethered turned their heads and whinnied for their companions, and one started to move after them.

'Go!' Luca ordered.

Freize kicked his cob into a canter, leading Ishraq's horse, with her clinging, half-conscious, to the horse's mane. Isolde snatched up her reins and urged her horse alongside them. Luca vaulted into his saddle as they heard the men shouting from behind. The first loose horse came out of the woods, trotting to catch up with him, and then all the others followed, their reins trailing. Freize yelled an incomprehensible word of warning to the horses as they clattered from the woods and came towards him. The gang of thieves scrambled after their runaway horses, then saw the little group on the road, and realised they had been robbed.

'Full gallop!' Luca yelled, and ducked as the first arrow whistled overhead. 'Go!' he shouted. 'Go! Go!'

They all hunched low over their horses' necks, thundering

down the road as the men spilled out of the wood, cursing and swearing, sending a shower of misdirected arrows after them. One of the stray horses bucked and screamed as it took an arrow in the rump, and raced ahead. The others weaved around them, making aim even more difficult. Luca held the pace as fast as he dared on the stony road, pulling up his frightened horse so it slowed to a canter and then a walk and then halted, panting when they were well out of range.

The stray horses collected around Freize. 'Gently, my loves,' he said. 'We're safe if we are all together.' He got down from his cob and went to the wounded horse. 'Just a scratch, little girl,' he said tenderly. 'Just a scratch.' She bowed her head to him and he pulled gently at her ears. 'I'll bathe it when we get to wherever in God's earth we are going, sweetheart.'

Ishraq was clinging on to the neck of her horse, exhausted and sick with her injury. Freize looked up at her. 'She's doing poorly. I'll take her up before me.'

'No,' Isolde said. 'Lift her up onto my horse. We can ride together.'

'She can barely stay on!'

'I'll hold her,' she said with firm dignity. 'She would not want to be held by a man, it is against her tradition. And I would not like it for her.'

Freize glanced at Luca for permission and, when the young man shrugged, he got down from his own horse and walked over to where the slave swayed in the saddle.

'I'll lift you over to your mistress,' he said to her, speaking loudly.

'She's not deaf! She's just faint!' Luca said irritably.

'Both as stubborn as each other,' Freize confided to the

slave girl's horse as her rider tumbled into his arms. 'Both as stubborn as the little donkey, God bless him.' Gently, he carried Ishraq over to Isolde's horse and softly set her in the saddle and made sure that she was steady. 'Are you sure you can hold her?' he asked Isolde.

'I can,' she said.

'Well, tell me if it is too much for you. She's no light-weight, and you're only a weakly little thing.' He turned to Luca. 'I'll lead her horse. The others will follow us.'

'They'll stray,' Luca predicted.

'I'll whistle them on,' Freize said. 'Never hurts to have a few spare horses, and maybe we can sell them if we need.'

He mounted his own steady cob, took the reins of Ishraq's horse, and gave a low encouraging whistle to the other four horses who at once clustered around him, and the little cavalcade set off steadily down the road.

'How far to the nearest town?' Luca asked Brother Peter.

'About eight miles, I think,' he said. 'I suppose she'll make it; but she looks very sick.'

Luca looked back at Ishraq, who was leaning back against Isolde, grimacing in pain, her face pale. 'She does. And then we'll have to turn her over to the local lord for burning when we get there. We've rescued her from bandits and saved her from the Ottoman galleys to see her burned as a witch. I doubt she will think we have done her a kindness.'

'She should have been burned as a witch yesterday,' Brother Peter said unsympathetically. 'Every hour is a gift to her.'

Luca reined back to bring his horse up alongside Isolde. 'How was she injured?'

'She took a blow from a cudgel while she was trying to

defend us. She's a clever fighter usually, but there were four of them. They jumped us on the road trying to steal from us and when they saw we were women without guards they thought to take us for ransom.' She shook her head as if to rid herself of the memory. 'Or for the galleys.'

'They didn't –' he tried to find the words '– er, hurt you?'

'You mean, did they rape us?' she asked, matter-of-factly. 'No, they were keeping us for ransom and then they got drunk. But we were lucky.' She pressed her lips together. 'I was a fool to ride out without a guard. I put Ishraq in danger. We'll have to find someone to travel with.'

'You won't be able to travel at all,' Luca said bluntly. 'You are my prisoners. I am arresting you under charges of witchcraft.'

'Because of poor Sister Augusta?'

He blinked away the picture of the two young women, bloodied like butchers. 'Yes.'

'When we get to the next town and the doctor sees Ishraq, will you listen to me, before you hand us over? I will explain everything to you, I will confess everything that we have done and what we have not done, and you can be the judge as to whether we should be sent back to my brother for burning. For that is what you will be doing, you know. If you send me back to him, you will sign my death warrant. I will have no trial worth the writing, I will have no hearing worth the listening. You will send me to my death. Won't that sit badly on your conscience?'

Brother Peter brought his horse alongside. 'The report has gone already,' he said with dour finality. 'And you are listed as a witch. There is nothing that we can do but release you to the civil law.'

'I can hear her,' Luca said irritably. 'I can hear her out. And I will.'

She looked at him. 'The woman you admire so much is a liar and an apostate,' she said bluntly. 'The Lady Almoner is my brother's lover, his dupe, and his accomplice. I would swear to it. He persuaded her to drive the nuns mad and blame it on me so that you would come and destroy my rule at the abbey. She was his fool and I think you were hers.'

Luca felt his temper flare at being called a fool by this girl, but gritted his teeth. 'I listened to her when you would not deign to speak to me. I liked her when you would not even show me your face. She swore she would tell the truth when you were – who knows what you were doing? At any rate, I had nothing to compare her with. But even so I listened out for her lies, and I understood that she was putting the blame on you when you did not even defend yourself to me. You may call me a fool – though I see you were glad enough for my help back there with the bandits – but I was not fooled by her – whatever you say.'

She bowed her head, as if to silence her own hasty words. 'I don't think you are a fool, Inquirer,' she said. 'I am grateful to you for saving us. I shall be glad to explain my side of this to you. And I hope you will spare us.'

The physician called to the Moorish slave as they rested in the little inn in the small town pronounced her bloodied and bruised but no bones broken. Luca paid for the best bed for her and Isolde, and paid extra for them not to have to share the room with other travellers.

'How am I to report that we are now paying for two women to travel with us?' Brother Peter protested. 'Known criminals?'

'You could say that I need servants, and you have provided me with two bonny ones,' Freize suggested, earning him a sour look from the clerk.

'No need to report anything at all. This is not an inquiry,' Luca ruled. 'This is just the life of the road, not part of our work.'

Isolde put Ishraq into the big bed, as if she were an equal, spooned soup into her mouth as if she were her sister, cared for her like her child and sat with her as she slept.

'How is the pain?'

'No better,' Ishraq grimaced. 'But at least I don't think I am doomed any more. That ride was like a nightmare, the pain went on and on. I thought I was going to die.'

'I couldn't protect you from the roughness of the road nor the stumbles of the horse. It jolted me, it must have been horrible for you.'

'It was hard to bear.'

'Ishraq, I have failed you. You could have been killed or murdered or enslaved. And now we are captured again. I have to let you go. You can go now, while I talk to them. Please – save yourself. Go south, get away to your homeland and pray to your god we will meet again one day.'

The girl opened her bruised eyes and gleamed at Isolde. 'We stay together,' she ruled. 'Didn't your father raise us as sisters of the heart, as companions who were never parted?'

'He may have done so, but my mother didn't give it her blessing, she fought against us being together every day of her life,' Isolde shrewdly reminded her. 'And we have had nothing but heartache since we lost my father.'

'Well, my mother blessed our friendship,' Ishraq replied. 'She told me: "Isolde is the sister of your heart". She was happy that I was with you all the day long, that we did our lessons together and played together, and she loved your father.'

'They taught you languages,' Isolde reminded her with pretended resentment. 'And medicine. And fighting skills. While I had nothing to learn but music and embroidery.'

'They prepared me to be your servant and companion,' Ishraq said. 'To serve and protect you. And so I am. I know the things I need to know to serve you. You should be glad of it.'

A quick tap of a finger on her cheek told her that Isolde was glad of it.

'Well, then,' Ishraq said. 'I need to sleep. You go to dinner. See if you can get him to release us. And if he does that, see if you can make him give us some money.'

'You think very highly of my powers of persuasion,' Isolde said ruefully.

'Actually, I do.' Ishraq nodded as her eyes closed. 'Especially with him.'

Luca sent for Isolde at dinnertime, planning to question her privately as they ate together, but then he found that both Brother Peter and Freize intended to be in the room with them.

'I shall serve the food,' Freize said. 'Better me than some wench from the inn, listening to everything you say, interrupting as like as not.'

'While you are notably reticent.'

'Reticent,' Freize repeated, committing the word to memory. 'Reticent. D'you know? I imagine that I am.'

'And I shall take a note. This is still an inquiry for murder and witchcraft,' Brother Peter said severely. 'Just because we found them in yet more trouble, does not prove their innocence. Quite the opposite. Good women stay at home and mind their manners.'

'We can hardly blame them for being homeless when their abbey was going to burn them for witches,' Luca said irritably. 'Or blame her for being expelled by her brother.'

'Whatever the reason, she and her servant are homeless and uncontrolled,' Brother Peter insisted. 'No man rules them and no man protects them. They are certain to get into trouble and to cause trouble.'

'I thought we had answered the questions of the abbey,' Luca said, looking from one determined face to the other. 'I thought we had concluded our inquiry and sent in our report? I thought they were innocent of most of the crimes? I thought we were satisfied as to their innocence?'

'We were satisfied as to the drugging, the poisoning and the murder,' Peter said. 'Satisfied that the great crimes were performed by the Lady Almoner. But what were the two of them doing in the mortuary that night? Don't you remember them tampering with the corpse, and the Lady Almoner saying they were having a Satanic Mass on the nun's body?'

Freize nodded. 'He's right. They have to explain.'

'I'll ask,' Luca said. 'I'll ask about everything. But if you remember her brother coming in, secretly hand in glove with that woman, and his readiness to see his sister burn before him – you can't help but pity her. And, anyway, if her answers are not satisfactory we can hand them over to the Lord Piccante who is the master here, and he can burn the two of them as the Lord Lucretili would have done. Is that your wish?' He looked at their glum faces. 'You want to see them dead? Those two young women?'

'My wish is to see justice done,' said Brother Peter. 'Forgiveness is for God.'

'Or I suppose we could just turn a blind eye and let them get away in the morning,' Freize suggested, as he headed out of the room.

'Oh, for goodness' sake!' Luca exclaimed.

Just then, Isolde came down the stairs for dinner, wearing

a gown she had borrowed from the innkeeper's wife. It was made of some coarse material, dyed a dark blue, and on her head she had a cap like countrywomen wore. It showed the golden fold of her hair where she had it twisted back into a plait. Luca remembered the tumble of gold when he had tackled her in the stable yard and the scent of rosewater when he had held her down. In the simple outfit her beauty was suddenly radiant and Luca and even Brother Peter were tongue-tied.

'I hope you are recovered,' Luca muttered as he set a chair for her.

Her eyes were downcast, her smile directed to her feet. 'I was not injured, I was only frightened. Ishraq is resting and recovering. She will be better in the morning, I am sure.'

Freize entered, banging the door, and started to slap down dishes onto the table. 'Fricassée of chicken – they killed an old rooster specially. Stew of beef with turnip, a pâté of pork – I wouldn't touch it myself. Some sausage which looks quite good and a few slices of ham.' He went back out and came in again with more dishes. 'Some marchpane from the local market which tastes almost like the real thing, but I wouldn't swear to its youth; some pastries which the goodwife made herself, I saw them come out of the oven and I tasted them for your safety and approve them. They have no fruit here at all but some apples which are so green that they are certain to half-kill you, and some sugared chestnuts which they have saved for visiting gentry for a good year. So I would not answer for them.'

'I am sorry,' Luca said to Isolde.

'No,' she said with a smile. 'He is very engaging and probably truthful, which matters more.'

'Some very good wine, that I took the liberty of tasting for you in the cellar, which would do my lady no harm at all.' Freize was encouraged by Isolde's praise into pouring the wine with a flourish. 'Some small ale to quench your thirst that they brew here from the mountain water, and is actually rather good. You wouldn't drink the water in any case, but you probably could here. And if you fancy a couple of eggs I can get them boiled or scrambled up as you wish.'

'He likes to think he is devoted to my service, and really he is very good to me,' Luca said in an undertone.

'And moreover,' Freize said, bearing down upon Isolde, 'there is a nice sweet wine for your voider course, and some good bread coming out of the oven now. They don't have wheat, of course, but the rye bread is sweet and light, being made with some kind of honey – which I established by a long conversation with the cook who is no other than the goodwife, and a very good wife, I would think. She says that the gown becomes you better than her, and so it does.'

'But sometimes, of course, he is quite unendurable,' Luca finished. 'Freize, please serve the meal in silence.'

'Silence, he says.' Freize nodded at Isolde with a con-spiratorial smile. 'And silent I am. See me: utterly silent. I am reticent, you know. Reticent.'

She could not help but laugh as Freize folded lip over lip, put all the remaining dishes on the table, bowed low, and stood with his back to the door, facing the room like a per-fect servant. Brother Peter sat down and started to help himself to the dishes, with his manuscript beside him and his ink pot adjacent to his wine glass.

'I see that you are questioning me, as well as feeding me,' she said to Luca.

'As the sacred Mass,' Brother Peter answered for him. 'Where you have to answer for your soul and your faith before you partake. Can you answer for your soul, my lady?'

'I have done nothing that I am ashamed of,' she said steadily.

'The attack on the dead woman?'

Luca shot a quelling look at Brother Peter but Isolde answered without fear. 'It was no attack. We had to know what she had been given to eat. And by discovering that she had been poisoned we saved the others. I knew Sister Augusta, and you did not. I tell you: she would have been glad that we did that to her – after death – so that we could save her sisters pain in their lives. We found the berries of belladonna in her belly, which proved that the nuns were being poisoned, that they were not possessed or going mad as we all feared. I hoped we could have given you the berries as evidence and saved the abbey from my brother and the Lady Almoner.'

Luca spooned the fricassée of chicken onto a big slice of rye bread and passed it to her. Daintily, she produced a fork from the sleeve of her gown and ate the meat from the top of the bread. None of them had seen such table manners before. Luca quite forgot his questions. Freize at the doorway was transfixed.

'I've never seen such a thing,' Luca remarked.

'It's called a fork,' Isolde said, as if it were quite ordinary. 'They use them in the court of France. For eating. My father gave me this one.'

'Never eaten anything that couldn't be speared on the tip of a dagger,' Freize offered from the doorway.

'Enough,' Luca advised this most interfering servant.

'Or sucked it up,' Freize said. He paused for a moment, to explain more clearly. 'If soup.'

'"If soup!"' Luca turned on him wrathfully. '"If soup!" For God's sake, be silent. No, better still, wait in the kitchen.'

'Keeping the door,' Freize said, motioning that his work was essential. 'Keeping the door from intruders.'

'God knows, I would rather have an intruder, I would rather have a band of brigands burst in, than have you commenting on everything that takes place.'

Freize shook his head in remorse and once again folded lower lip over upper lip to indicate his future silence. 'Like the grave,' he said to Luca. 'You go on. Doing well: probing but respectful. Don't mind me.'

Luca turned back to Isolde. 'You don't need an interrogation,' he said. 'But you must understand that we cannot release you unless we are convinced of your innocence. Eat your dinner and tell me honestly what happened at the abbey and what you plan for your future.'

'May I ask you what happened at the abbey? Have you closed it down?'

'No,' he said. 'I will tell you more later, but we left the abbey with the nuns in prayer and a new Lady Abbess will be appointed.'

'The Lady Almoner?'

'Dead,' was all he told her. 'Now you tell me all that you know.'

Isolde ate a little more and then put the slice of bread to one side. Brother Peter served the ragout onto her slice of bread, and dipped his pen in the ink.

'When I came to the abbey, I was grieving for my father and opposed to his wishes,' she said honestly. 'Ishraq came with me – we have never been parted since my father brought her and her mother home from the Holy Land.'

'She is your slave?' Brother Peter asked.

Vehemently, Isolde shook her head. 'She is free. Just because she is of Moorish descent everyone always thinks she is enslaved. My father honoured and respected her mother and gave her a Christian burial when she died when Ishraq was seven years old. Ishraq is a free woman, as her mother was free.'

'Freer than you?' Luca asked.

He saw her flush. 'Yes, as it turns out. For I was bound by the terms of my father's will to join the abbey, and now that I have lost my place I am a wanted criminal.'

'What were you doing with the body of Sister Augusta?'

She leaned forwards, fixing her dark blue gaze on him. Luca would have sworn she was speaking the truth. 'Ishraq trained with the Moorish physicians in Spain. My father took us both to the Spanish court when he was advising them about a new crusade. Ishraq studied with one of the greatest doctors: she studied herbs, drugs and poisons. We suspected that the nuns were being drugged, and we knew that I was having the most extraordinary dreams and waking with wounds in my hands.'

'You had the stigmata on your own hands?' Luca interrupted her.

'I believed that I did,' she said, suddenly downcast at the memory. 'At first I was so confused that I thought the marks were true: painful miracles.'

'Was it you that came to my room and showed me your hands?'

Silently, she nodded.

'There is no shame in it,' Luca said gently to her.

'It feels like a sin,' she said quietly. 'To show the wounds of Our Lord and to wake so troubled, after dreams of running and screaming . . .'

'You thought it was the drug belladonna that made you dream?'

'Ishraq thought it so. She thought that many of the nuns were taking the drug. Ishraq never ate in the refectory, she ate with the servants, and she never had the dreams. None of the servants were having dreams. Only the sisters who ate the refectory bread were affected. When Sister Augusta died so suddenly Ishraq thought that her heart had ceased to beat under the influence of the drug; she knew that if you have too much it kills you. We decided to open her belly to look for the berries.'

Brother Peter shaded his eyes with his hands, as if he could still see the two of them, bloodied to the elbow, about their terrible work.

'It was a very great sin to touch the body,' Luca prompted her. 'It is a crime as well as a sin to touch a corpse.'

'Not to Ishraq.' She defended her friend. 'She is not of our faith, she does not believe in the resurrection of the body. To her it was no greater sin than examining an animal. You can accuse her of nothing but of practising the craft of medicine.'

'It was a great sin for you,' he persisted. 'And surely unbearable? How could you – a young lady – do such a thing?'

She bowed her head. 'For me it was a sin. But I thought it had to be done, and I would not leave Ishraq to do it alone. I thought I should be ...' She paused. 'I thought I should be courageous. I am the Lady Lucretili. I thought I should be as brave as the name I bear. And at least we saw the berries in her belly, dark specks of the dried berries.' She put her hand into the pocket of her gown and brought out a couple of flecks of dark hard berries like peppercorns. 'We found these. This is proof of what we were doing, and what we found.'

Luca hesitated. 'You took these from the dead woman's belly?' he asked.

She nodded. 'It had to be done,' she said. 'How else could we prove to you that the nuns were being fed belladonna berries?'

Gingerly, Luca took them, and quickly passed them over to Brother Peter. 'Did you know the Lady Almoner was working with your brother?'

She nodded, sadly. 'I knew there was something between them, but I never asked. I should have demanded the truth – I always felt that she ...' She broke off. 'I didn't know, I saw nothing for sure. But I sensed that they were ...'

'Were what?'

'Could they possibly have been lovers?' she asked, very low. 'Is it possible? Or is it my jealous imagining? And my envy of her beauty?'

'Why would you say such a thing? Of the Lady Almoner?'

She shrugged. 'I sometimes think things, or see things, or almost smell things, that are not very clear, or not apparent to others ... in this case it was as if she belonged to him, as if she was ... his shirt.'

'His shirt?' Luca repeated.

Again she shook her head as if to shake away a vision. 'As if his scent was upon her. I can't explain better than that.'

'Do you have the Sight?' Brother Peter interrupted, staring at her over the top of his quill.

'No.' She shook her head in rapid denial. 'No, nothing like that. Nothing so certain, nothing so clear. I would not attend to it if I did have, I don't set myself up as some kind of seer. I have a sense of things, that is all.'

'But you sensed that she was his woman?'

She nodded. 'But I had no evidence, nothing I could accuse her of. It was just like a whisper, like the silk of her petticoat.'

A rumbling cough from the doorway reminded the men that it was Freize who had first noted the silk petticoat.

'It's hardly a crime to wear a silk petticoat,' Brother Peter said irritably.

'It was a suggestion,' she said thoughtfully. 'That she was not what she seemed, that the abbey under her command was not as it seemed. Not as it should be. But ...' She shrugged. 'I was new to the life, and she seemed in charge of everything. I did not question her and I did not challenge her rule of the abbey at first. I should have done so. I should have sent for an inquirer at once.'

'How did you get out of the cellar beneath the gate-house?' Brother Peter suddenly changed the course of questioning, hoping to throw her. 'How did you get out and escape when there were handcuffs and leg-cuffs and the cellar was dug into solid stone?'

Luca frowned at the harshness of his tone, but Brother Peter just waited for the answer, his pen poised. 'It's the major charge,' he remarked quietly to Luca. 'It's the only evidence of witchcraft. The work of the slave is the work of a heretic, she is not under the command of the Church. The attack on the body is the other woman's work also – we might think of it as evil but the heretic is not under our jurisdiction. The Lady Abbess has committed no crime, but her escape is suspicious. Her escape looks like witchcraft. She has to explain it.'

'How did you get out?' Luca asked her. 'Think carefully before you reply.'

She hesitated. 'You make me afraid,' she said. 'Afraid to speak.'

'You should be afraid,' Luca warned her. 'If you got out of the handcuffs and the cellar by magical means or with the assistance of the Devil then you will face a charge of witchcraft for that alone. I can acquit you of tampering with the dead woman, but I would have to charge you with invoking the Devil to aid your escape.'

She drew a breath. 'I can't tell you,' she started. 'I can't tell you anything that makes sense.'

Brother Peter's pen was poised over the page. 'You had better think of something; this is the one remaining charge against you. Getting out of the manacles and through the walls is witchcraft. Only witches can walk through walls.'

There was a terrible silence as Isolde looked down at her hands and the men waited for her answer.

'What did you do?' Luca said quietly.

She shook her head. 'Truly, I don't know.'

'What happened?'

'It was a mystery.'

'Was it witchcraft?' Brother Peter asked.

There was a long painful silence.

'I let her out,' Freize suddenly volunteered, stepping into the room from his post at the door.

Brother Peter rounded on him. 'You! Why?'

'Mercy,' Freize said shortly. 'Justice. It was obvious they had done nothing. It wasn't them panning for gold and swishing around in silk petticoats. That brother of hers would have burned her the moment he got his hands on her, the Lady Almoner had the pyres built ready. I waited till you were all busy in the yard, deciding what should be done, then I slipped down to the cell, released them, helped them up the ladder, got them into the stable yard on horses, and sent them on their way.'

'You freed my suspects?' Luca asked him, disbelievingly.

'Little lord.' Freize spread his hands apologetically. 'You were going to burn two innocent women, caught up in the excitement of the moment. Would you have listened to me? No. For I am well-known as a fool. Would you have listened to them? No. For the Lady Almoner had turned your head and this lady's brother was quick and ready with a torch. I knew you would thank me in the end, and here we are, with you thanking me.'

'I don't thank you!' Luca exclaimed, angry beyond measure. 'I should dismiss you from my service and charge you with interfering with a papal inquiry!'

'Then the lady will thank me,' Freize said cheerfully. 'And if she doesn't, maybe the pretty slave will.'

'She's not my slave,' Isolde said, quite at a loss. 'And you will find that she never thanks anyone. Especially a man.'

'Perhaps she will come to value me,' Freize said with dignity. 'When she knows me better.'

'She will never know you better for you are about to be dismissed,' Luca said furiously.

'Seems harsh,' Freize said, glancing at Brother Peter. 'Wouldn't you say? Given that it was me that stopped us from burning two innocent women, and then saved all five of us from the brigands. Not to mention gaining some valuable horses?'

'You interfered with the course of my inquiry and released my prisoners,' Luca insisted. 'What can I do but dismiss you and send you back to the monastery in disgrace?'

'For your own good,' Freize explained. 'And theirs. Saving you all from yourselves.'

Luca turned to Brother Peter.

'But why did you fasten up the handcuffs after you had released them?' Brother Peter asked.

Freize paused. 'For confusion,' he said gravely. 'To cause more confusion.'

Isolde, despite her anxiety, choked back a laugh. 'You have certainly caused that,' she said. A small smile exchanged between them made Luca suddenly frown.

'And do you swear you did this?' he asked tightly. 'However ridiculous you are?'

'I do,' Freize said.

Luca turned to Brother Peter. 'This vindicates them from the charge of witchcraft.'

'The report has gone,' Brother Peter ruled thoughtfully. 'We said that the captives were missing, accused of witchcraft, but that their accusers were definitely guilty. The matter is closed unless you want to reopen it. We don't have to report that we met them again. It is not our job to arrest them if we have no evidence of witchcraft. We're

He nodded. 'He was using the Lady Almoner to steal gold from your abbey lands. Now she is dead and you have run away, the abbey and the lands and the gold are all his.'

He saw her jaw harden. 'He has won my home, my inheritance, and a fortune as well?'

Luca nodded. 'He left the Lady Almoner to her death and rode away.'

She turned on Brother Peter. 'But you didn't charge *him*! You didn't pursue *him* for all the sins since Adam! Though I am responsible for everything done by Eve?'

He shrugged his shoulders. 'He committed no crime that we saw at the time. Now he pans for his own gold on his own land.'

'I will hold him to account. I will return and take back my lands. I am no longer bound by obedience to my father's will when my brother is such a bad guardian of our family honour. I will drive him out as he drove me away. I will go to my godfather's son and get help.'

'Was your godfather a man of substance? Your brother has his own castle and a small army to command.'

'He was Count Wladislaw of Wallachia,' she said proudly. 'His son is the new count. I will go to him.'

Brother Peter's head jerked up. 'You are the goddaughter of Count Wladislaw?' he asked curiously.

'Yes, my father always said to go to him in time of trouble.'

Brother Peter lowered his eyes and shook his head in wonderment. 'She has a powerful friend in him,' he said quietly to Luca. 'He could crush her brother in a moment.'

'Where does he live?'

'It's a long journey,' she admitted. 'To the east. He is at the court of Hungary.'

'That would be beyond Bosnia?' Freize abandoned any attempt at standing in silence by the door and came into the room.

'Yes.'

'Further east than that?'

She nodded.

'How are two pretty girls like you and the slave going to make that journey without someone stealing from you ... or worse?' Freize asked bluntly. 'They will skin you alive.'

She looked at Freize and smiled at him. 'Do you not think that God will protect us?'

'No,' he said flatly. 'My experience is that He rarely attends to the obvious.'

'Then we will travel with companions, with their guards, wherever we can. And take our chances when we cannot. Because I have to go. I have no-one else to turn to. And I will have my revenge on my brother, I will regain my inheritance.'

Freize nodded cheerfully at Luca. 'Might as well have burned them when you got the chance,' he observed. 'For you are sending them out to die anyway.'

'Oh, don't be ridiculous,' Luca said impatiently. 'We will protect them.'

'We have our mission!' Brother Peter objected.

Luca turned to Isolde. 'You may travel with us under our protection until our ways diverge. We are on a mission of inquiry, appointed by the Holy Father himself. We don't yet know our route but you may travel with us until our ways part.'

'Very important,' Freize supplemented, with a nod to the young woman. 'We are very important.'

'You can accompany us and when you find safe and reputable travellers on the road you can transfer to them, and travel with them.'

She bowed her head. 'I thank you. I thank you for myself and for Ishraq. And we will not delay nor distract you.'

'It is absolutely certain that they will do both,' Brother Peter remarked sourly.

'We can help them on their way at least,' Luca ruled.

'I should give you my name,' the young woman said. 'I am Lady Abbess no longer.'

'Of course,' Luca said.

'I am Lady Isolde of Lucretili.'

Luca bowed his head to her, but Freize stepped forwards, bowed low, his head almost to his knees, straightened up and thumped his clenched fist against his heart. 'Lady Isolde, you may command me,' he said grandly.

She was surprised, and giggled for a moment. Freize looked at her reproachfully. 'I would have thought you would have been brought up to understand a knight's service when it is offered?'

'He is a knight now?' Brother Peter asked Luca.

'Seems so,' came the amused response.

'Say a squire then,' Freize amended. 'I will be your squire.'

Lady Isolde rose to her feet and extended her hand to Freize. 'You do right to remind me to respond graciously to an honourable offer of service. I accept your service and I am glad of it, Freize. Thank you.'

With a triumphant glance at Luca, Freize bowed and touched her fingers with his lips. 'I am yours to command,' he said.

'I take it you will house and clothe and feed him?' Luca demanded. 'He eats like ten horses.'

'My service, as the lady well understood, is that of the heart,' Freize said with dignity. 'I am hers to command if there is a knightly quest or a bold venture. The rest of the time I carry on as your manservant, of course.'

'I am very grateful,' Isolde murmured. 'And as soon as I have a bold venture or knightly quest I will let you know.'

When Isolde entered the bedroom, Ishraq was sleeping, but as soon as she heard the soft footsteps, she opened her eyes and said, 'How was dinner? Are we arrested?'

'We're free,' Isolde said. 'Freize suddenly told his master that it was he who released us from the cellar under the gatehouse.'

Ishraq raised herself up onto one elbow. 'Did he say that? Why? And did they believe him?'

'He was convincing. He insisted. I don't think they wholly believed him but at any rate, they accepted it.'

'Did he say why he confessed to such a thing?'

'No. I think it was to be of service to us. And better than that, they have said that we can travel with them while our roads lie together.'

'Where are they going?'

'They follow orders. They go where they are told. But

there is only one way out of the village so we will all go east for the time being. We can travel with them and we will be safer on the road than with strangers or alone.'

'I don't like Brother Peter much.'

'He's all right. Freize swore to be my knight errant.'

Ishraq giggled. 'He has a good heart. You might be glad of him one day. He certainly served us tonight.'

Isolde stripped off the blue gown, and came in her chemise to the side of the bed. 'Is there anything you want? A small ale? Shall I sponge your bruises?'

'No, I am ready to sleep again.'

The bed creaked gently as Isolde got in beside her. 'Goodnight, my sister,' she said, as she had said almost every night of her life.

'Goodnight, dearest.'

VITTORITO, ITALY,
OCTOBER 1453

The little party lingered for two more days in the village while Ishraq's bruises faded and she grew strong again. Isolde and Ishraq bought light rust-coloured gowns for travelling, and thick woollen capes for the cold nights, and on the third day they were ready to set out at sunrise.

Freize had pillion saddles on two of the horses. 'I thought you would ride behind the lord,' he said to Isolde. 'And the servant would come up behind me.'

'No,' Ishraq said flatly. 'We ride our own horses.'

'It's tiring,' Freize warned her, 'and the roads are rough. Most ladies like to ride behind a man. You can sit sideways, you don't have to go astride. You'll be more comfortable.'

'We ride alone,' Isolde confirmed. 'On our own horses.'

Freize made a face and winked at Ishraq. 'Another time, then.'

'I don't think there will be any time when I will want to ride behind you,' she said coolly.

He unfastened the girth on the pillion saddle and swept it from the horse's back. 'Ah, you say that now,' he said confidently, 'but that's because you hardly know me. Many a lass has been indifferent at first meeting but after a while . . .' He snapped his fingers.

'After a while what?' Isolde asked him, smiling.

'They can't help themselves,' Freize said confidentially. 'Don't ask me why. It's a gift I have. Women and horses, they both love me. Women and horses – most animals really – just like to be close to me. They just like me.'

Luca came out to the stable yard, carrying his saddle pack. 'Are you not tacked up yet?'

'Just changing the saddles. The ladies want to ride on their own, though I have been to the trouble of buying two pillion saddles for them. They are ungrateful.'

'Well, of course they would ride alone!' Luca said impatiently. He nodded a bow to the young women, and when Freize led the first horse to the mounting block he went to Isolde and took her hand to help her up as she stepped to the top of the mounting block, put her foot in the broad stirrup and swung herself into the saddle.

Soon, the five of them were mounted and, with the other four horses and the donkey in a string behind them, they rode out onto the little track that they would follow through the forest.

Luca went first, with Isolde and Ishraq side by side just behind him. Behind them came Brother Peter and then

Freize, a stout cudgel in a loop at the side of his saddle and the spare horses beside him.

It was a pleasant ride through the beech woods. The trees were still holding their copper-brown leaves and sheltered the travellers from the bright autumn sun. As the path climbed higher they came out of the woods and took the stony track through the upper pastures. It was very quiet; sometimes they heard the tinkle of a few bells from a distant herd of goats, but mostly there was nothing but the whisper of the wind.

Luca reined back to ride with the two girls and asked Ishraq about her time in Spain.

'The Lord Lucretili must have been a most unusual man, to allow a young woman in his household to study with Moorish physicians,' he observed.

'He was,' Ishraq said. 'He had a great respect for the learning of my people, he wanted me to study. If he had lived I think he would have sent me back to Spanish universities, where the scholars of my people study everything from the stars in the sky to the movement of the waters of the sea. Some people say that they are all governed by the same laws. We have to discover what those laws might be.'

'Were you the only woman there?'

She shook her head. 'No, in my country women can learn and teach too.'

'And did you learn the numbers?' Luca asked her curiously. 'And the meaning of zero?'

She shook her head. 'I have no head for mathematics, though of course I know the numbers,' she said.

'My father believed that a woman could understand as well as a man,' Isolde remarked. 'He let Ishraq study whatever she wanted.'

'And you?' Luca turned to her. 'Did you attend the university in Spain?'

She shook her head. 'My father intended me to be a lady to command Lucretili,' she said. 'He taught me how to calculate the profits from the land, how to command the loyalty of people, how to manage land and choose the crops, how to command the guard of a castle under attack.' She made a funny little face. 'And he had me taught the skills a lady should have – love of fine clothes, dancing, music, speaking languages, writing, reading, singing, poetry.'

'She envies me the skills he taught me,' Ishraq said with a hidden smile. 'He taught her to be a lady and me to be a power in the world.'

'What woman would not want to be a lady of a great castle?' Luca wondered.

'I would want it,' Isolde said. 'I do want it. But I wish I had been taught to fight as well.'

At sunset on the first evening, they pulled up their horses before an isolated monastery. Ishraq and Isolde exchanged an anxious glance. 'The hue and cry?' she muttered to Luca.

'It won't have reached here. I doubt your brother sent out any messages once he was away from the abbey. I would guess he signed the writ only to demonstrate his own innocence.'

She nodded. 'Just enough to keep me away,' she said. 'Naming me as a witch and declaring me dead, leaves him with the castle and the abbey under his control, giving him the abbey lands and the gold. He wins everything.'

Freize dismounted and went to pull the great ring outside the closed door. The bell in the gatehouse rang loudly, and the porter heaved the double gates open. 'Welcome, travellers, in the name of God,' he said cheerfully. 'How many are you?'

'One young lord, one clerk, one servant, one lady and her companion,' Freize replied. 'And nine horses and one donkey. They can go in the meadow or in the stables as suits you.'

'We can put them out on good grass,' the lay brother said, smiling. 'Come in.'

He welcomed them into a big yard and Brother Peter and Luca swung down from their saddles. Luca turned to Isolde's horse and held up his arms to lift her down. She smiled briefly and gestured that she could get down on her own, then swung her leg and, lithe as a boy, jumped to the ground.

Freize went to Ishraq's horse and held out his arm. 'Don't jump,' he said. 'You'll faint the moment you touch the ground. You've been near to fainting any time this last five miles.'

She gathered her dark veil across her mouth and looked at him over the top of it.

'And don't look daggers at me either,' Freize said cheerfully. 'You'd have done better behind me with your arms around my waist and my back to lean on, but you're as stubborn as the donkey. Come on down, girl, and let me help you.'

Surprisingly, she did as he suggested and leaned towards him and let herself fall into his arms. He took her gently and set her on her feet with his arm around her to keep her steady. Isolde went to her and supported her. 'I didn't realise . . .'

'Just tired.'

The porter gave them a light to the guesthouse, indicated the women's rooms on one side of the high wall and the entry to the men's rooms on the other. He showed them the refectory and told them that they might get their dinner with the monks after Vespers, while the ladies would be served in the guesthouse. Then he left them with lit candles and a blessing.

'Goodnight,' Isolde said to Luca, bowing her head to Brother Peter.

'I'll see you in the morning,' Luca said to both women. 'We should leave straight after Prime.'

Isolde nodded. 'We'll be ready.'

Ishraq curtseyed to the two men and nodded at Freize.

'Pillion saddle tomorrow?' he asked her.

'Yes,' she said.

'Because you were overtired with the ride today?' Freize said, driving the point home.

She showed him a warm frank smile before she tucked her veil across her face. 'Don't gloat,' she said. 'I'm tired to my very bones. You were right, I was wrong, and foolishly proud. I'll ride pillion tomorrow and be glad of it; but if you mock me I will pinch you every step of the way.'

Freize ducked his head. 'Not a word,' he promised her. 'You will find me reticent to a fault.'

'Reticent?'

He nodded. 'It is my new ambition. It's my new word: reticent.'

They left immediately after Prime and breakfast, and the sun was up on their right-hand side as they headed north. 'Thing is,' Freize remarked to Ishraq quietly as she rode behind him, seated sideways, her feet resting on the pillion support, one hand around his waist, tucked into his belt, 'thing is, we never know where we are going. We just go along, steady as the donkey, who knows no more than us but plods along, and then that pompous jackal suddenly brings out a piece of paper and tells us we are to go somewhere else entirely and get into God knows what trouble.'

'But of course,' she said. 'Because you are travelling as an inquiry. You have to go and inquire into things.'

'I don't see why we can't know where we are going,' Freize said. 'And then a man might have a chance of making sure we stopped at a good inn.'

'Ah, it is a matter of dinner,' she said, smiling behind her veil. 'I understand now.'

Freize patted the hand that was holding his belt. 'There are very few things more important than dinner to a hard-working man,' he said firmly. Then, 'Hulloah? What's this?'

Ahead of them in the road were half a dozen men, struggling with pitchforks and flails to hold down an animal which was netted and roped and twisting about in the dirt. Freize halted and Isolde, Luca and Peter pulled up behind him.

'What have you got there?' Luca called to the men.

One of the men broke from the struggle and came towards them. 'We'd be glad of your help,' he said. 'If we could rope the creature to two of your horses we'd be able to get it along the road. We can't get forwards or backwards at the moment.'

'What is it?' Luca asked.

The man crossed himself. 'The Lord save us, it is a were-wolf,' he said. 'It has been plaguing our village and forests every full moon for a year but last night my brother and I, and our friends, and cousin, went out and trapped it.'

Brother Peter crossed himself, and Isolde copied him. 'How did you trap it?'

'We planned it for months, truly months. We didn't dare to go out at night – we were afraid his power would be too strong under the moon. We waited till it was a waning moon when we knew that his power would be weakened and shrunken. Then we dug a deep pit on the track to the village and we staked out a haunch of mutton on the far side. We thought he would come to the village as he always does and smell the meat. We hoped he would follow the track to the meat and he did. We covered the pit with light branches and leaves, and he didn't see it. It collapsed beneath him and he fell in. We kept him there for days, with nothing to eat so he weakened. Then we dropped the nets on him and pulled them tight and hauled him out of the pit. Now we have him.'

'And what are you going to do with him?' Isolde looked fearfully at the writhing animal, laden with nets, struggling on the road.

'We are going to cage it in the village till we can make a silver arrow, as only a silver arrow can kill it, and then we are going to shoot it in the heart and bury it at the cross-roads. Then it will lie quiet and we will be safe in our beds again.'

'Pretty small for a wolf,' Freize observed, peering at the thrashing net. 'More like a dog.'

'It grows bigger with the moon,' the man said. 'When the moon is full it waxes too – as big as the biggest wolf. And then, though we bolt our doors and shutter our windows, we can hear it round the village, trying the doors, sniffing at the locks, trying to get in.'

Isolde shuddered.

'Will you help us get it to the village? We're going to put it in the bear pit, where we bait the bears at the inn, but it's a good mile away. We didn't think it would struggle so, and we're afraid to get too close for fear of being bitten.'

'If it bites you, you turn into a werewolf too,' a man said from the back. 'I swore to my wife that I wouldn't go too close.'

Freize looked across their heads at Luca, and at a nod from his master, got down from his cob and went to the bundle in the road. Under the pile of nets and tangles of rope he could just see an animal crouched down and curled up. A dark angry eye looked back at him; he saw small yellow teeth bared in a snarl. Two or three of the men held their ropes out and Freize took one from one side and then one from the other side and tied them to two of the spare horses. 'Here,' he said to one of the men. 'Lead the horse gently. Did you say two miles to the village?'

'Perhaps one and a half,' the man said. The horse snorted in fear and sidled as the bundle on the road let out a howl. Then the ropes were tightened and they set off, dragging the helpless bundle along behind them. Sometimes the creature convulsed and rolled over, which caused the horses to jib in fear and the men leading them had to tighten their reins and soothe them.

'A bad business,' Freize said to Luca as they entered the

village behind the men, and saw the other villagers gather around with spades and axes and flails.

'This is the very thing that we were sent out to understand,' Brother Peter said to Luca. 'I shall open a report, and you can hold an inquiry. We can do it here, before continuing with our journey and our mission. You can find what evidence there is that this is a werewolf, half-beast, half-man, and then you can decide if it should be put to death with a silver arrow or not.'

'I?' Luca hesitated.

'You are the inquirer,' Brother Peter reminded him. 'Here is a place to understand the fears and map the rise of the Devil. Set up your inquiry.'

Freize looked at him; Isolde waited. Luca cleared his throat. 'I am an inquirer sent out by the Holy Father himself to discover wrong-doing and error in Christendom,' he called to the villagers. There was a murmur of interest and respect. 'I will hold an inquiry about this beast and decide what is to be done with it,' he said. 'Anyone who has been wronged by the beast or is fearful of it, or knows anything about it, is to come to my room in the inn and give evidence before me. In a day or two I shall tell you my decision, which will be binding and final.'

Freize nodded. 'Where's the bear pit?' he asked one of the farmers, who was leading a horse.

'In the yard of the inn,' the man said. He nodded to the big double doors of the stable yard at the side of the inn. As the horses came close, the villagers ran ahead and threw the doors open. Inside the courtyard, under the windows of the inn, there was a big circular arena.

Once a year, a visiting bear leader would bring his

chained animal to the village on a feast day and everyone would bet on how many dogs would be killed, and how close the bravest would get to the throat of the bear, until the bear leader declared it over, and the excitement was done for another year.

A stake in the centre showed where the bears were chained by the leg when the dogs were set on them. The arena had been reinforced and made higher by lashed beams and planks so that the inner wall was nearly as high as the first-floor windows of the inn. 'They can jump,' the farmer said. 'Werewolves can jump, everyone knows that. We built it too high for the Devil himself.'

The villagers untied the ropes from the horses and pulled the bundle in the net towards the bear pit. It seemed to struggle more vigorously and to resist. A couple of the farmers took their pitchforks and pricked it onwards which made it howl in pain and snarl and lash out in its net.

'And how are you going to release it into the bear pit?' Freize wondered aloud.

There was a silence. Clearly this stage had not been foreseen. 'We'll just lock it in and leave it to get its own self free,' someone suggested.

'I'm not going near it,' another man said.

'If it bites you once, you become a werewolf too,' a woman warned.

'You die from the poison of its breath,' another disagreed.

'If it gets the taste of your blood it hunts you till it has you,' someone volunteered.

Brother Peter and Luca and the two women went into the front door of the inn and took rooms for themselves and stables for the horses. Luca also hired a dining room that overlooked the bear pit in the yard and went to the window to see his servant, Freize, standing in the bear pit with the beast squirming in its net beside him. As he expected, Freize was not able to leave even a monster such as this netted and alone.

'Get a bucket of water for it to drink, and a haunch of meat for it to eat when it gets itself free,' Freize said to the groom of the inn. 'And maybe a loaf of bread in case it fancies it.'

'This is a beast from hell,' the groom protested. 'I'm not waiting on it. I'm not stepping into the pit with it. What if it breathes on me?'

Freize looked for a moment as if he would argue, but then he nodded his head. 'So be it,' he said. 'Anyone here have any compassion for the beast? No? Brave enough to catch it and torment it but not brave enough to feed it, eh? Well, I myself will get it some dinner, then, and when it has untied itself from these knots, and recovered from being dragged over the road for a mile and a half, it can have a sup of water and a bite of meat.'

'Mind it doesn't bite you!' someone said and everyone laughed.

'It won't bite me,' Freize rejoined stolidly. 'On account of nobody touches me without my word, and on account of I wouldn't be so stupid as to be in here when it gets loose. Unlike some, who have lived alongside it and complained that they heard it sniffing at their door and yet took months to capture the poor beast.'

A chorus of irritated argument arose at this, which Freize simply ignored. 'Anyone going to help me?' he asked again. 'Well, in that case I will ask you all to leave, on account of the fact that I am not a travelling show.'

Most of them left, but some of the younger men stayed in their places, on the platform built outside the arena so that a spectator could stand and look over the barrier. Freize did not speak again but merely stood, waiting patiently until they shuffled their feet, cursed him for interfering, and went.

When the courtyard was empty of people, Freize fetched a bucket of water from the pump, went to the kitchen for a haunch of raw meat and a loaf of bread, then set them down inside the arena, glancing up at the window where Luca and the two women were looking down.

'And what the little lord makes of you, we will know in time,' Freize remarked to the humped net, which shuffled and whimpered a little. 'But God will guide him to deal fairly with you even if you are from Satan and must die with a silver arrow through your heart. And I will keep you fed and watered for you are one of God's creatures even if you are one of the Fallen, which I doubt was a matter of your own choosing.'

Luca started his inquiry into the werewolf as soon as they had dined. The two women went to their bedroom, while the two men, Brother Peter and Luca, called in one witness after another to say how the werewolf had plagued their village.

All afternoon they listened to stories of noises in the night, the handles of locked doors being gently tried, and losses from the herds of sheep which roamed the pastures under the guidance of the boys of the village. The boys reported a great wolf, a single wolf running alone, which would come out of the forest and snatch away a lamb that had strayed too far from its mother. They said that the wolf sometimes ran on all four legs, sometimes stood up like a man. They were in terror of it, and would no longer take the sheep to the upper pastures but insisted on staying near the village. One lad, a six-year-old shepherd boy, told them that his older brother had been eaten by the werewolf.

'When was that?' Luca asked.

'Seven years ago, at least,' the boy replied. 'For I never knew him – he was taken the year before I was born, and my mother has never stopped mourning for him.'

'What happened?' Luca asked.

'These villagers have all sorts of tales,' Brother Peter said quietly to him. 'Ten to one the boy is lying, or his brother died of some disgusting disease that they don't want to admit.'

'She was looking for a lamb, and he was walking with her as he always did,' the boy said. 'She told me that she sat down just for a moment and he sat on her lap. He fell asleep in her arms and she was so tired that she closed her eyes for only a moment, and when she woke he was gone. She thought he had strayed a little way from her and she called for him and looked all round for him but she never found him.'

'Absolute stupidity,' Brother Peter remarked.

'But why did she think the werewolf had taken him?' Luca asked.

'She could see the marks of a wolf in the wet ground round the stream,' the boy said. 'She ran about and called and called, and when she could not find him she came running home for my father and he went out for days, tracking down the pack, but even he, who is the best hunter in the village, could not find them. That was when they knew it was a werewolf who had taken my brother. Taken him and disappeared, as they do.'

'I'll see your mother,' Luca decided. 'Will you ask her to come to me?'

The boy hesitated. 'She won't come,' he said. 'She grieves for him still. She doesn't like to talk about it. She won't want to talk about it.'

Brother Peter leaned towards Luca and spoke quietly to him. 'I've heard a tale like this a dozen times,' he said. 'Likely the child had something wrong with him and she quietly drowned him in the stream and then came back with a cock-and-bull story to tell the husband. She won't want to have us asking about it, and there's no benefit in forcing the truth out of her. What's done is done.'

Luca turned to his clerk and raised his papers so that his face was hidden from the boy. 'Brother Peter, I am conducting an inquiry here into a werewolf. I will speak to everyone who has any knowledge of such a satanic visitor. You know that's my duty. If along the way I discover a village where baby-killing has been allowed then I will inquire after that too. It is my task to inquire into all the fears of Christendom: everything – great sins and small. It is my task to know what is happening and if it foretells the end of days. The death of a baby, the arrival of a werewolf, these are all evidence.'

'Do you have to know everything?' Brother Peter demanded sceptically. 'Can we let nothing go?'

'Everything,' Luca nodded. 'And that is my curse that I carry just like the werewolf. He has to rage and savage. I have to know. But I am in the service of God and he is in the service of the Devil and is doomed to death.'

He turned back to the boy. 'I'll come to your mother.'

He got up from the table and the two men with the boy – still faintly protesting and crimson to his ears – led the way down the stairs and out of the inn. As they were going out of the front door, Isolde and Ishraq were coming down the stairs.

'Where are you going?' Isolde asked.

'To visit a farmer's wife, this young man's mother,' Luca said.

The girls looked at Brother Peter, whose face was impassive but clearly disapproving.

'Can we come too?' Isolde asked. 'We were just going out to walk around.'

'It's an inquiry, not a social call,' Brother Peter said.

But Luca said, 'Oh, why not?' and Isolde walked beside him, while the little shepherd boy, torn between embarrassment and pride at all the attention, went ahead. His sheepdog, which had been lying in the shadow of a cart outside the inn, pricked up its ears at the sight of him, and trotted at his heels.

He led them out of the dusty market square, up a small rough-cut flight of steps to a track that wound up the side of the mountain, following the course of a fast-flowing stream, and then stopped abruptly at a little farm, a pretty duck pond before the yard, a waterfall from the small cliff behind it. A ramshackle roof of ruddy tiles topped a rough wall of wattle and daub which had been lime-washed many years ago and was now a gentle buff colour. There was no glass in the windows but the shutters stood wide open to the afternoon sun. There were chickens in the yard and a pig with piglets in the walled orchard to the side. In the field beyond there were two precious cows, one with a calf, and as they walked up the cobbled track the front door opened and a middle-aged woman came out, her hair tied up in a scarf, a hessian apron over her homespun gown. She stopped in surprise at the sight of the wealthy strangers.

'Good day to you,' she said, looking from one to another. 'What are you doing, Tomas, bringing such fine folks here? I hope he has been no trouble, sir? Can I offer you some refreshment?'

'This is the man from the inn who brought the werewolf in,' Tomas said breathlessly. 'He would come to see you, though I told him not to.'

'You shouldn't have told him anything at all,' she observed. 'It's not for small boys, small dirty boys, to speak with their betters. Go and fetch a jug of the best ale from the still room, and don't say another word. Sirs, ladies – will you sit?'

She gestured to a bench set into the low stone wall before the house. Isolde and Ishraq took a seat and smiled up at her. 'We rarely have company here,' she said. 'And never ladies.'

Tomas came out of the house carrying two roughly carved three-legged stools and put them down for Brother

Peter and Luca, then dashed in again for the jug of small ale, one glass and three mugs. Bashfully, he offered the glass to Isolde and then poured ale for everyone else into mugs.

Luca and Brother Peter took their seats and the woman stood before them, one hand twisting her apron corner. 'He is a good boy,' she said again. 'He wouldn't mean to talk out of turn. I apologise if he offended you.'

'No, no, he was polite and helpful,' Luca said.

'He's a credit to you,' Isolde assured her.

'And growing very big and strong,' Ishraq remarked.

The mother's pride beamed out of her face. 'He is,' she said. 'I thank the Lord for him every day of his life.'

'But you had a previous boy.' Luca put down his mug and spoke gently to her. 'He told us that he had an older brother.'

A shadow came across the woman's broad handsome face and she looked suddenly weary. 'I did. God forgive me for taking my eye off him for a moment.' At the thought of him she could not speak; she turned her head away.

'What happened?' Isolde asked.

'Alas, alas, I lost him. I lost him in a moment. God forgive me for that moment. But I was a young mother and so weary that I fell asleep and in that moment he was gone.'

'In the forest?' Luca prompted.

A silent nod confirmed the fact.

Gently, Isolde rose to her feet and pressed the woman down onto the bench so that she could sit. 'Was he taken by wolves?' she asked quietly.

'I believe he was,' the woman said. 'There were rumours of wolves in the woods even then, that was why I was looking for the lamb, hoping to find it before nightfall.' She gestured at the sheep in the field. 'We don't have a big flock. Every beast counts for us. I sat down for a moment. My boy was tired so we sat to rest. He was not yet four years old, God bless him. I lay down with him for a moment and fell asleep. When I woke he was gone.'

Isolde put a comforting hand on her shoulder.

'We found his little shirt,' the woman continued, her voice trembling with unspoken tears. 'But that was some months later. One of the lads found it when he was bird's-nesting in the forest. Found it under a bush.'

'Was there any blood on it?' Luca asked.

She shook her head. 'It was washed through by rain,' she said. 'But I took it to the priest and we held a service for his innocent soul. The priest said I should bury my love for him and have another child – and then God gave me Tomas.'

'The villagers have captured a beast that they say is a werewolf,' Brother Peter remarked. 'Would you accuse the beast of murdering your child?'

He expected her to flare out, to make an accusation at once; but she looked wearily at him as if she had worried and thought about this for too long already. 'Of course when I heard there was a werewolf I thought it might have taken my boy Stefan – but I don't know. I can't even say that it was a wolf that took him. He might have wandered far and fallen in the stream and drowned, or in a ravine, or just been lost in the woods. I saw the tracks of the wolves but I didn't see my son's footprints. I have thought about it every day of my life; and still I don't know.'

Brother Peter nodded and pursed his lips. He looked at Luca. 'Do you want me to write down her statement and have her put her mark on it?'

Luca shook his head. 'Later we can, if we think there is need,' he said. He bowed to the woman. 'Thank you for your hospitality, goodwife. What name shall I call you?'

She rubbed her face with the corner of her apron. 'I am Sara Rossi,' she said. 'Wife of Raul Rossi. We have a good name in the village, anyone can tell you who I am.'

'Would you bear witness against the werewolf?'

She gave him a faint smile with a world of sorrow behind it. 'I don't like to talk of it,' she said simply. 'I try not to think of it. I tried to do what the priest told me and bury my sorrow with the little shirt, and thank God for my second boy.'

Brother Peter hesitated. 'We will certainly put it on trial and if it is proven to be a werewolf it will die.'

She nodded. 'That won't bring back my boy,' she said quietly. 'But I should be glad to know that my son and all the children are safe in the pasture.'

They rose up and left her. Brother Peter gave his arm to Isolde as they walked down the stony path, Luca helped Ishraq.

'Why does Brother Peter not believe her?' Ishraq asked him while she had her hand on his arm and was close enough to speak softly. 'Why is he always so suspicious?'

'This is not his first inquiry; he has travelled before and seen much. Your lady, Isolde, was very tender to her.'

'She has a tender heart,' Ishraq said. 'Children, women, beggars, her purse is always open and her heart is always going out to them. The castle kitchen gave away two dozen dinners a day to the poor. She has always been this way.'

'And has she ever loved anyone in particular?' Luca

208

asked casually. There was a big rock in the pathway and he stepped over it and turned to help Ishraq.

She laughed. 'Nothing to do with you,' she said abruptly. When she saw him flush she said, 'Ah, Inquirer! Do you really have to know everything?'

'I was just interested . . .'

'No-one. She was supposed to marry a fat indulgent sinful man and she would never have considered him. She would never have stooped to him. She took her vows of celibacy with ease. That was not the problem for her. She loves her lands, and her people. No man has taken her fancy.' She paused as if to tease him. 'So far,' she conceded.

Luca looked away. 'Such a beautiful young woman is bound to . . .'

'Quite,' Ishraq said. 'But tell me about Brother Peter. Is he always so miserable?'

'He was suspicious of the mother here,' Luca explained. 'He thinks she may have killed the child herself, and tried to blame it on a wolf attack. I don't think so myself; but of course, in these out-of-the-way villages, such things happen.'

Decisively, she shook her head. 'Not her. That is a woman with a horror of wolves,' she said. 'It's no accident she was not down in the village, though everyone else was there to see them bring it in.'

'How do you know that?' Luca said.

Ishraq looked at him as if he were blind. 'Did you not see the garden?'

Luca had a vague memory of a well-tilled garden, filled with flowers and herbs. There had been a bed of vegetables and herbs near to the door to the kitchen, and flowers and lavender had billowed over the path. There were some autumn pumpkins growing fatly in one bed, and plump grapes on the vine which twisted around the door. It was a typical cottage garden: planted partly for medicine and partly for colour. 'Of course I saw it, but I don't remember anything special.'

She smiled. 'She was growing a dozen different species of aconite, in half a dozen colours, and her boy had a fresh spray of the flower in his hat. She was growing it at every window and every doorway – I've never seen such a collection, and in every colour that can bloom, from pink to white to purple.'

'And so?' Luca asked.

'Do you not know your herbs?' Ishraq asked teasingly. 'A great inquirer like yourself?'

'Not like you do. What is aconite?'

'The common name for aconite is wolfsbane,' she said. 'People have been using it against wolves and werewolves for hundreds of years. Dried and made into a powder it can poison a wolf. Fed to a werewolf it can turn him into a human again. In a lethal dose it can kill a werewolf outright, it all depends on the distillation of the herb and the amount that the wolf can be forced to eat. For sure, no wolf will touch it; no wolf will go near it. They won't let their coats so much as brush against it. No wolf could get into that house – she has built a fortress of aconite.'

'You think it proves that her story is true and that she fears the wolf? That she planted it to guard herself against the wolf, in case it came back for her?'

Ishraq nodded at the boy who was skipping ahead of them like a little lamb himself, leading the way back to the village, a sprig of fresh aconite tucked into his hatband. 'I should think she is guarding him.'

A small crowd had gathered around the gate to the stable yard when Luca, Brother Peter and the girls arrived back at the inn.

'What's this?' Luca asked, and pushed his way to the front of the crowd. Freize had the gate half-open and was admitting one person at a time on payment of a half-groat, chinking the coins in his hand.

'What are you doing?' Luca asked tersely.

'Letting people see the beast,' Freize replied. 'Since there was such an interest, I thought we might allow it. I thought it was for the public good. I thought I might demonstrate the majesty of God by showing the people this poor sinner.'

'And what made you think it right to charge for it?'

'Brother Peter is always so anxious about the expenses,' Freize explained agreeably, nodding at the clerk. 'I thought it would be good if the beast made a contribution to the costs of his trial.'

'This is ridiculous,' Luca said. 'Close the gate. People can't come in and stare at it. This is supposed to be an inquiry, not a travelling show.'

'People are bound to want to see it,' Isolde observed. 'If they think it has been threatening their flocks and themselves for years. They are bound to want to know it has been captured.'

'Well, let them see it, but you can't charge for it,' Luca said irritably. 'You didn't even catch it, why should you set yourself up as its keeper?'

'Because I loosed its bonds and fed it,' Freize said reasonably.

'It is free?' Luca asked, and Isolde echoed nervously: 'Have you freed it?'

'I cut the ropes and got myself out of the pit at speed. Then it rolled about and crawled out of the nets,' Freize said. 'It had a drink, had a bite to eat, now it's lying down again, resting. Not much of a show really, but they are simple people and not much happens here. And I charge half price for children and idiots.'

'There is only one idiot here,' Luca said severely. 'And he is not from the village. Let me in, I shall see it.' He went through the gate and the others followed him. Freize quietly took coins off the remaining villagers and opened the gate wide for them. 'I'd wager it's no wolf,' he said quietly to Luca.

'What do you mean?'

'When it got itself out of the net I could see. It's curled up now in the shadowy end, so it's harder to make out, but it's no beast that I have ever seen before. It has long claws and a mane, but it goes up and down from its back legs to all fours, not like a wolf at all.'

'What kind of beast *is* it?' Luca asked him.

'I'm not sure,' Freize conceded. 'But it is not much like a wolf.'

Luca nodded and went towards the bear pit. There was

a set of rough wooden steps and a ring of trestles laid on staging, so that spectators to the bear baiting could stand all around the outside of the pit and see over the wooden walls.

Luca climbed the ladder and moved along the trestle so that Brother Peter and the two girls and the little shepherd boy could get up too.

The beast was huddled against the furthest wall, its legs tucked under its body. It had a thick long mane, and a hide tanned dark brown from all weathers, discoloured by mud and scars. On its throat were two new rope burns; now and then it licked a bleeding paw. Two dark eyes looked out through the matted mane and, as Luca watched, the beast bared its teeth in a snarl.

'We should tie it down and cut into the skin,' Brother Peter suggested. 'If it is a werewolf we will cut the skin and beneath it there will be fur. That will be evidence.'

'You should kill it with a silver arrow,' one of the villagers remarked. 'At once, before the moon gets any bigger. It will be stronger then, they wax with the moon. Better kill it now while we have it and it is not in its full power.'

'When is the moon full?' Luca asked.

'Tomorrow night,' Ishraq answered. The little boy beside her took the aconite from his hat and threw it towards the curled animal. It flinched away.

'There!' someone said from the crowd. 'See that? It fears wolfsbane. It's a werewolf. We should kill it right now. We shouldn't delay. We should kill it while it is weak.'

Someone picked up a stone and threw it. It caught the beast on its back and it flinched and snarled and shrank away as if it would burrow its way through the high wall of the bear pit.

One of the men turned to Luca. 'Your honour, we don't have enough silver to make an arrow. Would you have some silver in your possession that we might buy from you, and have forged into an arrowhead? We'd be very grateful. Otherwise we'll have to send to Pescara, to the money-lender there, and it will take days.'

Luca glanced at Brother Peter. 'We have some silver,' he said cautiously. 'Sacred property of the Church.'

'We can sell it to you,' Luca ruled. 'But we'll wait for the full moon before we kill the beast. I want to see the trans-formation with my own eyes. When I see it become a full wolf then we will know that it is the beast you report, and we can kill it when it is in its wolf form.'

The man nodded. 'We'll make the silver arrow now, so as to be ready.' He went into the inn with Brother Peter, dis-cussing a fair price for the silver, and Luca turned to Isolde and took a breath. He knew himself to be nervous as a boy.

'I was going to ask you, I meant to mention it earlier, there is only one dining room here . . . in fact, will you dine with us tonight?' he asked.

She looked a little surprised. 'I had thought Ishraq and I would eat in our room.'

'You could both eat with us at the large table in the dining room,' Luca said. 'It's closer to the kitchen, the food would be hotter, fresher from the oven. There could be no objec-tion.'

She glanced away, her colour rising. 'I would like to . . .'

'Please do,' Luca said. 'I would like your advice on . . .' He trailed off, unable to think of anything.

She saw at once his hesitation. 'My advice on what?' she asked, her eyes dancing with laughter. 'You have decided what to do with the werewolf, you will soon have orders as to your next mission. What can you possibly want with my opinion?'

He grinned ruefully. 'I don't know. I have nothing to say. I just wanted your company. We are travelling together, you and I, Brother Peter and Ishraq, Freize who has sworn himself to be your man – I just thought you might dine with us.'

She smiled at his frankness. 'I shall be glad to spend this evening with you,' she said honestly. She was conscious of wanting to touch him, to put her hand on his shoulder, or to step closer to him. She did not think it was desire that she felt; it was more like a yearning just to be close to him, to have his hand upon her waist, to have his dark head near to hers, to see his hazel eyes smile.

She knew that she was being foolish, that to be close to him, a novice for the priesthood, was a sin, that she herself was already in breach of the vows she had made when she had joined the abbey; and she stepped back. 'Ishraq and I will come sweet-smelling to dinner,' she remarked at random. 'She has got the innkeeper to bring the bathtub to our room. They think we are madly reckless to bathe when it's not even Good Friday – that's when they all take their annual bath – but we have insisted that it won't make us ill.'

'I will expect you at dinner, then,' he said. 'As clean as if it was Easter.' He jumped down from the platform and put out his hands to help her. She let him lift her down and as he put her on her feet he held her for a moment longer than was needed to make sure she was steady. He felt her lean slightly towards him, he could not have been mistaken; but then she stepped away and he was sure that he had been mistaken. He could not read her movements, he could not imagine what she was thinking, and he was bound by vows of celibacy to take no step towards her. But at any rate, she had said that she would come to dinner and she had said that she would like to dine with him. That at least he was sure of, as she and Ishraq went into the dark doorway of the inn.

Luca glanced up, self-consciously, but Freize had not observed the little exchange. He was intent on the werewolf as it turned around and around, as dogs do before they lie down. When it settled and did not move, Freize announced to the little audience, 'There now, it's gone to sleep. Show's over. You can come back tomorrow.'

'And tomorrow we'll see it for free,' someone claimed. 'It's our werewolf, we caught it, there's no reason that you should charge us to see it.'

'Ay, but I feed him,' Freize said. 'And my lord pays for his keep. And he will examine the creature and execute it with our silver arrow. So that makes him ours.'

They grumbled about the cost of seeing the beast as Freize shooed them out of the yard and closed the doors on them. Luca went into the inn and Freize to the back door of the kitchen.

'D'you have anything sweet?' he asked the cook, a plump dark-haired woman who had already experienced Freize's most blatant flattery. 'Or at any rate, d'you have anything half as sweet as your smile?' he amended.

'Get away with you,' she said. 'What are you wanting?'

'A slice of fresh bread with a spoonful of jam would be very welcome,' Freize said. 'Or some sugared plums, perhaps?'

'The plums are for the lady's dinner,' she said firmly. 'But I can give you a slice of bread.'

'Or two,' Freize suggested.

She shook her head at him in mock disapproval but then cut two slices off a thick rye loaf, slapped on two spoonfuls of jam and stuck them face to face together. 'There, and don't be coming back for more. I'm cooking dinner now and I can't be feeding you at the kitchen door at the same time. I've never had so many gentry in the house at one time before, and one of them appointed by the Holy Father! I have enough to do without you at the door night and day.'

'You are a princess,' Freize assured her. 'A princess in disguise. I shouldn't be surprised if someone didn't come by one day and snatch you up to be a princess in a castle.'

She laughed delightedly and pushed him out of the kitchen, slamming the door after him, and Freize climbed up on the viewing platform again and looked down into the bear pit where the werewolf had stretched out and was lying still.

'Here.' Freize waved the slice of bread and jam. 'Here – do you like bread and jam? I do.'

The beast raised its head and looked warily at Freize. It lifted its lips in a quiet snarl. Freize took a bite from the two slices, and then broke off a small piece and tossed it towards the animal.

The beast flinched back from the bread as it fell, but then caught the scent of it and leaned forwards. 'Go on,' Freize whispered encouragingly. 'Eat up. Give it a try. You might like it.'

The beast sniffed cautiously at the bread and then slunk forwards, first its big front paws, one at a time, and then its whole body, towards the food. It sniffed, and then licked it, and then gobbled it down in one quick hungry movement. Then it sat like a sphinx and looked at Freize.

'Nice,' Freize said encouragingly. 'Like some more?'

The animal watched him as Freize took a small bite, ate it with relish, and then once again broke off a morsel and threw it towards the beast. This time it did not flinch but followed the arc of the throw keenly, and went at once to where the bread landed, in the middle of the arena, coming closer all the time to Freize, leaning over the wall.

It gobbled up the bread without hesitation and then sat on its haunches, looking at Freize, clearly waiting for more.

'That's good,' Freize said, using the same gentle voice. 'Now come a little bit closer.' He dropped the last piece of bread very near to his own position, but the werewolf did not dare come so close. It yearned towards the sweet-smelling bread and jam, but it shrank back from Freize, though he stood very still and whispered encouraging words.

'Very well,' he said softly. 'You'll come closer for your dinner later, I don't doubt,' and he stepped down from the platform and found Ishraq had been watching him from the doorway of the inn.

'Why are you feeding him like that?' she asked.

Freize shrugged. 'Wanted to see him properly,' he said. 'I suppose I just thought I'd see if he liked bread and jam.'

'Everyone else hates him,' she observed. 'They are planning his execution in two nights' time. Yet you feed him bread and jam.'

'Poor beast,' he said. 'I doubt he wanted to be a werewolf. It must have just come over him. And now he's to die for it. It doesn't seem fair.'

He was rewarded with a quick smile. 'It isn't fair,' she

said. 'And you are right – perhaps it is just his nature. He may be just a different sort of beast from any other that we have seen. Like a changeling: one who does not belong where he happens to be.'

'And we don't live in a world that likes difference,' Freize observed.

'Now that's true,' said the girl who had been different from all the others from birth with her dark skin and her dark slanting eyes.

'Now then,' said Freize, sliding his arm around Ishraq's waist. 'You're a kind-hearted girl. What about a kiss?'

She stood quite still, neither yielding to his gentle pressure nor pulling away. Her stillness was more off-putting than if she had jumped and squealed. She stood like a statue and Freize stood still beside her, making no progress and rather feeling that he wanted to take his arm away, but that he could not now do so.

'You had better let me go at once,' she said in a very quiet even voice. 'Freize, I am warning you fairly enough. Let me go; or it will be the worse for you.'

He attempted a confident laugh. It didn't come out very confident. 'What would you do?' he asked. 'Beat me? I'd take having my ears boxed from a lass like you with pleasure. I will make you an offer: box my ears and then kiss me better!'

'I will throw you to the ground,' she said with a quiet determination. 'And it will hurt, and you will feel like a fool.'

He tightened his grip at once, rising to the challenge. 'Ah, pretty maid, you should never threaten what you can't do,' he chuckled, and put his other hand under her chin to turn up her face for a kiss.

It all happened so fast that he did not know how it had

been done. One moment he had his arm around her waist and was bending to kiss her, the next she had used that arm to spin him around, grabbed him, and he was tipped flat on his back on the hard cobbles of the muddy yard, his head ringing from the fall, and she was at the open doorway of the inn.

'Actually, I never threaten what I can't do,' she said, hardly out of breath. 'And you had better remember never to touch me without my consent.'

Freize sat up, got to his feet, brushed down his coat and his breeches, shook his dizzy head. When he looked up again, she was gone.

The kitchen lad toiled up the stairs carrying buckets of hot water, to be met at the door of the women's room by either Ishraq or Isolde who took the buckets and poured them into the bath that they had set before the fire in their bedroom. It was a big wooden tub, half of a wine barrel, and Ishraq had lined it with a sheet and poured in some scented oil. They closed and bolted the door on the boy, undressed, and got into the steaming water. Gently, Isolde sponged Ishraq's bruised shoulder and forehead, and then turned her around and tipped back her head to wash her black hair.

The firelight glowed on their wet gleaming skin and the girls talked quietly together, revelling in the steaming hot water, and the flickering warmth of the fire. Isolde combed Ishraq's thick dark hair with oils, and then pinned it on top of her head. 'Will you wash mine?' she asked, and turned so that Ishraq could soap her back and shoulders and wash her tangled golden hair.

'I feel as if all the dirt of the road is in my skin,' she said, as she took a handful of salt from the dish beside the bath, and rubbed it with oil in her hands and then spread it along her arms.

'You certainly have a small forest in your hair,' Ishraq said, pulling out little twigs and leaves.

'Oh, take it out!' Isolde exclaimed. 'Comb it through, I want it completely clean. I was going to wear my hair down tonight.'

'Curled on your shoulders?' Ishraq asked, and pulled a ringlet.

'I suppose I can wear my hair as I please,' Isolde said, flicking her head. 'I suppose it is nobody's business but mine, how I wear my hair.'

'Oh, for sure,' Ishraq agreed with her. 'And surely the inquirer has no interest in whether your hair is curled and clean and spread over your shoulders or pinned up under your veil.'

'He is sworn to the Church, as am I,' Isolde said.

'Your oaths were forced at the time, and are as nothing now; and for all I know his oaths are the same,' Ishraq said roundly.

Isolde turned and looked at her, soapsuds running down her naked back. 'He is sworn to the Church,' she repeated hesitantly.

'He was put into the Church when he was a child, before

he knew what was being promised. But now he is a man, and he looks at you as if he would be a free man.'

Isolde's colour rose from the level of the water, slowly to her damp forehead. 'He looks at me?'

'You know he does.'

'He looks at me . . .'

'With desire.'

'You can't say that,' she said, in instant denial.

'I do say it . . .' Ishraq insisted.

'Well, don't . . .'

In the yard outside, Luca had gone out to take one last look at the werewolf before dinner. Standing on the platform with his back to the inn, he suddenly realised he could see the girls in their bathtub as a reflection in the window opposite. At once he knew he should look away, more than that, he should go immediately into the inn without glancing upwards again. He knew that the image of the two beautiful girls, naked together in their bath, would burn into his mind like a brand, and that he would never be able to forget the sight of them: Ishraq twisting one of Isolde's blonde ringlets in her brown fingers, stroking a salve into each curl and pinning it up then gently sponging soap onto her pearly back. Luca froze, quite unable to look away, knowing he was committing an unforgivable trespass in spying on them, knowing that he was committing a terrible insult to them and worse, a venal sin, and, finally, as he jumped down from the platform and blundered into the inn, knowing that he had fallen far beyond liking, respect and interest for Isolde – he was burning up with desire for her.

Dinner was unbearably awkward. The girls came downstairs in high spirits, their hair in damp plaits, clean linen and clean clothes making them feel festive, as if for a party. They were met by two subdued men. Brother Peter disapproved of the four of them dining together at all, and Luca could think of nothing but the stolen glimpse of the two girls in the firelight, with their hair down like mermaids.

He choked out a greeting to Isolde and bowed in silence to Ishraq, then rounded on Freize at the door, who was fetching ale and pouring wine. 'Glasses! The ladies should have glasses.'

'They're on the table as any fool can see,' Freize replied stolidly. He did not look at Ishraq but he rubbed his shoulder as if feeling a painful bruise.

Ishraq smiled at him without a moment's embarrassment. 'Have you hurt yourself, Freize?' she asked sweetly.

The look he shot at her would have filled any other girl

with remorse. 'I was kicked by a donkey,' he said. 'Stubborn and stupid is the donkey, and it does not know what is best for it.'

'Better leave it alone then,' she suggested.

'I shall do so,' Freize said heavily. 'Nobody tells Freize anything a second time. Especially if it comes with violence.'

'You were warned,' she said flatly.

'I thought it might shy,' he said. 'This stupid donkey. I thought it might resist at first. I wouldn't have been surprised by a coy little nip by way of rebuke and encouragement, all at once. What I didn't expect was for it to kick out like a damn mule.'

'Well, you know now,' replied Ishraq calmly.

He bowed, the very picture of offended dignity. 'I know now,' he agreed.

'What is this all about?' Isolde suddenly asked.

'You would have to ask the lady,' Freize said, with much emphasis on the noun.

Isolde raised an eyebrow at Ishraq, who simply slid her eyes away, indicating silence, and no more was said between the two girls.

'Are we to wait all night for dinner?' Luca demanded, and then suddenly thought he had spoken too loudly and, in any case, sounded like a spoiled brat. 'I mean: is it ready, Freize?'

'Bringing it in at once, my lord,' Freize said with injured dignity, and went to the top of the stairs and ordered that dinner be served, by the simple technique of hollering for the cook.

The two girls did most of the talking at dinner, speaking

of the shepherd boy, his mother, and the prettiness of their little farm. Brother Peter said little, silent in his disapproval, and Luca tried to make casual and nonchalant remarks but kept tripping himself up as he thought of the dark gold of Isolde's wet hair, and the warm gleam of her wet skin.

'Forgive me,' he suddenly said. 'I am quite distracted this evening.'

'Has something happened?' Isolde asked. Brother Peter fixed him with a long slow stare.

'No. I had a dream, that was all, and it left my mind filled with pictures, you know how it does? When you can't stop thinking about something.'

'What was the dream?' Ishraq asked.

At once Luca flushed red. 'I can hardly remember it. I can only see the pictures.'

'Of what?'

'I can't remember them, either,' Luca stammered. He glanced at Isolde. 'You will think me a fool.'

She smiled politely and shook her head.

'Sugared plums,' Freize remarked, bringing them suddenly to the table. 'Great deal of fuss about these in the kitchen. And every child in the village waiting at the back door for any that you leave.'

'I'm afraid we cause a great deal of trouble,' Isolde remarked.

'Normally a party with ladies would go on to a bigger town,' Brother Peter pointed out. 'That's why you should be with a larger group of travellers who have ladies with them already.'

'As soon as we meet up with such a group we'll join

them,' Isolde promised. 'I know we are trespassing on your kindness by travelling with you.'

'And how would you manage for money?' Brother Peter asked unkindly.

'Actually, I have some jewels to sell,' Isolde said.

'And they have the horses,' Freize volunteered from the door. 'Four good horses to sell whenever they need them.'

'They hardly own them,' Brother Peter objected.

'Well, I'm sure *you* didn't steal them from the brigands, and the little lord would never steal, and I don't touch stolen horseflesh, so they must be the property of the ladies and theirs to sell,' Freize said stoutly.

Both girls laughed. 'That's kind of you,' Isolde said. 'But perhaps we should share them with you.'

'Brother Peter can't take stolen goods,' Freize said. 'And he can't take the fee for showing the werewolf, either, as it's against his conscience.'

'Oh, for heaven's sake!' Peter exclaimed impatiently and Luca looked up, as if hearing the conversation for the first time.

'Freize, you can keep the money for showing the werewolf but don't charge the people any more. It will only cause bad feeling in the village and we have to have their consent and good will for the inquiry. And of course the ladies should have the horses.'

'Then we are well provided for,' Isolde said with a smile to Brother Peter and a warm glance to Luca. 'And I thank you all.'

'Thank you, Freize,' Ishraq said quietly. 'For the horses came to your whistle and followed you.'

Freize rubbed his shoulder as if he was in severe pain, and turned his head away from her, and said nothing.

They all went to bed early. The inn had only a few candles and the girls took one to light themselves to bed. When they had banked in the fire in their bedroom and blown out the light, Ishraq swung open the shutter and looked down into the bear pit below the window.

In the warm glow of the yellow near-full moon she could make out the shape of Freize, sitting on the bear-pit wall, his legs dangling inside the arena, a fistful of chop bones from dinner in his hand.

'Come on,' she heard him whisper. 'You know you like chop bones, you must like them even more than bread and jam. I saved a little of the fat for you, it's still warm and crispy. Come on now.'

Like a shadow, the beast wormed its way towards him and halted in the centre of the arena, sitting on its back legs like a dog, facing him, its chest pale in the moonlight, its mane falling back from its face. It waited, its eyes on Freize, watching the chops in his hand, but not daring to come any closer.

Freize dropped one just below his feet, then tossed one a little further away, and then one further than that, and sat rock-still as the beast squirmed to the farthest bone. Ishraq could hear it lick, and then the crunching of the bone as it ate. It paused, licked its lips and then looked longingly at the next bone on the earthen floor of the bear pit.

Unable to resist the scent, it came a little closer, and took up the second bone. 'There you go,' Freize said reassuringly. 'No harm done and you get your dinner. Now, what about this last one?'

The last one was almost under his dangling bare feet. 'Come on,' Freize said, urging the beast to trust him. 'Come on now, what d'you say? What d'you say?'

The beast crept the last few feet to the last bone, gobbled it down and retreated, but only a little way. It looked at Freize, and the man, unafraid, looked back at the beast. 'What d'you say?' Freize asked again. 'D'you like a lamb chop? What d'you say, little beast?'

'Good,' the beast said, in the light piping voice of a child. 'Good.'

Ishraq expected Freize to fling himself off the arena wall and come running into the inn with the amazing news that the beast had spoken a word, but to her surprise he did not move at all. She herself clapped her hand over her mouth to stifle her gasp. Freize was frozen on the bear-pit wall. He neither moved nor spoke, and for a moment she wondered if he had not heard, or if she had misheard or deceived herself in some way. Still Freize sat there like a statue of a man, and the beast sat there like a statue of a beast, watching him; and there was a long silence in the moonlight.

'Good, eh?' Freize said, his voice as quiet and level as before. 'Well, you're a good beast. More tomorrow. Maybe some bread and cheese for breakfast. We'll see what I can get you. Goodnight, beast – or what shall I call you? What name do you go by, little beast?'

He waited, but the beast did not reply. 'You can call me Freize,' the man said gently to the animal. 'And perhaps I can be your friend.'

Freize swung his legs over to the safe side of the wall and jumped down, and the beast stood four-legged, listening for a moment, then went to the shelter of the furthest wall, turned around three times like a dog, and curled up for sleep.

Ishraq looked up at the moon. Tomorrow it would be full and the villagers thought that the beast would wax to its power. What might the creature do then?

A delegation from the village arrived the next morning saying respectfully but firmly that they did not want the inquiry to delay justice against the werewolf. They did not see the point of the inquirer speaking to people, and writing things down. Instead, all the village wanted to come to the inn at moonrise, moonrise tonight, to see the changes in the werewolf, and to kill it.

Luca met them in the yard, Isolde and Ishraq with him, while Freize, unseen in the stable, was brushing down the horses listening intently. Brother Peter was upstairs completing the report.

Three men came from the village: the shepherd boy's father, Raul Rossi; the village headman, Guglielmo Mugnaio; and his brother. They were very sure they wanted to see the wolf in its wolf form, kill it, and make an end to the inquiry. The blacksmith was hammering away in the village forge making the silver arrow even as they spoke, they said.

'Also, we are preparing its grave,' Guglielmo Mugnaio told them. He was a round red-faced man of about forty, as pompous and self-important as any man of great consequence in a small village. 'I am reliably informed that a werewolf has to be buried with certain precautions so that it does not rise again. So to make certain sure that the beast will lie down when it is dead and not stir from its grave, I have given orders to the men to dig a pit at the crossroads outside the village. We'll bury it with a stake through its heart. We'll pack the grave with wolfsbane. One of the women of the village, a good woman, has been growing wolfsbane for years.' He nodded at Luca as if to reassure him. 'The silver arrow and the stake through its heart. The grave of wolfsbane. That's the way to do it.'

'I thought that was the undead?' Luca said irritably. 'I thought it was the undead who were buried at crossroads?'

'No point not taking care,' Mr Miller said, glowingly confident in his own judgement. 'No point not doing it right, now that we have finally caught it and we can kill it at our leisure. I thought we would kill it at midnight, with our silver arrow. I thought we would make a bit of an event of it. I myself will be here. I thought I might hand over the silver arrow to the archer, and perhaps I might make a short speech.'

'This isn't a bear baiting,' Luca said. 'It's a proper inquiry, and I am commissioned by His Holiness as an inquirer. I can't have the whole village here, the death sentence agreed before I have prepared my report, and rogues selling seats for a penny.'

'There was only one rogue doing that,' Mr Miller pointed out with dignity. The noise of Freize grooming the horse and whistling through his teeth suddenly loudly increased. 'But the whole village has to see the beast and see its death. Perhaps you don't understand, coming from Rome as you do. But we've lived in fear of it for too long. We're a small community, we want to know that we are safe now. We need to see that the werewolf is dead and that we can sleep in peace again.'

'I beg your pardon, sir, but it's thought that my first son was taken by the beast. I'd like to see an end to it. I'd like to be able to tell my wife that the beast is dead,' Raul Rossi, the shepherd boy's father, volunteered to Luca. 'If Sara knew that the beast was dead then she might feel that our son Tomas can take the sheep out to pasture without fear. She might sleep through the night again. Seven years she has wakened with nightmares. I want her to be at peace. If the werewolf was dead, she might forgive herself.'

'You can come at midnight,' Luca decided. 'If it is going to change into a wolf then it will do so then. And if we see a change, then I shall be the judge of whether it has become a wolf. Only I shall make that judgement, and only I will rule on its execution.'

'Should I advise?' Mr Miller asked hopefully. 'As a man of experience, of position in the community? Should I consult with you? Help you come to your decision?'

'No.' Luca crushed him. 'This is not going to be a matter of the village turning against a suspect and killing him out of their fear and rage. This is going to be a weighing of the evidence and justice. I am the inquirer. I shall decide.'

'But who is going to fire the arrow?' Mr Miller asked. 'We have an old bow which Mrs Louisa found in her loft, and we have restrung it, but there's nobody in the village who is trained to use a longbow. When we're called up to war we go as infantry with billhooks. We haven't had an archer in this village for ten years.'

There was a brief silence as they considered the difficulty. Then: 'I can shoot a longbow,' Ishraq volunteered.

Luca hesitated. 'It's a powerful weapon,' he said. He leaned towards her. 'Very heavy to bend,' he said. 'It's not like a lady's bow. You might be skilled in archery, ladies' sports, but I doubt you could bend a longbow. It's a very different thing from shooting at the butts.'

Freize's head appeared over the stable door to listen, but he said nothing.

In answer, she extended her left hand to Luca. On the knuckle of the middle finger was the hard callous, the absolute mark of an archer that identified him like a tattoo. It was an old blister, worn hard by drawing the arrow shaft across the guiding finger. Only someone who had shot arrow after arrow would have his hand marked by it.

'I can shoot,' she said. 'A longbow. Not a lady's bow.'

'However did you learn?' Luca asked, his hand withdrawing from her warm fingers. 'And why do you practise all the time?'

'Isolde's father wanted me to have the skills of the women of my people, even though I was raised far from them,' she said. 'We are a fighting people – the women can fight as well as the men. We are a hard people, living in the desert, travelling all the time. We can ride all day. We can find water by smell. We can find game by the turn of the wind. We live by hunting, falconry and archery. You will learn that if I say I can shoot, I can shoot.'

'If she says she can, she probably can,' Freize commented from inside the stable. 'I, for one, can attest that she can fight like a barbarian. She could well be a time-served archer. Certainly, she is no lady.'

Luca glanced from Freize's offended face, looming over the stable door, to Ishraq. 'If you can do it, then I shall appoint you executioner and give you the silver arrow. It's not a skill that I have. There was no call for it in the monastery. And I understand that no-one else here can do it.'

She nodded. 'I could hit the beast, though it is only a little beast, from the wall of the arena, shooting across to where it cowers, at the far side.'

'You're sure?'

She nodded with quiet confidence. 'Without fail.'

Luca turned to the headman and the two others. 'I will watch the beast through the day and as the moon rises,' he said. 'If I see it transform into a full wolf I will call you, and in any case you can come at midnight. If I judge that it is a wolf in shape as well as nature then this young woman here

233

will serve as executioner. You will bring the silver arrow and we will kill it at midnight, and you can bury it as you see fit.'

'Agreed,' the headman said. He turned to go and then he suddenly paused. 'But what happens if it does not turn? If it does not become wolf? What if it remains as it is now, wolfish but small and savage?'

'Then we will have to judge what sort of beast it is and what might be done with it,' Luca said. 'If it is a natural beast, an innocent animal ordained by God to run free, then I may order it to be released in the wild.'

'We should try it with tortures,' someone volunteered.

'I will try it with the Word,' Luca said. 'That is my inquiry, that I am appointed to do. I will take evidence and study the scriptures and decide what it is. Besides, I want to know for my own satisfaction what sort of beast it is. But you can be assured: I will not leave you with a werewolf at your doors. Justice will be done; your children will be safe.'

Ishraq glanced to the stable, expecting Freize to say that it was a speaking beast, but the look he showed her over the stable door was that of the dumbest servant who knows nothing and never speaks out of turn.

At midday the bishop of the region arrived after a day's journey from the cathedral town of Pescara, accompanied by four attending priests, five scholars, and some servants.

Luca greeted him on the doorstep of the inn and welcomed him with as good a grace as he could muster. He could not help but feel that he was completely outclassed by a fully-fledged bishop, dressed all in purple and riding a white mule. He could not help but feel diminished by a man of fifty who had with him nine advisors and what seemed like endless servants.

Freize tried to cheer the cook by explaining that it would all be over one way or another by tonight and that she would have to provide only one great dinner for this unique assembly of great men.

'Never have I had so many lords in the house at any one time,' she fretted. 'I will have to send out for chickens and Jonas will have to let me have the pig that he killed last week.'

'I'll serve the dinner, and help you in the kitchen too,' Freize promised her. 'I'll take the dishes up and put them before the gentry. I'll announce each course and make it sound tremendous.'

'The Lord knows that all you do is eat, and steal food for that animal in the yard. It's causing more trouble to me out there than ever it did in the forest.'

'Should we let it go, d'you think?' Freize asked playfully.

She crossed herself. 'Saints save us, no! Not after it took poor Mrs Fairley's own child and she never recovered from the grief. And last week a lamb, and the week before that a hen right out of the yard. No, the sooner it's dead the better. And your master had better order it killed or there will be a riot here. You can tell him that, from me. There are men coming into the village, shepherds from the highest farms, who won't take kindly to a stranger who comes here and says that our werewolf should be spared. Your master should know that there can only be one ending here: the beast must die.'

'Can I take that ham bone for it?' Freize asked.

'Isn't that the very thing that was going to make soup for the bishop's dinner?'

'There's nothing on it,' Freize urged her. 'Give it to me for the beast. You'll get another bone anyway when Jonas butchers the pig.'

'Take it, take it,' she said impatiently. 'And leave me to get on.'

'I shall come and help as soon as I have fed the beast,' Freize promised her.

She waved him out of the kitchen door into the yard and Freize climbed the platform and looked over the arena wall. The beast was lying down, but when it saw Freize it raised its head and watched him.

Freize vaulted to the top of the wall, swung his long legs over, and sat in comfort there, his legs dangling into the bear pit. 'Now then,' he said gently. 'Good morning to you, beast. I hope you are well this morning?'

The beast came a little closer, to the very centre of the pit, and looked up at Freize. Freize leaned into the pit, holding tightly on to the wall with one hand, leaned down so far that the ham bone was dangling just below his feet. 'Come,' he said gently. 'Come and get this. You have no idea what trouble it cost me to get it for you, but I saw the ham carved off it last night and I set my heart on it for you.'

The beast turned its head a little one way and then the other, as if trying to understand the string of words. Clearly, it understood the gentle tone of voice, as it yearned upwards to the silhouette of Freize, on the wall of the bear pit. 'Come on,' said Freize. 'It's good.'

Cautious as a cat, the beast approached on all fours. It came to the wall of the arena and sat directly under Freize's feet. Freize stretched down to it and slowly the beast uncurled, put its front paws on the walls of the arena and reached up. It stood tall, perhaps more than four feet. Freize fought the temptation to shrink back from it, imagining it would sense his fear; but also he was driven on to see if he could feed this animal by hand, to see if he could bridge the divide between this beast and man. And he was driven, as always, by his own love of the dumb, the vulnerable, the hurt. He stretched down a little lower and the beast stretched up its shaggy head and gently took the ham bone in its mouth, as if it had been fed by a loving hand, all its life.

The moment it had the meat in its strong jaws, it sprang back from Freize, dropped to all fours and scuttled to the other side of the bear pit. Freize straightened up – and found Ishraq's dark eyes on him.

'Why feed it if I am to shoot it tonight?' she asked quietly. 'Why be kind to it, if it is nothing but a dead beast waiting for the arrow?'

'Perhaps you won't have to shoot it tonight,' Freize answered. 'Perhaps the little lord will find that it's a beast we don't know, or some poor creature that was lost from a fair. Perhaps he will rule that it's an oddity, but not a limb of Satan. Perhaps he will say it is a changeling, put among us by strange people. Surely it is more like an ape than a wolf? What sort of a beast is it? Have you, in all your travels, in all your study, seen such a beast before?'

She looked uncertain. 'No, never. The bishop is talking with your lord now. They are going through all sorts of books and papers to judge what should be done, how it should be tried and tested, how it should be killed, and how it should be buried. The bishop has brought in all sorts of scholars with him who say they know what should be done.' She paused. 'If it can speak like a Christian, then that alters everything. Your lord, Luca Vero, should be told.'

Freize's glance never wavered. 'Why would you think it could speak?' he said.

She met his gaze without coquetry. 'You're not the only one who takes an interest in it,' she said.

All day Luca was closeted with the bishop, his priests, and his scholars, the dining table spread with papers which recorded judgements against werewolves and the histories of wolves going back to the very earliest times: records from the Greek philosophers' accounts, translated by the Arabs into Arabic and then translated back again into Latin. 'So God knows what they were saying in the first place,' Luca confided in Brother Peter. 'There are a dozen prejudices that the words have to get through, there are half a dozen scholars for every single account, and they all have a different opinion.'

'We have to have a clear ruling for our inquiry,' Brother

Peter said, worried. 'It's not enough to have a history of anything that anyone thinks they have seen, going back hundreds of years. We are supposed to examine the facts here, and you are supposed to establish the truth. We don't want antique gossip – we want evidence, and then a judgement.'

They cleared the table for the midday meal and the bishop recited a long grace. Ishraq and Isolde were banned from the councils of men and ate dinner in their own room, looking out over the yard. They watched Freize sit on the wall of the bear pit, a wooden platter balanced on his knee, sharing his food with the beast that sat beneath him, glancing up from time to time, watching for scraps, as loyal and as uncomplaining as a dog, but somehow unlike a dog – a sort of independence.

'It's a monkey for sure,' Isolde said. 'I have seen a picture of one in a book my father had at home.'

'Can they speak?' Ishraq asked. 'Monkeys? Can they speak?'

'It looked as if it could speak, it had lips and teeth like us, and eyes that looked as if it had thoughts and wanted to tell them.'

'I don't think this beast is a monkey,' Ishraq said, carefully. 'I think this beast can speak.'

'Like a parrot?' Isolde asked.

They both watched Freize lean down and the beast reach up. They saw Freize pass a scrap of bread and apple down to the beast and the beast take it in his paw, not in his mouth – take it in his paw and then sit on his haunches and eat it, holding it to his mouth like a big squirrel.

'Not like a parrot,' Ishraq said. 'I think it can speak like a

Christian. We cannot kill it, we cannot stand by and see it killed until we know what it is. Clearly it is not a wolf, but what is it?'

'It's not for us to judge.'

'It is,' Ishraq said. 'Not because we are Christians – for I am not. Not because we are men – for we are not. But because we are like the beast: outsiders that other people dread. People don't understand women who are neither wives nor mothers, daughters nor confined. People fear women of passion, women of education. I am a young woman of education, of colour, of unknown religion and my own faith, and I am as strange to the people of this little village as the beast. Should I stand by and see them kill it because they don't understand what it is? If I let them kill it without a word of protest, what would stop them coming for me?'

'Will you tell Luca this?'

Ishraq shrugged. 'What's the use? He's listening to the bishop, he's not going to listen to me.'

At about two in the afternoon the men agreed on what was to be done and the bishop stepped out to the doorstep of the inn to announce their decision. 'If the beast transforms into a full wolf at midnight then the heretic woman will shoot it with a silver arrow,' he ruled. 'The villagers will bury it in a crate packed with wolfsbane at the crossroads and the blacksmith will hammer a stake through its heart.'

'My wife will bring the wolfsbane,' Raul Rossi volunteered. 'God knows she grows enough of it.'

'If the beast does not transform . . .' The bishop raised his hand, and raised his voice, against the murmur of disbelief. 'I know, good people, that you are certain that it will . . . but just suppose that it does not . . . then we will release it to the authorities of this village, the lord and yourself, Master Miller, and you may do with it what you will. Man has dominion over the animals, given to him by God. God Himself has decreed that you can do what you want with this beast. It was a beast running wild near your village, you caught it and held it, God has given you all the beasts into your dominion – you may do with it what you wish.'

Mr Miller nodded grimly. There was little doubt in anyone's mind that the beast would not last long after it was handed over to the village.

'They will hack it to pieces,' Ishraq muttered to Isolde.

'Can we stop them?' she whispered back.

'No.'

'And now,' the bishop ruled, 'I advise you to go about your business until midnight when we will all see the beast. I myself am going to the church where I will say Vespers and Compline and I suggest that you all make your confessions and make an offering to the church before coming to see this great sight which has been wished upon your village.' He paused. 'God will smile on those who donate to the church tonight,' he said. 'The angel of the Lord has passed among you, it is meet to offer him thanks and praise.'

'What does that mean?' Ishraq asked Isolde.

'It means: "pay up for the privilege of a visit from a bishop",' Isolde translated.

'You know, I thought it did.'

There was nothing to do but to wait until midnight. Freize fed the beast after dinner and it came and sat at his feet and looked up at him, as if it would speak with him, but it could find no words. In turn Freize wanted to warn the beast, but with its trusting brown eyes peering at him through its matted mane he found he could not explain what was to happen. As the moon rose, man and beast kept a vigil with each other, just as the bishop was keeping vigil in the church. The beast's leonine head turned up to Freize as he sat, darkly profiled against the starlit sky, murmuring quietly to it, hoping that it would speak again; but it said nothing.

'It would be a good time now for you to say your name, my darling,' he said quietly. 'One "God bless" would save your life. Or just "good" again. Speak, beast, before midnight. Or speak at midnight. Speak when everyone is looking at you. But speak. Make sure you speak.'

The animal looked at him, its eyebrows raised, its head on one side, its eyes bright brown through the tangled hair. 'Speak, beast,' Freize urged him again. 'No point being dumb if you can speak. If you could say "God bless" they would account it a miracle. Can you say it? After me?"God bless"?'

At eleven o' clock the people started to gather outside the stable door, some carrying billhooks and others scythes and axes. It was clear that if the bishop did not order the animal shot with the silver arrow then the men would take the law into their own hands, cleave it apart with their tools or tear it apart with their bare hands. Freize looked out through the door and saw some men at the back of the crowd levering up the cobbles with an axe head, and tucking the stones into their pockets.

Ishraq came out of the inn to find Freize, reaching down into the bear pit to give the beast a morsel of bread and cheese.

'They are certain to kill it,' she said. 'They have not come for a trial; they have come to see it die.'

'I know,' he nodded.

'Whatever sort of beast it is, I doubt that it is a werewolf.'

He shrugged. 'Not having seen one before, I couldn't say. But this is an animal which seeks contact with humans, it's not a killer like a wolf, it's more companionable than that. Like a dog in its willingness to come close, like a horse in its shy pride, like a cat in its indifference. I don't know what sort of beast it is. But I would put my year's wages on it being an endearing beast, a loving beast, a loyal beast. It's a beast that can learn, it's a beast that can change its ways.'

'They're not going to spare it on my word or yours,' she said.

He shook his head. 'Not on any word from either of us. Nobody listens to the unimportant. But the little lord might save it.'

'He's got the bishop against him, and the bishop's scholars.'

'Would your lady speak up for it?'

She shrugged. 'Who ever listens to a woman?'

'No man of any sense,' he replied instantly and was pleased to see the gleam of her smile.

She looked down at the beast. It looked up at her and its ugly truncated face seemed almost human. 'Poor beast,' she said.

'If it was a fairytale you could kiss it,' Freize volunteered. 'You could bend down and kiss it and it would be a prince. Love can make miracles with beasts, so they say. But no! Forgive me, I remember now, that you don't kiss. Indeed, you throw a good man down in the mud for even thinking that you might.'

She did not respond to his teasing, but for a moment she looked very thoughtful. 'You know, you're right. Only love can save it,' she said. 'That is what you have been showing from the moment you first saw it. Love.'

'I wouldn't say that I . . .' Freize started, but in that moment she was gone.

In a very little while, the head of the village, Mr Miller, hammered at the gate of the inn and Freize and the inn servant opened the great double doors to the stable yard. The villagers flooded in and took their places on the tables that surrounded the outer wall of the arena, just as they would for a bear baiting. The men brought strong ale with them, and their wives sipped from their cups, laughing and smiling. The young men of the village came with their sweethearts, and the cook in the kitchen sold little cakes and pies out of the kitchen door, while the maids ran around the stable yard selling mulled ale and wine. It was an execution and a party: both at once.

Ishraq saw Sara Rossi arrive, a great basket of wolfsbane in her arms, and her husband followed behind, leading their donkey loaded with the herb. They tied the donkey in the archway and came into the yard, their boy with his usual sprig of wolfsbane in his hat.

'You came,' Isolde said warmly, stepping forwards. 'I am glad that you are here. I am glad that you felt you could come.'

'My husband thought that we should,' Sara replied, her face very pale. 'He thought it would satisfy me to see the beast dead at last. And everyone else is here. I could not let the village gather without me, they shared my sorrow. They want to see the end of the story.'

'I am glad you came,' Isolde repeated. The woman clambered up on the trestle table beside Ishraq, and Isolde followed her.

'You have the arrowhead?' the woman asked Ishraq. 'You are going to shoot it?'

Without a word, the young woman nodded and showed her the longbow and the silver-tipped arrow.

'You can hit it from here?'

'Without fail,' Ishraq said grimly. 'If he turns into a wolf, then the inquirer will see him turn, he will tell me to kill him, and I will do so. But I think he is not a wolf, nor anything like a wolf, not a werewolf nor any animal that we know.'

'If we don't know what it is, and can't tell what it is, it's better dead,' the man said firmly, but Sara Rossi looked from the beast to the silver arrowhead and gave a little shiver. Ishraq gazed steadily at her and Isolde put her hand over the woman's trembling fingers. 'Don't you want the beast dead?' Isolde asked her.

She shook her head. 'I don't know. I don't know for sure if it took my child, I don't know for sure if it is the monster that everyone says. And there is something about it that moves me to pity.' She looked at the two young women. 'You will think me a fool; but I am sorry for it,' she said.

She was still speaking as the doors of the inn opened and Luca, Brother Peter and the bishop, the scholars, and the priests came out. Isolde and Ishraq exchanged one urgent glance. 'I'll tell him,' Isolde said swiftly and jumped down from the stand and made her way to the door of the inn, pushing through the crowd to get to Luca.

'Is it near to midnight?' the bishop asked.

'I have ordered the church bell to be tolled on the hour,' one of the priests replied.

The bishop inclined his head to Luca. 'How are you going to examine the supposed werewolf?' he asked.

'I thought I would wait till midnight, and watch it,' Luca said. 'If it changes into a wolf we will clearly be able to see it. Perhaps we should douse the torches so that the beast can feel the full effect of the moon.'

'I agree. Put out the torches!' the bishop ordered.

As soon as the darkness drowned the yard, everyone was silent, as if fearful of what they were doing. The women murmured and crossed themselves, and the younger children clung to their mothers' skirts. One of them whimpered quietly.

'I can't even see it,' someone complained.

'No, there it is!'

The beast had shrunk back into its usual spot as the yard had filled with noisy people; now, in the darkness it was hard to see, its dark mane against the dark wood of the bear-pit wall, its dark skin concealed against the mud of the earth floor. People blinked and rubbed their eyes, waiting for the dazzle of the torches to wear off, and then Mr Miller said, 'He's moving!'

The beast had risen to its four feet and was looking around, swinging his head as if fearful that danger was coming but not knowing what was about to happen. There was a whisper like a cursing wind that ran around the arena as everyone saw him move, and most men swore that he should be killed at once. Freize saw people feeling for the cobbles they had tucked into their pockets, and knew that they would stone the beast to death.

Isolde got to Luca's side and touched his arm; he leaned his head to listen. 'Don't kill the beast,' she whispered to him.

At the side of the arena, Freize exchanged one apprehensive look with Ishraq, saw the gleam of the silver arrowhead and her steady hand on the bow, and then turned his gaze back to the beast. 'Now gently,' he said, but it could not hear his voice above the low curses that rumbled around it, and it pulled back its head and hunched its shoulders as if it was afraid.

Slowly, ominously, as if announcing a death, the church bell started to toll. The beast flinched at the noise, shaking its mane as if the sonorous clang was echoing in its head. Someone laughed abruptly, but the voice was sharp with fear. Everyone was watching as the final notes of the midnight bell died on the air and the full moon, bright as a cold sun, rose slowly over the roof of the inn and shone down on the beast as it stood at bay, not moving, sweating in its terror.

There was no sign of hair growing, there was no sign of the beast getting bigger. Its teeth did not grow, nor did it sprout a tail. It stayed on four legs, but the watchers, looking intently, could see that it was shivering, like a little deer will shiver when chilled by frost.

'Is it changing?' the bishop asked Luca. 'I can't see anything. I can't see that it is doing anything.'

'It's just standing, and looking round,' Luca replied. 'I can't see any hair growing, and yet the moon is full on it.'

Somebody in the crowd cruelly howled in a joking impression of a wolf, and the beast turned its head sharply towards the sound as if it hoped it were real, but then shrank back as it realised that it was a harsh jest.

'Is it changing now?' the bishop asked again, urgently.

'I can't see,' Luca said. 'I don't think so.' He looked up. A cloud, no bigger than a clenched fist, was coming up over the full moon, wisps of it already darkening the arena. 'Maybe we should get the torches lit again,' Luca said anxiously. 'We're losing the light.'

'Is the beast changing to wolf?' the bishop demanded even more urgently. 'We will have to tell the people our decision. Can you order the girl to shoot it?'

'I can't,' Luca said bluntly. 'In justice, I cannot. It's not turning to wolf. It's in full moon, it's in moonlight, and it's not turning.'

'Don't shoot,' Isolde said urgently to him.

It was getting swiftly darker as the cloud came over the moon. The crowd groaned, a deep, fearful sound. 'Shoot it! Shoot it quickly!' someone called.

It was pitch black now. 'Torches!' Luca shouted. 'Get some torches lit!'

Suddenly there was a piercing terrible scream, and the sound of someone falling: a thud as she hit the ground and then a desperate scrabbling noise as she struggled to her feet.

'What is it?' Luca fought to the front of the crowd and strained his eyes, peering down into the darkness of the arena. 'Light the torches! In God's name what has happened?'

'Save me!' Sara Rossi cried out in panic. 'Dear God, save me!' She had fallen from the wall into the bear pit and was alone in the arena, her back pressed against the wooden wall, her eyes straining into the darkness as she looked for the beast. The animal was on its feet now, peering towards her with its amber eyes. It could see well in the darkness, though everyone else was blind. It could see the woman, her hands held out before her, as if she thought she could fend off fangs and pouncing claws.

'Ishraq! Shoot!' Luca shouted at her.

He could not see her dark hood, her dark eyes, but he could see the glint of the silver of the arrow, he could see the arrow on the string pointed steadily towards the dark shadow, which was the beast scenting the air, taking one hesitant step forwards. And then he heard her voice; but she was not calling to him, she was shouting down to Sara Rossi as she froze in terror, pinned against the wall of the arena.

'Call him!' Ishraq shouted to Sara. 'Call the beast.'

The white blur of Sara's frightened face turned up to Ishraq. 'What?' She was deaf with terror: too afraid to understand anything. 'What?'

'Don't you know his name?' Ishraq demanded gently, the silver arrow pointing unwaveringly at the beast slowly creeping closer.

'How should I know the name of the beast?' she whispered up. 'Get me out! Get me up. For the love of God! Save me!'

'Look at him. Look at him with your love. Who have you missed for all this time? What was his name?'

Sara stared at Ishraq as if she were speaking Arabic, and then she turned to the beast. It was closer still, head bowed, moving its weight from one side to the other, as if readying for a pounce. It was coming, without a doubt. It snarled, showing yellow teeth. Its head raised up, smelling fear; it was ready to attack. It took three stiff-legged steps forwards; now it would duck its head and run and lunge for her throat.

'Ishraq! Shoot the beast!' Luca yelled. 'That's an order!'

'Call him,' Ishraq urged the woman desperately. 'Call him by the name you love most in the world.'

Outside the arena, Raul Rossi dashed to the stables shouting for a ladder, leaving his son frozen with horror on the bear-pit fence, watching his mother face the beast.

Everyone was silent. They could just see the beast in the flickering light of the two torches, could see it slowly coming towards the woman, in the classic stalk of a wolf, its head down, level with its hunched shoulders, its eyes on the prey, sinuously moving forwards.

Freize thrust one torch into Luca's hand and readied himself to jump down into the bear pit with another flaming in his grip as Sara spoke: 'Stefan?' she asked in a hushed whisper. 'Stefan? Is that you?'

The beast stopped, putting its head on one side.

'Stefan?' she whispered. 'Stefan, my son? Stefan – my son?'

Freize froze on the side of the arena, silently watching as the beast rose from his four legs to his hind legs, as if he was remembering how to walk, as if he was remembering the woman who had held his hands for every step that he took. Sara pushed herself off the arena wall and moved towards him, her legs weak beneath her, hands outstretched.

'It's you,' she said wonderingly, but with absolute certainty. 'It's you ... Stefan. My Stefan, come to me.'

He took a step towards her, then another, and then in a rush which made the watching people gasp with fear but which made his mother cry out with joy, he dashed at her and flung himself into her arms. 'My boy! My boy!' she cried out, wrapping her arms around his scarred body, pulling his matted head to her shoulder: 'My son!'

He looked up at her, his dark eyes bright through his

matted mane of hair. 'Mama,' he said in his little boy's voice. 'Mama.'

The bishop got hold of Luca for a whispered angry consultation. 'You knew of this?'

'Not I.'

'It was your servant who had an arrow on the bow and didn't shoot. It was your servant who has been feeding the beast and coaxing it. He must have known, but he led us into this trap.'

'She was ready with the arrow, you saw her yourself. And my servant was about to jump into the arena and get between the woman and the beast himself.'

'Why didn't she shoot? She said that she could shoot. Why didn't she do so?'

'How would I know? She is no servant of mine. I will ask her what she thought she was doing and I will write it up in my report.'

'The report is the last of our worries!'

'Forgive me, your eminence, it is my principal concern.'

'But the beast! The beast! We came to kill it and show a triumph for the Church over sin. There can be no killing of the beast now.'

'Of course not,' Luca said. 'As my report will show. He is no beast. His mother has claimed him back. She will take him and bathe him and cut his hair and nails and teach him to wear clothes again and to speak.'

'And what do you think you will say in your report?' the bishop said acidly. 'You had a werewolf in your keeping and behold now you have nothing but a dirty wild boy. You don't come out of this very well, any more than we do.'

'I shall say that your scholarship revealed to us what happened here,' Luca said smoothly. 'Among the other accounts that your scholars prepared, you brought us the classical story of Romulus and Remus, who were raised by a wolf and founded the City of Rome, our rock. You told us of other stories of children who had been lost in the forest and were found again, raised by wolves. Your library held these stories, your scholarship recognised them, your authority warned us what might have happened here.'

The bishop paused, mollified, his rounded belly swelling with his vanity. 'The people were waiting for an execution,' he warned. 'They won't understand the miracle that has happened here. They wanted a death, you are offering them a restoration.'

'That is the power of your authority,' Luca said quickly. 'Only you can explain to them what happened. Only you have the scholarship and the skill to tell them. Will you preach now? It is the theme of the Prodigal Son, I think: the return of the lost one whose father sees him afar off and runs to greet him, loving him dearly.'

The bishop looked thoughtful. 'They will need guidance,' he considered, one plump finger to his lips. 'They were expecting a trial to the death. They will want a death. They are a savage unlearned people. They were expecting an execution and they will want a death. The Church shows its power by putting evil-doers to death. We have to be seen to conquer over sin. There is nothing that brings more people to the church than a witch-burning or an execution.'

'Your Grace, they are lost in the darkness of their own confusion. They are your sheep; lead them to the light. Tell them that a miracle has taken place here. A little child was lost in the wood, he was raised by wolves, he became like a wolf. But as your eminence watched, he recognised his mother. Who can doubt that the presence of a bishop made all the difference? These are an ignorant and fearful people but you can preach a sermon here that people will remember forever. They will always remember the day that the Bishop of Pescara came to their village and a miracle took place.'

The bishop rose up and straightened his cape. 'I will preach to them from the open window of the dining room,' he said. 'I will preach now, while they are gathered before me. I shall preach a midnight sermon, extempore. Get torches to shine on me. And take notes.'

'At once,' Luca said. He hurried from the room and gave the order to Freize. The balcony glowed with torchlight, the people, abuzz with speculation and fear, turned their faces upwards. As their attention went to the bishop, glorious in his purple cope and mitre at the window, Freize and Ishraq, Raul Rossi and his younger son, unbarred the single entrance door into the arena, and went in to fetch Sara Rossi, her eldest son held tightly in her arms.

'I want to take him home,' she said simply to her husband. 'This is our son Stefan, returned to us by a miracle.'

'I know it,' Raul replied. His wind-burned cheeks were

wet with tears. 'I knew him too. As soon as he said "Mama", I knew it. I recognised his voice.'

Stefan could barely walk; he stumbled and leaned on his mother, his dirty head on her shoulder.

'Can we put him on the donkey?' Freize suggested.

They lifted the panniers of wolfsbane from the donkey's back but the herb was still in its mane and clinging to the animal's back. Sara helped him up, and he did not flinch either at the touch of the herb or the smell of the flowers. Ishraq, watching quietly in the darkness, gave a quick affirmative nod.

Freize led the donkey away from the village, up the twisting little steps, as Sara walked beside her son cooing soothingly to him. 'Soon we will be home,' she said. 'You will remember your home. Your bed is just as it was, the sheets on the bed, the pillow waiting for you. Your little poppet Roos – do you remember him? – still on your pillow. In all these years I have never changed your room. It has always been waiting for you. I have always been waiting for you.'

On the other side of the donkey, Raul Rossi held his son steady, one hand on his little tanned leg, one hand on his scarred back. Ishraq and Isolde came behind with his little brother Tomas, his dog at his heels.

The farmhouse was shuttered for the night, but they brought the wolf-boy into the hall and he looked around, his eyes squinting against the firelight, without fear, as if he could just remember, as in a dream, when this had been his home.

'We can care for him now,' Raul Rossi said to the girls and Freize. 'My wife and I thank you from our hearts for all you have done.'

Sara went with them to the door. 'You have given me my son,' she said to Ishraq. 'You have done for me what I prayed the Virgin Mary would do. I owe you a debt for all my life.'

Ishraq made a strange gesture: she put her hands together in the gesture of prayer and then with her finger-tips she touched her own forehead, her lips, and her breast, and then bowed to the farmer's wife. '*Salaam*. It was you who did a great thing. It was you who had the courage to love him for so long,' she said. 'It was you who lived with grief and tried to bury your sorrow and yet kept his room for him, and your heart open to him. It was you that did not accuse the beast – when the whole village howled for vengeance. It was you who had pity for him. And then it was you who had the courage to say his name when you thought you faced a wolf. All I did was throw you down into the pit.'

'Wait a moment,' Freize said. 'You threw her down into the bear pit to face a beast?'

Isolde shook her head, in disapproval, but clearly she was not at all surprised.

Ishraq faced Freize. 'I'm afraid I did.'

Raul Rossi, one arm around his wife, one around Tomas's shoulders, looked at Ishraq. 'Why did you do it?' he asked simply. 'You took a great risk, both with my wife's life and with your own. For if you had been wrong, and she had been hurt, the village would have mobbed you. If she had died there, attacked by the beast, they would have killed you and thrown your body down for the wolf to eat.'

Ishraq nodded. 'I know,' she said. 'But in the moment –

when I was sure it was your son, and I was certain they would order me to shoot him – it was the only thing I could think of doing.'

Isolde laughed out loud, put her arm around her friend's shoulders and hugged her close. 'Only you!' she exclaimed. 'Only you would think that there was nothing to do but throw a good woman into a bear pit to face a beast!'

'Love,' Ishraq said. 'I knew that he needed love. I knew that she loved her son.' She turned to Freize. 'You knew it too. You knew that love would see through the worst of appearances.'

Freize shook his head, and stepped outside into the moonlight. 'I'll be damned,' he said to the changing sky. 'I will be damned and double damned if I ever understand how women think.'

The next morning they saw the bishop leave in his pomp, his priests before him on their white mules, his scholars carrying the records, his clerks already writing up and copying his sermon on 'The Prodigal Son', which they said was a model of its kind.

'It was very moving,' Luca told him on the doorstep. 'I have mentioned it in my report. I have quoted many of the passages. It was inspirational, and all about authority.'

As soon as he was gone, they ate their own midday

dinner and ordered their horses brought out into the stable yard. Freize showed Ishraq her horse, saddled and bridled. 'No pillion saddle,' he said. 'I know you like to ride alone. And the Lord knows, you can handle yourself and, I daresay, a horse as well.'

'But I'll ride alongside you, if I may,' she said.

Freize narrowed his eyes and scrutinised her for sarcasm. 'No,' he said after a moment's thought. 'I'm just a servant, you are a lady. I ride behind.'

His smile gleamed at the consternation on her face.

'Freize – I never meant to offend you . . .'

'Now you see,' he crowed triumphantly. 'Now you see what happens when you throw a good man down on his back on the cobbles – when you go tipping good women into bear pits. Too strong by half, is what I would say. Too opinionated by half, is what I would propose. Too proud of your opinion to make any man a good sweetheart or wife. Bound to end in a cold grave as a spinster, I would think. If not burned as a witch, as has already been suggested.'

She raised her hands as if in surrender. 'Clearly I have offended you—' she began.

'You have,' Freize said grandly. 'And so I shall ride behind, like a servant, and you may ride ahead, like an opinionated overly powerful lady, like a woman who does not know her place in the world, nor anyone else's. Like a woman who goes chucking men onto their backs, and women into bear pits, and causing all sorts of upset. You shall ride ahead, in your pomp, as vain as the bishop, and we know which of us will be the happier.'

Ishraq bowed her head under his storm of words, and

mounted her horse without replying. Clearly, there was no dealing with Freize in his state of outrage.

Isolde came out of the inn and Freize helped her into the saddle and then Luca came out followed by Brother Peter.

'Where to?' Ishraq asked Luca.

He mounted his horse and brought it alongside hers. 'Due east, I think,' he said. He looked to Brother Peter. 'Isn't that right?'

Brother Peter touched the letter in his jacket pocket. 'North-east it says on the outside of the letter, and at breakfast tomorrow, at Pescara, if we get there, God willing, I am to open our orders.'

'We will have another mission?' Luca asked.

'We will,' Brother Peter said. 'All I have is the directions to Pescara, but I don't know what the instructions will say nor where they will take us.' He looked at Isolde and Ishraq. 'I take it that the ladies will be travelling with us to Pescara?'

Luca nodded.

'And leaving us there?' Brother Peter prompted.

'Can't go soon enough for me,' Freize said from the mounting block as he tightened his girth and got on his horse. 'In case she takes it into her head to throw me into a river – or into the sea when we get there, which clearly she might do if she takes it into her own wilful head.'

'They will leave us when they find safe companions,' Luca ruled. 'As we agreed.' But he brought his horse alongside Isolde and reached out to put his hand on hers, as she held her reins. 'You will stay with us?' he asked quietly. 'While our roads go together?'

The smile that she gave him told him that she would. 'I

will stay with you,' she promised. 'While our roads lie together.'

The little cavalcade of Luca and Isolde, Brother Peter and Ishraq, with Freize behind them, surrounded by his beloved extra horses, clattered out of the gateway of the inn, not yet knowing where they were going, nor what they had to do, and headed north-east for Pescara – and for whatever lay beyond.

AUTHOR NOTE

This has been a joy to write, and I hope that you've enjoyed reading it as much as I have loved working on it. The character of Luca Vero is entirely imaginary, as are Isolde and Freize. The character of Ishraq, though invented, is based on the many courageous and adventurous men and women who moved between the world of Christendom and the worlds of the other religions: Jews, Muslims, and even those farther afield.

What the book means to you, the reader, will be for you to decide. Most people will read it, I hope, for pleasure and with pleasure, and have the fun of joining young, passionate characters on a journey into an unknown world, where they face their fears and experience their powers. Some readers may want to know a little more about the world of the Order of Darkness.

The Order of Darkness is based on the fifteenth-century Order of the Dragon, which was created to defend Christendom against the apparently unstoppable rise of the Muslim Ottoman Empire. One of the characters who will arrive in the story in subsequent books, was introduced to this Order by his father when he was just a little boy and rose to become its commander, fighting at the very outpost of Christendom.

The investigation entrusted to Luca – to find the signs of the end of times – is a fictional version of the anxiety felt by most people after the fall of Constantinople. The rise of all sorts of strange phenomena in Europe at this time shows that many people were fearing that anything could happen – and was happening. Also, these were deeply superstitious times. People genuinely believed that there was another, unseen, world sometimes glimpsed but often bearing down upon their lives. For those of us who now live in a world where we try to measure and understand every-thing, it is hard to imagine what it would have been like to have no explanation for everyday events like illness, thun-der, or an eclipse, yet having your world rocked by the death of a loved one, your house shaken by a thunderclap or your day turning into night as a dark moon eats up the sun.

Isolde is typical of the girls of her time in that her life would be completely determined by her father and, on his death, her brother or any male kinsman. Legally, she could not buy or sell land or property, and anything she inherited would automatically belong to her husband on marriage.

She would have no rights of her own at all: a father or husband was legally allowed to beat her; he could care for her as well or as badly as he liked. In these sorts of circumstances life in a nunnery was probably preferable to a bad marriage – as Isolde decides. In the nunnery there was the possibility of a career (like the Lady Almoner, who joins as a little girl and rises in authority) and the chance to organise your own life inside the strict rules of the order. Many women relished the education, and many had a deep religious experience.

Poor boys had a similar chance at improving their lives if they were accepted into a monastery and someone like Luca – who has exceptional abilities – would have had a good chance of rising to be a clerk or secretary to a great lord, who would find his administrators in the ranks of the Church. If Luca had stayed inside the Church, he might have risen to become a senior cleric. Brother Peter is a career churchman like this; he came from a poor family but is rising up through the Church. Luca does not take this route because he uncovers the many frauds that were going on in medieval churches. People wanted to see miracles, and dishonest churchmen produced relics of saints that could not possibly be genuine, and faked mechanical toys like weeping statues. This was part of the superstitions of the times, but was promoted by the Church, which made its money from the payments of the faithful.

Freize is, at first sight, a more normal poor boy. He joins the monastery as a lay worker – not a priest but someone simply working in the monastery as he might have worked in a big house. He has a gift for handling animals, and for common sense. He would have been very poor in the medieval world. If he had not won a place in a monastery, he would probably have had to work in the fields and would have been regarded as the servant, almost the property, of the local lord, who ruled everything.

Ishraq is perhaps the most unusual character of the four. Brought into Europe from the Middle East by Lord Lucretili, she was raised as his daughter's companion and protector, and he had her trained in fighting skills, medicine and other disciplines. She remains half in and half outside of the society as a heretic. Medieval Christians thought that anyone who did not accept the Bible just as they did was a non-believer and their soul was damned to hell. If someone chose to prosecute her for heresy, then she could be burned by the Church – but as long as she made no enemies she might pass through society with people showing little more than curiosity. There were probably far more heretics, Moors, Africans and other races and religions in Europe than have been counted.

If you are interested in the background history to the story, including some lovely medieval details on shoes, clothes, food, washing, courtship – almost everything! – you can visit my site orderofdarkness.com. Or you can do your own research; most of the things that I mention can be found in books or on the Internet, and also there is a pack of teachers' notes available to share in the classroom, which can be downloaded from orderofdarkness.com or simonandschuster.co.uk.

I hope you enjoy the illustrations throughout the book. It's not an author photo at the top of this note but a version of Christine de Pizan, a wonderful medieval woman, one of the first commercial writers in Europe.

Why is this book different from my historical novels? Mostly my historical fictions are based on everything that we know about a real person, her life and her times. This novel is based on four purely fictional young people, and the world they live in. It reflects the historical reality of their times, but of course nobody but a fictional heroine has such an exciting day-to-day life! And why did I write it? Not because I have finished writing fictional biographies at all – my new novel, *The Kingmaker's Daughter*, is just out – but I thought it would be fun to write something less rooted in the historical record. I wrote it for the pleasure that it has given to me and in the hope that you will like it too.

PHILIPPA GREGORY

Read on for an
exclusive extract from
Order of Darkness 2: *Stormbringers*,
coming soon!

Freize soon found a master who was prepared to take them across the sea to the town of Split. But he would not go until midday. 'I have been fishing half the night, I want a hot meal and dry clothes and then I'll come with you,' he says. 'Sail at noon. You'll hear the church bells for Sext.'

They shook hands on the agreement and Freize went back to the inn, pausing at the stables to order the grooms to have the horses ready for sailing at midday. It seemed to him that the crowds at the quayside had grown busier, even though the market had finished trading. There were a lot of young people at the front door, peering into the inn, and in the stableyard about a dozen children were sitting on the mounting block and the wall of the well. One or two of them had hauled up the dripping bucket from the well and were drinking from their cupped hands.

'What are you doing here?' he asked a group of about six boys, none of them more than twelve years old. 'Where are your parents?'

They did not answer him immediately, but solemnly crossed themselves. 'My father is in heaven,' one of them said.

'Well, God bless you,' Freize said, assuming that they were a party of begging children, travelling together for safety. He crossed the yard and went into the inn through the kitchen door, where the landlady was lifting half a dozen good-sized loaves of rough rye bread from the oven.

'Smells good,' Freize said appreciatively.

'Get out of the way,' she returned. 'There is nothing for you until breakfast.'

He laughed and went on to the small stone hall at the front of the inn and found Luca and Brother Peter talking with the inn keeper.

Luca turned as he heard Freize's step. 'Oh, there you are. Are there many people outside?' he asked.

'It's getting crowded,' Freize replied. 'Is it a fair or something?'

'It's a crusade,' the inn keeper explained. 'And we're going to have to feed them somehow and get them on their way.'

'Oh, is that what it is? Your wife said she was expecting some pilgrims,' Freize volunteered.

'Pilgrims!' the man explained. 'Aye, for that was all that someone told us. But now they are starting to come into town and they say there are hundreds of them, perhaps thousands. It's no ordinary pilgrimage, for they travel all together as an army will march.'

'Where are they going?' Brother Peter asked.

The inn-keeper shook his head. 'I don't know. Their leader walks with them. He must have some idea. I have to go and fetch the priest, he will have to see that they are housed and fed. I'll have to tell the lord of the manor, he'll want to see them moved on. They can't all come here, and besides half of them have no money at all, they're begging their way along the road.'

'If they are in the service of God then He will guide them,' Brother Peter said. 'I'll come with you to the priest.'

Luca said to Freize, 'Let's take a look outside.'

The two young men stepped out of the front door of the inn and found the quayside now crowded with boys and girls, some of them barefoot, some of them dressed in little more than rags, all of them travel-stained and weary. Most were seated exhausted on the cobblestones, though some of them stood looking out to sea. There were more than a hundred children, none of them older than sixteen, some as young as six or seven, and more of them all the time, coming in through the town gate at the far end of the quay, as the gatekeeper watched in bewilderment.

'God save us!' Freize exclaimed. 'What's going on here? They're all children.'

'There's more coming,' Isolde called from the open window above them. She pointed north, over the roofs of the little town where the road wound down the hill. 'I can see them. There must be hundreds.'

'Is anyone leading them? Any adult in charge?' Luca called up to her.

Isolde shaded her eyes with her hand. 'I can't see anyone. No-one on horseback, no cart, just hundreds of children walking slowly.'

Almost under their feet, a small girl sat down abruptly and started to sob quietly. 'I can't walk,' she wept. 'I just can't.'

Freize knelt down beside her, saw that her little feet were bleeding from blisters and cuts. 'Of course you can't,' he said. 'And I don't know what your father was doing letting you out. Where do you live?'

Her face was illuminated at once, sore feet forgotten. 'I live with Johann the Good,' she said.

Luca bent down. 'Johann the Good?'

She nodded. 'He has led us here. He will lead us to the Promised Land.'

The two young men exchanged one anxious glance. 'This Johann,' Luca started, 'where does he come from?'

She frowned. 'Switzerland, I think. God sent him to lead us.'

'Switzerland?' exclaimed Freize.

'And where did he find you?'

'I was working on a farm outside Verona.' She reached for her little feet and chafed them as she spoke. At once her hands became stained with her blood but she paid no attention. 'Johann the Good and his followers came to the farm to ask for food and a barn to sleep in for the night, but my master was a hard man and drove them away. I waited till he was asleep and then my brother and I ran away after them.'

'Your brother's here?' Freize asked looking round. 'An older brother? Someone to look after you?'

She shook her head. 'No, he's dead now. He took a fever and he died one night and we had to leave him in a village; they said they would bury him in the churchyard.'

Freize put a hand on Luca's shoulder, and pulled him back from the child. 'What sort of fever?' he asked.

'I don't know, it was weeks ago.'

'Where were you? What was the village?'

'I don't know. It doesn't matter for I will see my brother again. Johann said that he will meet us in the Promised Land where the dead live again and the wicked burn.'

'Johann said that the dead will rise?' Luca asked. 'Rise from their graves, and we will see them?'

Freize had his own question. 'So who takes care of you, now that your brother is dead?'

She shrugged her little shoulders, as if the answer was obvious. 'God takes care of me,' she said. 'He called me and He guides me. He guides all of us and Johann tells us what He wants.'

Luca straightened up. 'I'd like to speak with this Johann,' he said.

She rose to her feet, wincing with the pain. 'There he is,' she said simply and pointed to a thick crowd of young boys who had come through the town gate and were leaning their sticks against the harbour wall and dropping their knapsacks down.

'Get Brother Peter,' Luca said shortly to Freize. 'I'm going to need him.'

Freize nodded, and placed a gentle hand on the little girl's shoulder. 'You stay here,' he said. 'I'll wash your feet when I get back and find you some shoes. What's your name?'

'Rosie,' she said. 'My feet are all right. God will heal them.'

'I'll help Him,' Freize said firmly.

Luca stood waiting, as Freize went up the narrow stone steps from the quayside to the market square where the church stood, raised above the square by another flight of broad steps. As Freize went upwards, taking the steps two at a time, the door of the church above him opened, and Brother Peter came out.

'Luca needs you,' Freize said shortly. 'There are hundreds of child pilgrims here, led by a youth they call Johann the Good.'

Brother Peter followed Freize back to the quayside to find it even more crowded. Every moment brought new arrivals in through the main gate at the top of the town and through the little quayside gate from the north. Some of them were children of nine or ten, others young men – apprentices who had run away from their masters or farm boys who had left the plough. A group of little girls trailed in last, holding hands in pairs as if on their way to school. Luca guessed that at every halt the smaller, weaker children caught up with the others; some never caught up at all.

Brother Peter spoke to Luca. 'The priest is a good man and has money to buy food for them, and the monastery is baking bread and the brothers will bring it down to the market.'

'It seems to be a pilgrimage of children led by a young man,' Luca said. 'I thought we should question him.'

Brother Peter nodded. 'He might have a calling,' he said cautiously. 'Or he might have been tempted by Satan himself to steal these children from their parents. Either way, the Lord of our Order would want to know. This is something we should understand.'

'He says that the dead will rise,' Luca emphasized to Peter. It was a key sign of the end of days: when the graves should give up their dead.

Brother Peter looked startled. 'He is preaching of the end of days?'

'Exactly,' Luca said grimly.

'Which one is he?'

'That one, called Johann,' Luca said, and started to make his way through the weary crowd to the boy who stood alone, his head bowed in prayer. 'The little girl called him Johann the Good.'

There were so many children pouring through the gate and down the quayside now that Luca could only wait and watch as they passed. He thought there were about a thousand of them in all, most of them looking exhausted and hungry, but all of them looking hopeful, some even inspired, as though driven by some determination to press on. Luca saw Freize take the little girl to the inn kitchen to bathe her feet, and thought that there were probably several hundred little girls like her, barely able to keep up, with no-one looking after them.

'It could be a miracle,' Brother Peter said, struggling through the sea of young people to get to Luca's side. 'I have seen such a thing only once before. When God calls for a pilgrimage and His people answer, it is a miracle. We have to know how many there are, where they are going, and what they hope to achieve. They may be healers, they may have the Sight. Milord will want to know about their leader, and what he preaches.'

'Johann the Good,' Luca repeated. 'That's him there.'

As if he felt their gaze on him the young boy waiting at the gate as his followers passed, raised his head and gave them a brilliant smile. He was about fifteen years old, with long blond hair that fell in untidy ringlets down to his shoulders. He had piercing blue eyes and was dressed like a Swiss goatherd, with a short robe over thick leggings tied crisscross, and strong sandals on his feet. In his hand he had a crook, like a shepherd's crook, carved with a series of crosses. As they watched, he kissed a cross and whispered a prayer, then turned to them.

'God bless and keep you, Masters,' he said.

Brother Peter, who was more accustomed to dispensing

blessings than receiving them, said stiffly, 'And God bless you too. What brings you here?'

'God brings me here,' the youth answered. 'And you?'

Luca choked on a little laugh at Brother Peter's surprise at being questioned by a boy. 'We too are engaged on the work of God,' he said. 'Brother Peter and I are enquiring into the well-being of Christendom. We are commissioned by the Holy Father himself,'

'The end of days is upon us,' the boy said simply. 'I have seen the signs. Does the Holy Father know that?'

'What signs have you seen?' Luca asked.

'Enough to be sure,' the lad replied. 'That's why we are on our journey.'

To be continued . . .

BOOK GROUP NOTES

Changeling is the first book in the Order of Darkness series. Visit www.orderofdarkness.com for more information.

About the Book:

It is 1453 and the terrifying news comes that the headquarters of the Church in the East, Constantinople, has fallen to the besieging armies of the Ottoman Empire, a seemingly unstoppable Muslim force which looks likely to overrun all of Europe. To many people this will signal the 'end of days' – literally the end of the world and the second coming of Christ. Novice priest Luca Vero, aged seventeen, is recruited into a secret Order to discover all the occurrences of evil in the Christian world. The Order believes that an understanding of all the mysteries of the world will reveal the devil and his works.

At the same time, recently-orphaned Lady Isolde of Lucretili, also seventeen, is banished to the local nunnery, as her brother inherits all the great lands of Lucretili. Isolde and her Moorish servant and best friend, Ishraq, immediately suspect that something is not right at the Abbey: nuns are fainting in chapel, seeing visions, sleepwalking, even finding bloody stigmata on their palms. Is it the work of the devil? Her worst fears seem confirmed when the Abbey receives a visitor: investigator Luca Vero, accompanied by his servant, Friczc, and a dour clerk, Brother Peter. What dark force is terrifying the nuns and causing them to act this way? Can Luca and Isolde uncover the true source of the problem?

About the Author:

Philippa Gregory was an established historian and writer when she discovered her interest in the Tudor period and wrote the international bestseller *The Other Boleyn Girl* which became a major film starring Natalie Portman and Scarlett Johansson. She has written several bestselling novels set in the Tudor period and The Cousins' War series, which is to be a major TV production. *Changeling* is the first of a new series of novels set in medieval Europe, titled Order of Darkness. Philippa lives with her family on a small farm in Yorkshire where she keeps horses, hens and ducks. Her other great interest is the charity that she founded nearly twenty years ago: Gardens for The Gambia. She has raised funds and paid for 160 wells in the primary schools of this very dry and poor African country, and thousands of school children have been able to learn market gardening in the school gardens watered by the wells. The charity also provides wells for women's collective gardens and for The Gambia's only agricultural college at Njawara. A past student of Sussex University, and a PhD and Alumna of the Year at Edinburgh University, her love of history is the hallmark of her writing. She also reviews for the *Washington Post*, the *LA Times*, and for UK newspapers, and is a regular broadcaster on television, radio, and webcast.

Character Guide:

Luca: Luca is in training to join the priesthood, not because he feels a call from God (the official criteria) but because it is a promising profession for bright young people. His parents put him in the monastery because it was virtually the only way they could give Luca an education. After his parents disappeared, it made sense for Luca, who had no property, to remain and pursue a career in the priesthood. But wanting an education is not the same as wanting to devote himself and swear unswerving obedience to the church, as Luca's hunger for knowledge and for adventure makes clear. Luca, the Italian version of Luke, means light, and Vero is the Italian for truth, thus Luca's name is a metaphor for his role in casting light on superstition and the inexplicable.

Frieze: Luca's companion Frieze was also a young boy living at the monastery, but his situation was very different: he was a kitchen boy, a lowly servant. While Frieze is older and stronger than Luca, the fact that he is less educated and lived at the monastery as a servant, not a student, places him lower on the social hierarchy than Luca – no matter how protective he is of the friend he calls the 'little lord'.

Peter: As a clerk, Peter holds an administrative position in the church and so is (presumably) loyal to it – one reason Frieze is so suspicious of him.

Isolde: As a young noblewoman, Isolde has wealth and privilege: she wears beautiful gowns and people stop what they are doing to bow low when she enters a room. But she also chafes under many limitations: the only options open to her as an adult are a life as a wife, or as a nun. Women who refused to marry, or who failed to receive proposals, could not continue on forever (or for very long) as unmarried adult women, because that category made no sense in their society. They had no choice but to enter a nunnery, no matter how weak their devotion to religion. Noblewomen could read and write, but beyond that were taught only the skills that would make them elegant and entertaining – how to dance, sing, and play musical instruments; how to decorate a home and to dress themselves well; and how to do decorative arts such as sketching and embroidery. Some ladies also learned other European languages (though not ancient Latin or Greek, the languages of higher learning), but Isolde did not. Meaning beautiful, Isolde is a name redolent of Malory's iconic *Tristan and Isolde* (1470). It is the Celtic version of the name that has other variants such as Isoletta in Italian.

Ishraq: Ishraq is the only character in the book who is not white or Christian. As such, she is a puzzle to many around her. Isolde, who was raised alongside her, sees her as a friend, even a sister, but most who meet her do not understand who or what she is. Ishraq is a Moor, which means that she is a Muslim of African or Arab descent, raised somewhere in the Ottoman Empire. Muslims lived in Asia, Africa, and the Arab regions of the world; in Europe, the only significant Muslim population was in southern Spain. Isolde's father brought Ishraq and her mother back with him from a Crusade. However Lord Lucretili treated Ishraq and her mother well. Although many Moors living in Europe were slaves, Ishraq and her mother were not. Lord Lucretili raised Ishraq so that she would fit in with her own culture, rather than with his own, making sure she could ride horses, fight, shoot a bow and arrow, and hunt. He also sent her to Islamic centres of learning, where she studied medicine and anatomy and the advanced Arabic learning. Ishraq dresses in Moorish clothes and refrains from following Christian rites, and both practices make her an outsider. The Arabic name Ishraq means sunrise – so another name that is suggestive of metaphorically bringing light to the dark.

Giorgio: Isolde's brother and the new Lord Lucretili. Because he is male, Giorgio enjoys many social and legal privileges denied to Isolde. When his father dies, he becomes the head of the household; Isolde knows that she must obey her brother's will, just as she obeyed her father's. Giorgio inherits his father's title and his lands and other property. He need not marry if he does not wish to. He alone has seen his father's will, the contents of which he communicates to Isolde.

Sister Ursula, the Lady Almoner: The term 'almoner' refers to a church official who is responsible for giving out alms (money) to the poor. However, Sister Ursula's main job is to manage the abbey/convent – she is a sort of a manageress who controls the work schedule and the storeroom, and who lives separately and better than the other sisters (let alone the mere lay sisters). She is suspicious and resentful of Isolde and Ishraq – with, as it turns out, good reason.

Pope Nicholas V: Born 1397, he served as Pope from 1447 until his death in 1455. He established the Vatican library and began an ambitious building programme in Rome. A great patron of the humanists, he is considered the first Renaissance pope.

Period Overview and Background Information:

Life in fifteenth-century Europe: In the period before industrialisation or urbanisation, let alone computers or the digital age, the majority of Europeans were poor and illiterate. Most people worked on farms, tending crops or animals. A tiny minority formed a wealthy aristocracy that owned most of the land and wielded all of the political power. But more powerful even than them was the Church.

The Church: In the fifteenth century, the Church – no one called it the Catholic Church, because until the Reformation there were no other churches in the west – was extremely important. Most governments were small, weak, or fragmented. The Church was not only the spiritual institution of most Europeans, but was also the largest, wealthiest, and most powerful institution in all of western Europe.

Abbey, Monastery, Nunnery: Abbeys, monasteries, convents and nunneries are all Catholic institutions in which monks and nuns lived and worshipped, under the authority of the Abbot or Abbess. A monastery is a male community; convent and nunnery are synonyms for female communities. Usually, either one can be referred to as an Abbey; in *Changeling*, a shared central Abbey is set between a monastery and a nunnery. Abbeys were common in Europe. They offered food and shelter to strangers and travellers.

Prayer times: Life in a monastery or convent was highly regulated and included frequent prayer. Monks and nuns daily prayed the "Liturgy of the Hours," a list of prayers recited at different times of day. In the fifteenth century the Liturgy of the Hours had eight scheduled prayer times: Matins (at midnight), Lauds (at dawn), Prime (in the early morning), Terce (at mid-morning), Sext (at noon), None (in mid-afternoon), Vespers (at dusk), and Compline (at night before going to bed).

Lay sister: in the fifteenth century, convents had a social hierarchy that reflected that of the larger society. Elite women who could bring a dowry to the convent became sisters, but poorer women, from illiterate peasant families, came to the convent penniless, and became lay sisters. Lay sisters did menial work – domestic chores, agricultural work, spinning – while the sisters spent their time in prayer. In places where sisters avoided contact with the world, lay sisters were the nunnery's link to the outside – they would take the convent's products to market, talk to outsiders, and greet visitors. In other words, while on paper a convent was a house of God in which all were equal, in practice convents – like the rest of Europe – had ladies who did not work, and servants who did.

Numbering systems: today, we use what are called Arabic numerals. These are the digits 0, 1, 2, 3, 4, 5, 6, 7, 8, 9, used in a place-value notation system in which the same numeral can have different values depending on where it is placed; for example, the numeral '1' would have a value of 1 in the right-hand column, but a value of 10 in the next column to the left. In Luca and Isolde's time, however, most people in the West still used Roman numerals, where the numerals are I, V, X, L, C, D, and M, and they always have the same value no matter where in a figure they are located. Arabic numerals first appeared in the West in the tenth century, and were spreading quickly through Europe after the invention of moveable-type print in the mid-fifteenth century – the very time that *Changeling* takes place. Arabic numerals permit much more advanced types of calculations; they would be very exciting to someone who "thinks about numbers", as Luca does.

Changeling: In the village he grew up in, Luca was rumoured to be a changeling, a fairy baby that had been switched with a human child and left to be raised in its place by human parents (though changelings could also be troll or elf babies, and the term could also refer to the human baby that had been spirited away). Changeling stories were often used to explain a child with abilities or looks that did not run in the family, as when Luca's poor, illiterate, and apparently infertile parents suddenly found themselves the mother and father of a handsome and clever son. Sometimes, rumours of changelings also circulated about wealthy or powerful families; that the heir to the fortune, or the throne, was not the true heir.

Fall of Constantinople: After its decline in the fifth century, the

Roman Empire had divided into two parts: the eastern half – called the Byzantine Empire – used Greek as its learned language, and had Constantinople as its capital, while the western part – western Europe – used Latin as its scholarly language, and had Rome as its capital. The two parts had their tensions, but both were Christian areas. Then in the spring of 1453, the Ottoman (or Turkish) empire laid siege to and captured the city of Constantinople. To fifteenth-century Christians, the fall of Constantinople to the Ottomans – which spelled the end of the Byzantine empire – was a catastrophe. They feared that the Muslim Ottomans might go on to conquer the rest of Europe and to stamp out Christianity. Many thought that the fall of Constantinople was a sign that the end of days was coming.

End of days: Medieval Christians believed that Christ's second coming was imminent. They were always on the lookout for signs that the 'end of days', in which a series of major disasters would strike and Christ would return to earth, was approaching. Some took the fall of Constantinople to be a harbinger of the end of days – Constantinople was, after all, a major centre of Christian authority, the 'Rome of the east' – and became extremely anxious about the fate of the Church, humanity, and the world.

Stigmata: Stigmata are marks that miraculously appear, without any physical cause, on a person's body, in the places where Jesus's body would have been marked by his crucifixion. The most common stigmata appear on the palms of the sufferer's hands, but they can also be on the feet, the chest, or the brow (where Jesus wore a crown of thorns during his crucifixion). Throughout history, most people with stigmata – called stigmatics – have been women. When *Changeling* takes place, one well-known stigmatic was Catherine of Siena, a nun who lived in the 1300s and was declared a saint by Pope Pius II in 1461.

Golden fleece: In Greek mythology, the Golden Fleece is the fleece of a sheep or ram that was winged and had golden wool; it is part of the story of Jason and his Argonauts. But there are also many stories about ways that one can use a regular sheep's fleece to collect tiny particles of gold from running streams. One very old account is from Georgia, in eastern Europe and dates from the 5th century BCE. Fleeces were submerged in a stream, and would catch tiny flecks of gold from deposits upstream. The fleeces would then be hung to dry before the gold was combed out. In parts of Georgia, people still pan for gold using fleece.

Children raised by wolves: there are many myths and stories about feral or wild children, said to have been raised by wolves or other animals. In Roman mythology, the city of Rome was founded by twin brothers, Romulus and Remus, who were nursed and raised by a she-wolf. Throughout human history there have been other stories of children raised in the wild by wolves or other animals. Few have ever been documented as factual, but the compelling notion that animal parents could raise human children, along with the hope that children lost in the wilderness might still be alive, means that these stories flourish even today.

Themes of the Book:
Eastern and western traditions: religion, medicine, mathematics
Freedom and imprisonment
Belief and superstition
The role of women in society
Children and families
Loyalty, companionship, trust
Difference and outsiders

Discussion Questions:
1 Isolde's brother tells her that her father's will left her two options: to marry the drunken and brutish Prince Roberto, or to renounce her wealth and live her entire life as a nun, with no husband or family. Why does Isolde choose the nunnery? Which option would you choose? Why?
2 How does the relationship between Luca and Frieze change over the course of the book?
3 Luca and Isolde both have some of the qualities a monk or nun should possess, but lack others. What do you think were the most important requirements for the religious life? What would you do if you found yourself poorly suited for the career your parents chose for you, or the one you planned to pursue? Why do you think Isolde tries to obey her father's wishes?
4 How do various characters – Isolde, the Lady Almoner, Frieze, and others – perceive Ishraq? In what ways is she different from others in her society? How do people today react to those they perceive as different from themselves?
5 What are some of the explanations that the nuns, the villagers, and others offer for the strange goings-on at the nunnery, and for the wild creature they capture? How do people today seek to explain phenomena they cannot understand?

6　We never learn how Isolde and Ishraq escaped the Abbey's gate-house cellar. How do you think they escaped? Why do you think Frieze claims that he released them?

7　What are the differences between the way that Isolde's father raised her and the education he provided for Ishraq? Why were the two trained differently? Whose knowledge and skills do you think are more useful? Whose position in society would you prefer to occupy?

8　The villagers think that Sara Rossi's son Stefan was taken by a werewolf; Brother Peter thinks that Sara had a hand in his disappearance. What do you think actually happened?

9　What do you think the merits of the different life options available to a noble woman like Isolde were – marriage or the convent? What advantages/disadvantages did each have?

10　In the book, we see a wide variety of relationships start, change, or end, based on revelations about trustworthiness. Can you pinpoint some key moments in the text where one character realises s/he cannot trust another? Think about moments in your own life when you realised that someone was not worthy of the trust you gave them, or when you decided to offer someone new your trust.

For more information, visit www.orderofdarkness.com

Scan the QR code to take you there now!

Get the free mobile app at
http://gettag.mobi